# GABRIELA'S CHASE

## A Novel

SHERILYN FAITH

Published by Verlag
Newport Beach, California

Library of Congress Control Number: 2025905168

ISBNs:
979-8-9926809-0-4  (paperback)
979-8-9926809-3-5  (eBook)
979-8-9926809-2-8  (audiobook)

Cover art by Sam Sutton
Interior layout by Kimberly Martin, Jera
Editing Candice L. Davis

# ENDORSEMENTS

Life can be simply difficult, with dangers, losses, and failures we can't avoid. *Gabriela's Chase* is a character-driven and well-plotted adventure centered on a young woman who encounters major obstacles to reach her dream. But it is also a message for the trials that everyone faces, providing inspiration, focus, relational and spiritual support, and hope. It's a book for all of us. I highly recommend it.

—John Townsend, PhD, *New York Times* bestselling
author of *Boundaries* series

If there's a theme that springs from this fascinating, often gritty novel of a young woman finding her passion in life, it's this line near the end of *Gabriela's Chase: I knew what I was fighting for.* Gabriela is a fighter, and not just on the streets of her hometown, where a wrong look or misplaced affiliation can put your life at risk. She trains to become a skilled boxer and eventually applies her skills to rescuing young women in another country. This is a story of redemption and grace that will inspire you to answer the whisper that Gabe hears more than once, giving her the courage to do the right thing: *Homegirl, I hear your prayer.*

—Stan Jantz, co-author of international
bestseller, *God Is in the Small Stuff*

As a native to Orange County—*Gabriela's Chase* is the real deal. A young woman who fights against all odds to rise above in life and inspire others to achieve in education and career. It's the kind of story we need youth to hear so that they too can reach for the stars.

—Martha Trujillo, UC Irvine
Master's of Criminology, law, and society

This is an exciting and poignant novel about teenage Gabe and her early years as a boxer among dangerous street gangs. A desperate escape to Colombia allows her surcease, including a touching romantic encounter. Her life is again shaken with dangers that involve intimations of trafficking but also offer a choice that may save her. Along this journey of redemption, Gabe encounters a gallery of characters that will, like her, stay long with the reader.

—John Rechy, author of *City of Night* and first novelist to
receive PEN USA West's Lifetime Achievement Award,
Texas Institute of Letters Lifetime Achievement Award

Sherilyn's book tells the gripping story of Gabriela (Gabe) and her life transformation despite the most challenging of circumstances. Thought-provoking and compelling, as Sherilyn takes readers on a powerful journey of hope and resilience from Santa Ana, California, to Cartagena, Colombia. Stories help us connect our story and God's story, and this story stirs reflection and awe.

—Eric Geiger, PhD, author of bestseller *Simple Church*, former vice president of Lifeway Books, Senior Pastor Mariners Church

*Gabriela's Chase* is a powerful, faith-filled adventure of hope and resilience. Follow Gabriela as she overcomes the struggles of street life, pursuing her calling in medicine, and embarks on a daring mission to rescue trafficked girls—all guided by faith and the belief in a greater purpose. A suspenseful and inspiring must-read!

—Kim Campbell, author of *Gentle on My Mind: In Sickness and in Health with Glen Campbell*

Elevating stories of women growing up in under-resourced communities shines light on the extenuating circumstances and incredible resilience that is often birthed from adversity.

—Gloria Bashara, former Santa Ana Lighthouse community center director

Sherilyn has written a compelling story of coming of age for a young woman living in a difficult society, neighborhood, and family circumstances. She relates how life is not easy and how decisions we make have such impactful and lifelong results. Written for young adults, the lessons are for all of us.

—Greg Campbell, author of *The Surprising Power of The Coil*

The baking heat of Santa Ana, California. The wooden huts and shacks of Cartagena, Colombia. Sex trafficking. Sherilyn Faith beautifully tracks the journey of the young boxer Gabriela who navigates it all, gloves on, gloves off, fighting both for others and for herself.

—Adrienne Sharp, winner of *Booklist's* ten best first novels for *The Sleeping Beauty*

*To my family*
*and the memory*
*of my father and mother*
*with love*

*There is always something left to love.*
—Gabriel García Márquez

# PROLOGUE

ON GRACE STREET, GIRLS wear red-and-black jackets. Their hair is short, cropped—buzzed if they're cool. Long, teased hair works, too, and is good for hiding razor blades. The girls give each other hard looks—eyes steely, lips pressed cold and hard like a door slammed in juvie—and every look a specific signal. If you're not careful, they'll start mad dogging you, staring at you hard and long, real mean, and then you got trouble, a real fight on your hands.

# PART I

## SANTA ANA, CALIFORNIA

*The endurance of darkness is the
preparation for great light.*
—St. John of the Cross

## chapter 1

"GET LOST," GABRIELA'S HOMEGIRL said to her. "Don't tell that girl your secrets." She knew Gabriela, nicknamed Gabe, earnestly wanted out of this dark lifestyle. Gabe's homegirls teased her for boxing at the community center gym and talking to Petra, the counselor. Homegirls lied to Petra, but what they said about girl fights was true.

Sweeping gusts of the Santa Ana winds were oven hot. It was school lunch break in the quad, and Ramón, handsome, slow-moving, and tall, walked toward Gabe. He gave her a dry, fiery look. She wondered if he got on campus through the back door and if he was coming on to her.

A couple of her homegirls pulled in close. Ramón was the leader of the Middle Towners, the pack she and her brother jumped into together a year before. She hadn't realized Ramón was so enticing.

She stared back at him, squinting to see if his earnest, dark eyes held a secret invitation for her. She hadn't had much time for homeboys, with studying and assisting at the clinic, so nineteen-year-old Ramón's reputation frightened her. She couldn't let him tug at her feelings, using those eyes to draw her down deep into gang life. Fika, his sometimes girlfriend and leader of the vicious Las Locas Latinas, caught their hungry looks. She appeared to try to lock eyes with Gabe, but Gabe turned her head away quickly so she couldn't.

Surely, Fika couldn't blame her for looking at Ramón. Who wouldn't? It was common knowledge in the hood Ramón was muscular, rugged, and had a scar on his face that made him look even more intriguing—the kind of guy a girl would look at twice but didn't dare to because of Fika's probable retaliation.

Wearing a flannel shirt over a mini dress and army boots, Gabe lifted her chin to bravely signal Ramón with a secret smile and flashed their gang sign.

Ramón grinned smugly, seemingly basking in the attention directed his way from both Fika and Gabe. Shoulders thrown back, he chuckled. Gabe's eyes widened as she enjoyed seeing Ramón's full chest rise with pride, but Fika looked mortified. Gabe's homegirl nudged her. As Gabe dared to look at Fika and held her eye, Fika's face sparked like flint.

While her eyes were still fixed on Gabe, mad dogging her, three of the Las Locas Latinas—the homies Fika called for—flanked her. They looked poised for action. In the next moment, all five feet, ten inches of Fika came charging across the quad toward Gabe. Fika's orange-streaked brown hair flamed out behind her.

Fika, with two mean-looking girls, burst into Gabe's group of homegirls. Gabe moved back quickly—a move she learned from her boxing coach at the community center ring—stepping on the foot of *su hermana*, her sisterly homegirl Rosa. Fika pulled a knife from her teased hair and slowly slid her clenched fingers up and down the shaft. The knife was the fold-and-lock kind, pressed from the end so you could close and hide it. The sharp edge of the blade was on top for cutting up—damaging. *No knives, just scalpels!* Gabe tensed. She'd given up her fighting knife in exchange for a dissection tool in anatomy class, as part of her commitment to get top grades and learn about the human body.

"Girls are crazy to fight over me." Gabe heard Ramón mutter through tightly drawn lips.

Gabe knew Fika was a dangerous rival as rumors about fights spiraled around the hood.

She looked at her smartwatch and then blinked at a familiar face across the schoolyard. Her gringa wannabe-friend Candy was watching her, and even worse, so were a couple of her freshmen self-defense students, Carina and Lupe. *Not my students. Not here.* Gabe grimaced and stepped back.

Shaking his head at Gabe and Fika, Ramón turned his back and left the quad.

"What were you doing staring at my homeboy Ramón?" Fika's face contorted into a bulldog-like mask as she screeched.

"Huh?" Gabe was stunned. Instinctively, she knew not to fight but to flee. Her Converse tennis shoes went into high gear as she retreated behind two big girls in her group who tried to back her up but couldn't move fast enough.

Fika lunged toward her, red-eyed like a mad dog, her knife at gut level projecting swiftly from her hand.

"Watch out for Fika!"

Fika thrust the knife out to wound her, but Gabe stepped back, jaguar swift. Off balance, Fika, with her left hand, grabbed a handful of thick, dark hair from Gabe's innocent Afro-Cuban homegirl Rosa and, with her right hand, wielded the sharp blade of her knife, slicing superficially across the arm. Rosa screamed and grabbed her wound. Trickles of blood dripped from the cut onto her shirt as Fika darted under the eaves of a building. Gabe stripped off her flannel shirt and followed student medic protocol, pressing it to Rosa's injury, and the bleeding lessened.

"Fika." The homegirl Rosa hissed in a private whisper as the tuft of dark hair that Fika pulled swirled out into the sweltering Santa Ana inversion layer.

When the school resource officers—brawny men in Bermuda shorts—rushed to the scene, the other girls stared at them blankly. Gabe looked around. Her self-defense students Carina and Lupe were now away from the fracas.

No one would rat on Fika unless she wanted to be next.

The guards held Rosa and stopped all bleeding; then they took her to the school medical unit. The nurse would treat her, but no perpetrator's name would be cited. Soon it would be as if the action had never occurred—only an accident report and a scar left to show for it.

Now Fika might send the Locas homegirls and barrio dogs after Gabe, who might have to change territories to protect her own life. This time, when Gabe talked to Petra at the center, she might rat and tell the social worker what happened to bring some heat down on the Locas.

Grace Street had a life all its own. As it turned to dusk on a stifling hot night, Gabe left her home for the boxing ring and Petra's counseling office at the community center. She walked straight ahead, eyes down, making sure to avoid a tough-looking weight lifter (or what her boxing coach, Al, called a meathead) sitting on the hood of someone's car. His huge pythons, a tattoo of snakes on each bicep, were folded across his chest as he joked with two young men hanging out on the sidewalk.

Mothers with babies in their laps sat on doorsteps of houses or stairs of apartments, waiting for it to cool down before making dinner. Cruisers in mobs, sets, cliques, and crews drove by in everything from lowered Chevys to sports SUVs. Yesterday she'd seen two men in a tricked-out black-and-gray SUV, almost running down a woman before jumping onto the curb. Word in the hood was the speedsters robbed the hardware company, injured the owner, and still hadn't been found.

The hood felt different when dark descended on the city, like death all too soon covering the deeds of the day. On the busy street corner, people staked out the sidewalk in front of the local grocery store. The hot air brought out the true scents of the nearby restaurants: Asian food and Vietnamese meats blended with oil-fried tortillas and beans. Fathers, mothers, and children circled around, laughing with drinks in hand, while on other streets of the city, bandits and bangers set the night's agenda in human lives to win or lose.

Even though Grace Street residents felt like *familia*, when Gabe walked on the crumbly sidewalk, she didn't forget some ten gangs had carved up a forty-block radius of Santa Ana.

Now, eager footsteps sounded close behind her as she walked to the community center, but when she turned around, she saw only the shadow of a tall willowy woman against a building.

"What's going on, girlfriend?" No one answered Gabe's attempt to sound fearless.

What if it was Fika or one of the Locas? She rubbed her eyes from the dust of the tenacious Santa Ana winds.

Gabe darted into Grace Community Center, nodding at the teenage and adult boxers in the entry, who smiled back respectfully. No big sign out front or bright lights to draw attention, the doorway leading into the lobby could just as well take you into an artist's garret, seedy apartment complex, or any other type of business you'd expect to see on this slightly stealth section of Grace Street. No poster of a model in full makeup hitting a heavy bag. The vast majority of singles looking for boutique glam couture athletics wouldn't even know this place existed, nor would any Instatweet sponsor listings. Sections of paint missing from the walls with dings in the baseboards would probably weed out anyone looking for a luxury exercise experience. Trash, needles, and condoms left by squatters gave way to a converted abandoned location—the community center's covert boxing facility with hardcore ring, bags, and workout equipment.

Coach Al, a former state champion, told boxers he'd rather DIY to make sure the gym was up to his standards. Here in her familiar escape scene, Gabe donned tape, gloves, shoes, ducked under the ropes, and pranced until Coach Al squared up to oppose her in the ring.

Sidestepping Coach's right cross, Gabe came back with a left jab. Coach's large frame tilted slightly, and Gabe moved in. Gabe's red glove met Coach's glove with a controlled swing. He countered with a short jab. She thrust forward, and then Coach stepped back and let Gabe fade forward ever so slightly off balance.

Coach snickered, but Gabe collected her strength. This time her upper right landed.

"Nailed me in the collarbone."

"Clavicle."

"Take this," Coach said and tapped her glove with a full-on punch capable of maiming her had he not stopped mid-punch.

"Don't go easy on me."

Coach thrust out a left cross Gabe might have missed had she not practiced night after night. She faded back before repeating a left cross back at him. After flinching a nanosecond, the coach stabbed at Gabe with a serious right.

She ducked and then recovered with consecutive punches as if Coach were a punching bag. She backed Coach up toward the ropes. He retaliated with a series of jabs and counterpunches. But Gabe kept up with the best Coach could muster, her footwork blazing as he'd taught her. The sparring gave Gabe a shot of confidence.

Coach tried to back her up against the ropes, but she fought back with a series of punches she'd practiced at home in front of the mirror. Coach scowled and grabbed his shoulder.

He stepped aside. "I give. I thought you were in the doctor business, not the destruct-o business."

"How about both? You good?" Gabe panted between breaths. She placed her gloves on her hips and half smiled, looking to see if he was kidding.

"Of course. Think I can't take a short round?" Coach tried to hide his gasps.

She motioned for him to let her see his shoulder.

"Nah, nothing a few stretches won't fix."

"You're tough, Coach. By the way, I've got another fight ahead. With my demons."

"Petra's in." He glared. "You have a welt on your arm?"

She blinked at the skin over her biceps. "From school."

"School fight? Go talk with Petra."

"Sure, Coach." *Had a shadow of distrust flit across Coach's eyes?*

He nodded and gave a grunt.

# chapter 2

AFTER CHANGING BACK TO her bloodied school clothes in the dank locker room, picking up essentials, including her piece, and splattering on some perfume, Gabe took the stairs to the counseling office on the second floor, two at a time. Straightening and pulling down her mini dress under the flannel shirt, she plopped down on the worn chair and made every effort to give Petra the hurt look she'd given her before. Only this time, Gabe was not acting. Her helplessness and the full-bodied scent of her fake Chanel seemed to get Petra's attention. Today she really felt like a sixteen-year-old, soon to be seventeen, on a broken-down, rickety roller coaster.

Gabe knew her problem needed more immediate attention than Petra's average community center client. Yet she felt unsure of her because Petra had left the barrio and gotten "pedicured." She'd like to trust her, but Petra might be too nosey.

Serene and professional, Petra nodded with the enthusiasm of a woman in her early twenties. She peeked at the tattoo revealed when Gabe's mini dress hiked up, then smiled when Gabe scrunched her skirt down apologetically. Her tattoo. A monarch, the regal butterfly emblazoned with cheerful majesty—everything she wanted but nothing she had. She thought Petra must have a soft spot for losers, for people with excuses and apologies.

Petra wore an appropriately stylish designer pantsuit and wedges, but with only a government paycheck, she must have picked them up at the factory outlets. The seams on the suit didn't quite match. It was subtle, but Petra wasn't as put together as Gabe had thought, and that gave her a small hope that she would understand her tinny-feeling, off-kilter emotions.

"Is that blood on your shirt? What happened?"

"Locas are after me! I can't teach your self-defense class!" Gabe felt embarrassed at her outburst.

"The good you're doing, don't let it go." Petra lost her usual coolness and looked chagrined at Gabe's dismissal of her assignment.

"It's not my fault this time." Gabe parted Petra's home-made curtains with a quick hand to look outside at the usual high-density buzz of Grace Street. Hot air and two flies slipped in through the screen.

She waved a big fly out of her face. "The Locas will come after me. Both Lupe and Carina saw it too."

Petra looked disappointed.

Gabe squirmed in her seat.

"Do you want to fight Fika?" Petra put down her pencil.

"What do you think? No trouble, and in two more weeks, I box in a national fight.

"Principal says he's coming to the match because he heard I got a scholarship to take AP bio and physio tests."

"Are you an AP Scholar with honors?"

13

"Yeah, guess so. First time I've looked forward to seeing the principal." Gabe gave an easy laugh and leaned back in the tattered Goodwill shop chair. Petra always acted relieved when the makeshift springs held up under her one-hundred-thirty-pound strain.

Gabe started to light one of her borrowed cigarettes but stopped as if she remembered Petra's aversion to tobacco.

"Training rules." Petra nodded as Gabe put away the cigarette. "Talk around town is you have the skills to be a doctor."

"Yeah. Maybe." Gabe pushed her long, thick, wavy brown hair away from her sweaty face. Even at five-nine, with her lush hair and brown eyes, she'd never be Miss Latina. Yet Gabe's face was attractive when she wasn't fighting. Homeboys teased her. They called her "Brick House" because of her solid build, a show of respect for her firm, muscular look.

Fika can rip her shanks somewhere else. *And who leaked my dream to be a doctor?*

Petra reached over the desk and, with a nudge, pulled the curtain over and looked down to the street below. "Is Fika big, very tall, and has brown hair with orange streaks?" she asked.

"Yeah, I told you she'd still be waiting for me. She cut up my homegirl Rosa. Then she stalked me here." Gabe fixed her glare on Petra to see that she understood the threat and the enemies.

"Who are you afraid of?" Petra nodded toward the street.

"Fika. I'm also afraid of Big Mama Java with her hair extensions."

"Who's that, Gabe?"

"Fika's bodyguard. Ha, I made it up. I can't get to sleep at night."

"You could always count sheep."

"I've tried. They get shot one by one as they try to jump." She blinked to make out the blur of Petra's university diploma and pointed to it on the wall.

"Your paper helps you here on the streets?" Gabe goaded, a tactic to draw Petra briefly away. Gabe wiggled uneasily on the couch. She wasn't sure if she wanted to tell her about the trouble. The lump of metal inside her jacket pocket felt reassuring.

"I worked hard for that diploma, but my Navajo grandmother thinks it's worthless too. She wanted me to teach on the reservation." Gabe liked Petra's persistence enough to try for one or more of those parchment papers with the shiny seal herself, but she knew Petra's endurance wouldn't help her with the personal vendettas going down in the streets.

"I have a personal stake in you," Petra continued. "Teach self-defense. Take the girls on field trips. You know what's more powerful than your devastating left hook? The message of your life."

"My life? At least you have an *abuelita*. Before my *abuelita* left us, she'd take me to church downtown, and we'd sing hymns. For lunch, we'd make *sopa de tomate albahaca* steaming hot. The spicy smells wafted all up and down the street. When she wrapped her arms around me, snuggling, I felt loved. Cuddling up with her, taking in her floral scent, is my favorite memory. Then … disappeared. She didn't even come back when my niece Luz was born. Then Luz's *padre*, my brother Sal died. My *padre* was deported. Mamacita can't get across the border."

"I'm sorry. Yet I see there's hope, Gabe. You're so persistent about your pre-med and the boxing, and you're the one who can walk out a free woman if you choose."

Gabe knew Petra considered her one of her girls—one of the few who were improving, if only she could keep clean. But sometimes reality didn't look so good without a kick—a fight, a vice—like now.

Petra looked at her with those amber and green-speckled eyes as if Gabe could overcome it all. Months ago, with Petra's help, Gabe had agreed to give up her vices: forty ouncers, Night Train, and worse.

This jam, though, wasn't just fighting her personal demons; it was Fika fighting her and her homies. Fika acted like Gabe disrespected her by watching Ramón, and their turf could ignite in a heartbeat. She patted her jacket pocket where she'd hidden the piece. It was still there.

Petra cocked her head.

Gabe gave her long hair a flick and decided to toss Petra some private information to see how she'd react. "Fika tried to kill me today. She saw me look at her *novio*, and she knows I want out of the gangs, so she wants to settle up. I need to get out of here."

"Who else is in on this?" Petra probed.

Gabe bounced on the springs. "We tell you family *peccadillos*, but you talk to the wrong people, and I'm dead."

"I'm professionally required to keep our conversations confidential. And I'm not the one with a gun."

Gabe gulped. "Fika's going to cut my throat. Can you help?"

Petra looked inconspicuously out the window and shook her head.

"She won't leave until I do. I dare you to do something, Petra. Give me the keys to your car!"

Petra reached into her drawer, pulled out a metal ring with keys, took off the house key, and threw the rest at Gabe.

They landed square on the lap of her miniskirt, slipping down into the opening between her legs.

"Your car keys?" Gabe gasped.

"Leave by the back stairs and don't look back tonight."

Gabe stood and moved toward the back door. "Is this a game, like Trust Me or something?"

"Just teach self-defense."

"Yeah, I got it."

Looking out the window, Petra brushed her hair away from her face, and Gabe was surprised to see the counselor's forehead glisten.

"Drive my Hyundai ... to the high school, Gabe. Leave the car there and run. Fika will never see you."

"You'll let me drive your car?"

"The indicator says check engine, but it's okay."

"Didn't know you were so cool."

"I'm not." Petra looked at the sweat marks on the underarms of her discount sleeveless top. "There goes my dry-cleaning budget," she sighed. Her face screwed up, and Gabe thought she might chase after her down the steps and through the alley with a hawk-eye on her car.

# chapter 3

IN THE LOCKER ROOM, Gabe opened her gym bag and applied a protective layer of cream, then she brushed her hand against her face, glistening smooth with the Vaseline she'd smeared on to protect her complexion from fisticuffs and knife cuts.

She then reached into her inside pocket, checking, and walked outside. Good, the borrowed gun felt strange but reassuring, just in case she was followed.

"Fika, where are you, girl?" Gabe whispered loud enough to compete with the hiss of steam rising from a manhole cover. No reply greeted her, and no outline of Fika in dusk's shadows. Everything was still in the parking lot except for the scuffling sounds of boxing shoes and Al's coaching commands coming from the gym.

Lunging behind the wheel of Petra's Hyundai, she gripped the locked leather-covered steering wheel and forced it to the right.

She remembered it'd be time for the late shift at Shin's garment factory if the inspector hadn't closed the factory up. Her earnings for sewing seams and hems only factored a little toward her college savings and med-training goals.

The car radio sounded like tin compared to the full, quadrophonic speakers of José's Chevy. A gold Cadillac minivan with white trim zipped by, its stereo blaring:

*"Homies, get racked.*
*Through the clear white haze, my troop*
*and I were talking trash on the down low in the*
*downtown,*
*And the Main Street bangers tallied up ..."*

Then, cruising by slowly, a lowered black Volkswagen bug with black tinted windows and a license plate stating: "IT BE LOW."

"Low down, feeling low," she sighed. A car like that would be an easy mark. She knew how to pry open door locks on the older model bugs and some newer sedans. A year ago, she and her homegirls would have stalked it, dropping two cars back, then staking out where it parked.

It was simple. She knew how from her street training: stealing earlier models, using screwdrivers to put a hole right through the side of the lock, sometimes hot-wiring them. She and her friends would drive around, get their weed, gulp their brew, and then they would ditch the car, feeling like they were on top of the world. No one ever got caught. Ever. She was fifteen, almost sixteen then, but almost seventeen, felt a whole lot wiser.

She thought she saw someone in the black bug staring at her, so she turned her head so as not to be seen by the anonymous silhouette behind the smoke-tinted windows. No way did she want to be recognized by Fika's or Ramón's men.

She took a breath. Petra believed in her.

She looked up to see the black bug had made a U-turn and pulled beside her.

Two tough males from another gang, the Mean Gangstas, MGs, had rolled down their windows. They looked ready for a fight. The Volkswagen came closer, forcing Gabe to the side of the road.

Gangsta got out of the car and came toward her. Taunting her, the tall guy pulled out a .38 and waved it. "Where are you from?"

"What you need?" She deflected and hid her Middle Town affiliation. With a quick rush of anger, she felt herself doing the unimaginable. Stepping out of the passenger side of the car, she felt for the gun still tucked inside her shirt.

"Sit down!" The tall MG pushed her to the ground with the other strong arm not holding the gun, to hold her down while she screamed and wiggled.

"Nobody pushes Gabe!" She kicked hard to get free.

"She's a wild one. Trouble. Not worth it." He let her up.

She jumped to her feet, pulled the gun out from her shirt, and pointed it at him.

"Stop!" He shouted then backed up a few steps and then ran.

Gabe ducked into the car.

"The broad is the only one in the car!" the tall one relayed to the other. "Doesn't know what she's into."

"Yeah. Not worth the risk." The short one stared at her.

She couldn't stop shaking and hoped it didn't show. She shot the gun in the air then dropped down.

"Hey, you!" The tall one was still angry. "No one shoots, then drops." She heard them start their car and tear out. A gunshot rang out, and the almost noiseless sound of a hole cleanly blasted a parting blast at an angle through the Hyundai's front windshield.

Curled up in the seat, she did something she thought she would never do. She whimpered.

"I never used a gun before. I never did, never."

"Whose windshield got wasted?" her brother José asked when Gabe pulled up in the Hyundai.

"Petra's. At the center."

"We don't need nothing from that gringa. You good?"

"Good, but I need these wheels to shake off Fika."

"Ramón wants me."

"Listen, José. I'll only take you if you tell Ramón you're through."

"Can't tell Ramón anything."

At dusk, Ramón was waiting at the top of the park. As night shadows swept along the asphalt, Gabe watched as homies appeared from all directions. He would size up the toughest hombres, puff out his chest, and chicken-chest them, bat chest-on-chest until they cracked.

"Sizing me up?" a gang member would banter back to Ramón. When José stared at Ramón, he cowered. Gabe slammed her hand angrily against the dashboard.

She turned her head away, hoping Ramón didn't see her waiting in the car. Even from a distance, she felt he was looking at her.

Ramón stood unflinching, unmovable on the hillside, a fixture in the neighborhood as long as she could remember. Nineteen years old, the same age as her dead brother Sal, who was a year ahead of José and three years older than Gabe, Ramón seemed to be revered by all the homeboys, and his family went way back with Gabe's family, the Almas.

Yet, Gabe knew that Ramón, unlike her good-hearted older brother Sal, was like a corrupt politician who didn't have his people's best interests in mind. Gabe remembered Petra saying Ramón was the highest functioning in a group of psychopaths. Sal left behind his daughter, Luz, who Gabe adored. Ramón, returning from jail, gained power by eliminating his rivals.

José trotted halfway up the hill as Ramón came down to meet him, and they talked. José nodded a couple of times, and she saw him go behind the picnic tables.

"*Cholo.*" Gabe watched José act like a yes-man, even though they'd agreed to tell Ramón they were through.

A year ago, past those elm trees, in a Middle Town initiation the homies jumped in José and Gabe together. She remembered the jumping-in ritual when gang members formed a circle around the two. Ramón said brother and sister had to last five minutes fighting against some pretty tough hombres, but when time was up, they didn't want to stop, so they kicked for longer. Ramón said the fierce brother-sister team passed the initiation better than anybody, going strong for ten long minutes. Sometimes girls got trained in, but José didn't let her—she was, after all, his younger sister.

Older brother Sal had blocked Ramón's power, then backed out and settled down with his wife and daughter, Luz. That was, until his murder. Although no one was arrested, their family couldn't be sure Ramón's followers didn't do the hit.

When José came down the hill, Ramón was next to him with a package wrapped in brown paper—probably Ramón's substances. She wasn't down for this. She was wearing the wrong color; she was wearing red, the rival's color. José had told her to always wear Middle Town's blue so as not to look like the Latin Pumas and get caught in friendly fire.

*Turn the key, and you're out of here.* Take off with nothing holding you back. She looked up at José, and he eyed her as if she should stay, as if he wanted Gabe to save him, to deliver a package.

"*Loco*, José, I've stopped! You said you'd get out too!" Gabe put the key in the ignition to go when a large, sinewy brown arm holding a cigarette reached in to grab her.

"I'd jump in on five men to kiss a face like yours." Ramón. He maneuvered his way next to her in the passenger's seat with a masculine grace that belied his size. She couldn't help but like the way his dark hair curled around the nape of his neck into a ponytail.

"I like a fresh face that doesn't get kissed a lot."

Gabe winced.

"Angel Gabe—in a fight, I'd want you by my side."

"Don't be stupid. I never shot anyone."

"What about when Fika hit you? I saw you reach up close to all near six feet of her, take her by the shoulders, slam her head down on the bar. Gabe, you were beautiful."

"She was drinking ... swung at me. You forget, Fika cut up my homegirl." What was Ramón doing, taking the chance of enraging Fika?

"I didn't forget. I saw you ready to fight for me. You're crazy, and you're my homeboy's sister, an untouched beauty."

Gabe pouted.

"Come here, gorgeous." Ramón pulled her toward him. He put his hand behind her head and planted a firm kiss. It had been a long time since a kiss had made her flush.

She started to push him away, but one of his thighs pressed hard against hers through the baggy gang clothes, the ones her aunt warned her not to wear. He gave her a hard look.

"Your friend, the one you got the car from, she's in trouble." Ramón held her shoulders.

"Petra." Gabe identified the counselor.

"There's action coming soon at her workplace from Fika and the girls because she protects you."

"What do I care?" she covered.

"Do this job, carry this, and I'll protect your Petra." Ramón pulled out another package wrapped in brown paper and thrust it into the space between them.

She took it, hating herself. She knew the scenario well: *chicas* do the dirty work and the time.

"I'll have more for you." Ramón was stern. Gabe's brain clicked on—he's dealing.

Gabe looked at José standing helpless nearby. "My brother, dragging me down again," she muttered. Petra had helped her stay away, stay clean. How did she ever think she'd ever get free? Did she dare to dream or think she was different than anyone else trapped in this life?

"Bring Gabe to my place later tonight." Ramón motioned to José.

*Ramón is hell's jester, an evil clown.*

José whispered something in Ramón's ear while looking over his shoulder at her. Ramón looked angry and shook his head. "I own you."

José looked around uneasily. He put the items in Petra's glove compartment.

"Snitch, and I'll get you," Ramón blared out.

Gabe quaked in her tennis shoes.

# chapter 4

RAMÓN COULD TELL YOU to go to hell, and you'd look forward to the journey. His place was halfway down Governor Street, half a block from the busy traffic scene at Fifth and Grand. She and José parked on Grand and walked to the front of the main house. Like many of the large, old homes, this one had iron gates posted as sentinels where the driveway and sidewalk met. The creaky noise of the gate opening startled Gabe. She frowned. Then the sudden backpedaling of her brother sent her grabbing his sleeve.

"You need to go in alone. Ramón wants you because it looks like boyfriend-girlfriend to cops casing him out."

*I'll have more for you. Dealing? Suddenly Ramón's words made sense.*

José waved at her to go forward. She inhaled the scent from an outdoor barbeque next door where she heard a family preparing dinner.

"Wait here for me!"

"No. Post office on Grand in fifteen minutes. Bring the package."

"José, I'll be out in five."

José shrugged.

She mumbled under her breath and shuffled onto the cobblestone driveway. A waning crescent moon crept over the brick house roof, lighting it to look strangely austere and traditional. Actually, the main house looked like not a bad place to live. The large jutting cornerstone atop made her recall Heathcliff's home in *Wuthering Heights* she read in lit class.

Ramón stepped out of his small side unit, a shabby hovel, and walked up the driveway to meet her. His navy plaid flannel flapped open in the wind to reveal his biceps through a white sleeveless T-shirt, making his physique looked massive in the night. A sensuality radiated from his brisk confidence and evenly measured stride. Strength emanated from his direct eye contact and smile. She decided to play into it.

"*Cómo estás*, Gabe?" He took her hand and led her through the door into his squalid, windowless unit.

"Not bad."

"Sit down." He gestured to the long, worn couch that faced a giant television set, the most prominent possession in the dusty studio setup. From the kitchenette, Ramón fetched a Lemonade Light. He had a Corona Extra for himself.

"It's a Light. No alcohol, no calories for you." He smirked.

Gabe placed her drink on the serape he used for a rug, a multi-color blanket made of natural fibers like they made in Mexico years ago, unlike the acrylic fabrics they sold everywhere today. "You say you'll give Petra protection."

"Yes." The sight of his flexed arm muscles alerted her. She gulped. Then sounds of a pro boxing match on the television turned her head. She liked the underdog. She followed Ramón's gaze to the set. For minutes, Ramón acted like she wasn't even in the room, making him enticing, unattainable.

When he didn't give her his attention, she wanted it. She wondered how his muscles felt to the touch and decided to count to ten. If he didn't talk, she'd walk.

At the count of seven, he spoke. "I hear you're quite the boxer."

"Yeah, who says?"

"Not your brother. The word is out. You're the only girl the hombres ask to fight them."

*Was he mocking her?*

On the screen, the contender took a sharp right and fell against the ropes. She stared as he struggled to regain his balance.

"Like you don't know. Ramón, you plan to use me like you do José. Like you did Sal!" The boxing celebrity rallied and was back in control of the round with a crisp right hook to the new competitor's ear. The ear began to bleed.

"No, Gabe, I tried to protect your brother Sal. Another group put a hit on him. I keep José close so he's safe."

"Right."

"What, Gabe?"

"Right, that's a powerful right punch."

"Don't evade me. I help my people." He stomped his foot on the serape. "This hole is a castle compared to my home." His mobile rang, and he crooned into it though his lip had a cruel upturn. A female on the line. Like a wild coyote, he smelled weakness, stared, prepared to strike.

The top-ranked boxer mounted an offensive. She had to make a quick comeback.

He hung up, moved over, and put his arm around her. She slid away.

He tried to put his hand on her back and massage it. She pushed it down. Undeterred, his hands moved up to her neck as he worked out a knot. The gentle pressure of fingers powered by sculpted arms caught her off guard. She half-sighed. He closed in on her lips. Then the roar of the TV crowd rallied her to be alert.

"You were raised in a dump, so what else?"

"All right. You're the scrappy one."

"How many rounds do you have in you?"

"The home in Mexico where I grew up was a shack. A couple of the steps leading to the porch were only loose, crumbled-up concrete. Inside, me and my sisters and brothers, four kids in all, were tied up with a rope. Some days handcuffs. My *padre* secured us and went to work drunk. My *madre* left because of him."

"Padre drew a line between him on the couch and us kids. He'd drunkenly bellow, 'If you're a man, you'll come across this line; if you're not, you'll come with me.' He'd beat us if we came toward him, and he'd beat us if we didn't."

"He beat you anyway?"

Ramón nodded. "Right before I came to California at age eleven, I was tortured in a Mexican jail for a drug deal gone bad—"

She looked at the boxing on the screen. Ramón was known for fakes and feints.

"Mexican police had me down. One sat on my head. Another held my neck. Then a third poured soda down my nose, filled up my whole freaking nose. I'd pass out, then wake up again. Until I almost drowned in my own boogers."

She felt a tug. Could she tell him she also felt helpless when the enormity of her dreams and expectations pressed down on her? No. He was a coyoté, with scary connections, seducing more than just her. "You've come far from that. Now your illegal deals are north of the border."

Ramón looked as if she'd given him her lethal left hook.

Never would she be the *novia del jefe*, the leader's girl, but she admired his resilience.

"Gabe, don't dance like you're in the ring with me." He pressed a six-inch-long, brown paper package in her hand. "Tell José I'll call."

Stunned, she pushed the stuff back at him too late and opened the door.

The evening was cooling off, and the breeze felt good. She looked down and fingered the package. She might throw it in a dumpster, and no one would be the wiser. She knew the boxing match was over. They both missed seeing who won the fight.

# chapter 5

*R*AT-A-TAT-TAT. THE SOUND OF gunfire was an intermittent rhythm in her mind. Gabe tapped her foot at a bus stop near the Grand Street Post Office, one of the last remaining pay phone booths in the county, and a stop-sign intersection with billboards gang members used for target practice. She and José waited for Ramón's buyers to pick up the package.

The government billboard and the one for Colgate toothpaste were evenly punctured with bullet holes. Gabe felt a certain dark satisfaction that the perfect female models now had deep, glaring cavities in their teeth, even though their mouths might whisper intriguing secrets.

She tapped her foot. At the downtown studio gallery, Rosa was waiting to show Gabe her original sculpture works and paintings by the blacklisted Cuban abstract expressionist artists. Gabe had said she may stop by. Rosa may be worried about her.

She flinched, remembering Ramón grabbing her. She didn't know much about love, but she knew you didn't have to know someone before you kissed them because you got to know them better once you did.

José was shaking. What was up with him? Had he sampled the merchandise? "I'll go to college. Get José free." She spoke the vows aloud. "Be an example for my niece, Luz."

"You're valuable to yourself and others—you're loved." She frowned as she recalled one of the affirmations Petra had given her. What would Petra think of her now? She'd parked the community center counselor's car around the corner.

A loud yellow sedan with its muffler dragging and some new homies inside bounced around a corner. José bumped out from the bus stop into the street to see who.

The white wannabe homegirl, Candy, leaned out of the SUV's back window and waved. She wore big gold hoop earrings with her hair up in a pop-diva twist. "Hey, Gabe, listen to this. It's your favorite!" She turned up the volume of one of the rap songs they cranked up real high at the center to make Coach Al mad.

Gabe had to laugh even though she didn't want to. Another of Candy's attempts to make Gabe like her.

"See you at the concert!" Candy looked hurt for a second when Gabe only gave a nod, and Gabe winced. Gabe wanted to help her, but she couldn't show weakness on the street. Candy's single mom worked long hours and didn't give her much attention. Her mom tried but couldn't get her out of the mostly Latinx school district.

A silver SUV with big wheels honked to get Candy's yellow wheels moving along.

José's smartphone rang in her hand. "Answer it!" José back-pedaled to see the silver SUV.

Gabe shivered, listening, waiting. The phone line was dead. A voice seemed to mumble the instructions. Did she imagine it, or was it the breeze? She heard only the faint sound of a voice whispering, "Luz, Luz," in an eerie lullaby with Spanish guitar. A quiet whisper again, reminding her of her lovely yet faraway niece named Luz. Was it their contact, or was the wind fooling her?

José ran over to her and stuck out his hand. His hand shook, and he almost dropped the package on the ground. His gaze begged Gabe to take it, but she turned to run away. Over her shoulder, Gabe saw José grab it and sprint over to shove the parcel in through the silver SUV's tinted window.

When Gabe was two blocks away from the drop point, she checked her watch. She planned before tomorrow's festival to prep for teaching self-defense class—chasing after her new life.

She could hear a faint voice inside, but she couldn't calm herself to listen.

"It starts in the mind." Gabe remembered Petra's counsel. Breathe. Pray. Her mentor's words broke through. Gabe could make a significant contribution.

"The contribution I made today isn't like the person I want to be. For me or my niece Luz." Where was her abuelita when she needed her? She whiffed at the air with her fist.

# chapter 6

"CIRCLE UP. I MEAN, bring it in." Gabe took a deep breath, placing her Everlast-gloved hand on slender hip as she quickly exhaled, snapping out of her surly mood to welcome the chattering young women into the drab, dimly lit community center room. With deep-set, moody eyes, she scanned through a printed packet of material, pursing her full lips and tossing brunette hair back.

Lifting an eyebrow at the giggling homegirls, she recalled the glint in Petra's eye when the community center counselor found Gabe working on the punching bag and pleaded the girls needed a self-defense teacher. She'd never let up. And Gabe fell for it.

She wiggled her toes enclosed in a worn version of the latest ankle-high boxer's shoe.

More than a sprinkling of feisty junior high age and older participants brushed by her, complaining about their math teachers, and she tensed her sculpted biceps and then focused to match her wits to her whereabouts. Teens, sisters, mothers—many younger than Gabe's sixteen-going-on-seventeen years—seemed to ignore the dusty wood floors and leftover potato chip bags in the corner. They noisily scraped chairs on the ground, dragging them forward to form a circle.

"Circle? I like rows," Carina raised her voice to get the students' attention.

"People get information in rows, but lives change in circles," Gabe spoke, glancing at her cheat notes. While at ease as the top student in her anatomy class, she now flinched at leading a self-defense workshop.

"A circle will work." One mother slid into her chair.

"I'm Gabriela. Call me Gabe, pronounced like Abe."

"Gabe, like Honest Gabe?"

Gabe ignored the heckler.

"What are those gloves for?" a student asked.

"Boxing." A respectful titter came from the girls. "First, you learn self-defense. Now, let's close our eyes and breathe."

A few girls slumped against the chairs.

"Don't lean back against the seat. Move toward the middle." She gave commands to "breathe in for five counts, out for five counts," and Gabe led warm-up exercises while stifling a resigned, sultry yawn from staying up late the night before.

"Who can tell me what is the root of violence against girls and women and the mindset that encourages it?" Gabe read from her notes.

"Anger," a girl puffed out between breaths.

"Meanness, Gabe?" Mamacita asked. Gabe's mother shifted in her seat. Gabe could tell she'd just had a good talk with Petra. Gabe's twenty-five-year-old aunt Olivia nodded nearby.

"Power ... and rape!" Carina shouted.

"Yeah." A shy teen let the word escape her mouth.

"You all know as well as I do." Gabe nodded. "Now, what is the first point in self-defense? Alertness. Close your eyes. Visualize how many windows in the room."

"Ah, four?" one tried.

"No. Anyone else?"

The women seemed stumped.

"Six. Observation is a key to your safety." Gabe firmly planted her foot. "Maybe you can do better here. Keep your eyes closed and describe the clothes of the *mujer* seated to your left."

"Jeans and a T-shirt." Carina kept up her snarky attitude.

"How'd you guess?" The young women laughed at each other for wearing the same combination. "It was a good answer based on previous knowledge. Now try to your right."

"Blue shirt and black skirt," Aunt Olivia said.

A girl garbed in a yellow top shook her head no and laughed hoarsely.

"I'm the one in the blue shirt!" Lupe chuckled.

"This class is nonthreatening. You weren't attuned to your surroundings—the room, your classmates' dress." Gabe lifted her arms. "On the streets, you better be wary. Goes for me too."

Another murmur in the crowd. *Had some heard about her troublemaking or emergency-assisting the clinic doctor?*

"Be your own ally. Some women are on power-and-shaming trips," Gabe shakily half read and then spoke out. "It comes from us blaming ourselves and each other. Feeling shame for our pasts—job failures, broken relationships, abortions, substances—"

Lupe looked up.

"We don't want to find self-destructive ways trying to handle shame by being uncooperative and quiet. We women have to understand the thinking of the culture, defend our-selves, promote change."

"Did you do this?!"

"Yes, Lupe, my brother José attended a breakout group to help with self-esteem, centering. Without violence. With God."

"God? On these mean streets?" A middle-schooler drew herself up to her full height.

"Who would this help?" Lupe looked around to read the room, landing on Carina, who joked, "What name do I offer up first?"

"You know it, Carina." Gabe laughed. "Lupe, a skit. You're babysitting after school at night. You have to walk home a long distance." Gabe circled her arm overhead lasso-like.

Acting like a babysitter, Lupe pretended she was headed home, walking around the circle.

"Hey, girl." Carina whistled. Lupe laughed.

"Yeah, babe." Gabe put on a cap and impersonated a male truck driver. "How would you like a ride home?"

Lupe looked behind her, and Gabe noticed her flushed face. She rushed away from Gabe acting as a driver, but Gabe closed in on her.

"Think you're going to get away?!" Lupe laughed at Carina's impression.

"Get in!" Gabe grabbed her. "What would prevent this?"

"The kid's parent should walk me home," Lupe said.

"Knowing bus routes. Save money for rides," Mamacita added.

"A car!" Rosa, the Afro-Cuban artist, added. She waved her scar from Fika's jab.

"Yes! A car." The women joined in.

"Never, never get in the car of someone you don't know. If you get pushed in, jump out." Gabe looked adamant. "Your survival odds drop a lot once you enter the vehicle."

At the door, Petra nodded and startled Gabe. Gabe surmised Petra had stuck her head in the door to affirm her for taking time away from the medical assisting internship and boxing. Then the mentor glided away mostly unnoticed.

"*Ten cuidado* be careful on the night shift. I can only imagine what you're going through."

"*Mi hija*, my friend was taking trash out in an office after midnight when a man stepped in, closed the door, grabbed her, but the woman hit him until the night shift rescued her."

"Bring her to class, Mamacita."

Mamacita nodded shyly.

Gabe pulled out a scowling dummy with straw hair and button eyes sewn on and placed it in the front of the room. "This is Bill."

"Bill or Willy?" a girl asked sassily.

"Give the dummy your own name, a name that makes you angry!"

"Yay, that'll work," Lupe agreed. A few women half cheered.

"Everybody, up. Find some space where you can move," Gabe said. "Think this is real. A bad guy is coming to hurt you. A man's weak spots are the nose and you know. Line up. Take turns kicking the guy right in the breadbasket."

"Oh!" Mamacita covered her face.

"My turn." A girl kicked too high and fell off balance.

"Keep your balance. Save your life, save someone's life."

Carina stared at Gabe and elbowed her friend. *Had they heard Gabe helped the clinic doctor save a homeboy's life? It was a secret.*

The young mother tiptoed up and whacked the dummy, which swung around backward.

The students squealed.

Gabe shook her ready legs and offered coaching to a participant who clamored for her.

"What about defense against a girl gangster? Show us the moves!"

"Can you, Gabe?"

*No. They didn't hear about her past with gangs?*

"All right! Is my kick high enough to hurt someone?" a kickboxer asked.

"Yes. You're a good kicker." Gabe looked pleased.

Carina and the kickboxer jumped up and down, empowered by kicking their assailant. Gabe gave a low chuckle at how eagerly the women completed the attack assignment and dismissed them.

After Mamacita left, Carina and a few junior high girls came up to ask Gabe if she'd train them again. A surprised smile spread across Gabe's face.

"Soon, please. We really need it," the youngest one begged. The other girls nodded. One winked, but Carina looked pained as if she'd had a dangerous run-in. Their mother winced hopefully.

"Yes, girls." Chattering excitedly, the girls left Gabe. What kind of predators were these girls running up against? What dark shadows might they face on the streets? She stared at them as they walked away. She knew exactly.

Gabe stood against the wall. "They seem so open." She was not always the professional they saw today. She didn't want them hurt for anything she may do.

# chapter 7

AT THE DÍA DE la Raza Freedom Day, a festival cele-brating a Latin American revolution, the jovial weekend crowd at the community college stirred restlessly. Warm-up bands didn't sound warmed up themselves, but the hot, peppery taste of steaming homemade chicken tamales ped-dled by student groups made the eaters salivate and clamor for more spicy fun. Even Gabe's wannabe homegirl, the blond gringa Candy, and Gabe's beautiful aunt Olivia looked excited by the momentum building in the crowd. Gabe had another reason to look forward to the next Spanish rock group invited for Rock *en Español,* Los Mixers. Ramón was the lead guitar player. She felt a rush followed by shame.

Ramón and a woman walked through the crowd toward the stage. Tall, lean, and dramatic, she looked about five-ten with long, straight, dark hair and a beautiful face. She had a burnished complexion and angular cheekbones, and the black lace of a bodysuit poked through the holes in the rear and knee of her jeans. Under the top of the lace bodysuit was a black bra barely visible underneath her red-and-plaid shirt.

Adjacent to her stood a marvelous-looking young man, six-plus feet, with long, dark hair and a nose that evoked a Mayan god. Silver jewelry draped him from his neck to his wrists, and the detailed tattoo on his upper arm was of the same branch-like design as the image of a garish black head on his gray muscleman T-shirt. He wore gold cross earrings and snakeskin boots. Ramón was always a knockout, but this time, the woman eclipsed him. When the lead singer had worked with the microphone cords, Gabe thought she was just part of the crew. Now, as the female vocalist jumped up on stage, it was easy to see she'd be the highlight of the act.

"Whoa. *Sí*," the singer breathed into the microphone, yanking it off the stand. She addressed the audience with a kick and an undulating move of the hips.

Long-legged, too tall to be a gymnast but possibly a jazz dancer, the artist's gently sloping rear showed no line between her hips and rump through the black lace bodysuit, and she rocked with the grace of a Mayan temple priestess. She was the lead singer, and he the lead guitar player. Gabe realized Ramón didn't see her. She had watched him flirt with a young woman in a T-shirt and jeans in the audience, but when he grabbed his guitar and worked his way toward the leggy singer, his electricity with her shot through the crowd even before he touched a note.

"*Buenos días!*" The female vocalist's dark eyes glaring out through hair parting, falling over her eyes, and cascading down past her shoulders to her curves. Her seductive gaze fell upon the crowd, compelling them to watch her every move. One buff janitor in the audience leaned around a pole to see and hear the band better.

"*Sí, bueno!*" Cheering picked up through the crowd, and they clapped and whistled in praise of her charisma even before the music began. She was the sensual charge, the sound muse.

Over on the side, Candy watched, obviously appreciating the sisterhood, the chemical connection between light and dark leaping from the stage. Her head ducked and weaved, whipping golden locks around her face, almost hiding her elation.

Down on one knee, the singer sprang up and, with a toss of her hair, turned to the second guitarist, wearing a black cap with skull and crossbones. With a playful pull, she yanked the cap off his head and placed it atop her head.

"Wow," she sizzled. She ripped off the plaid shirt, tearing it as she did, and worked it up with Ramón. She touched, almost grabbed, her own rear, dancing fast. The bass guitarist came crazily toward her with a cigarette dangling from his mouth when she sang about the *chichanga*, stubborn woman, running her fingers up her own neck, then on the black lace all the way down to her thigh. He tore the black cap back from her. Their sensual moves excited the drinking, dancing crowd.

Candy signaled to Gabe that she was enjoying the music, blending into the crowd now that she'd donned her black-and-white Cinco de Mayo baseball cap. She looked almost as uninhibited as the lead singer, copying every move of the vocalist's dance steps. Gabe smiled back at her, feeling happy about the joyful intersection of the cultural hoopla of street music and dance. Then she saw a homeboy push his novia down to the ground, yelling, "Sniper!" Others reacted with scream-filled shuffling.

Gabe jumped. Her heart fell. *A gun? Not here.* The band stopped abruptly. There was no stopping her as she ran forward. Her ears buzzed from the gunshots and the amps.

She and the bass player knelt beside Ramón, collapsed flat over his guitar.

Hands reached in to help her lift Ramón's crimson-spotted T-shirt from the wounds where the bullets had entered his head and neck. A band member tossed her a thick flannel shirt. Gabe pressed it hard over the open wound. Ramón was half conscious, sucking air, straining to speak.

"Get a blanket! Call 911!" Gabe yelled.

Candy indicated she had 911 on the line. A buff on-site janitor and some students ran to the health center. Men and women glanced nervously over to the street corner, where a group of loud homies flashed gang signs.

Preteen and elementary school children who had been close to the stage quickly got up from the ground where they had fallen flat when the hail of bullets burst.

"Payback." A young homie dusted dirt from his baggies.

"It could have been anybody." His girlfriend wrapped her arms around him.

*Why hasn't the world stopped turning? Would life end when Ramón was shot?*

A gang of six or seven homies moved over to the quad, a scary, strange battalion. One short homie carried a boom box blaring Mexican songs. The oldest had a swagger and a scar on his face that ran from ear to chin. In the back of the ranks, a young man sat tall in a wheelchair, rapidly spinning his wheels and moving at an even pace with the group.

One of the bicyclist's pursuers jogged up to the stage carrying the gunman's vehicle, a yellow bicycle. "Dudes in a black Chevy caught him at the corner and tried to rub him out."

Gabe took Ramón's brown hand and felt for his pulse like she'd been taught in CPR.

Gabe looked around. "Why aren't paramedics here?" All the while, Ramón's warning sparked her fears. Had Fika hired the hitman, Middle Town rivals?

"911 said they're coming!" Candy shouted, backed away and ran for safety. Gabe was grateful to her for once.

People stared at Gabe, and it occurred to her that she must look like a qualified medic while attending Ramón. Medicine was second nature to her. The YouTube videos on how to treat gunshot victims flashed through her mind. She'd meticulously studied the human body in anatomy and physiology, so she knew she'd done everything she could. The shirt tourniquet held back the blood from the neck.

A face pressed in. Gabe flinched and her shaking hand let go of the bandage.

# chapter 8

JUST THE OTHER NIGHT, Gabe dreamt she was stepping around land mines with her brother José. Then her nightmare took her to a Mexican jail, where Ramón was imprisoned in a clean, hotel-like room complete with fresh flowers on the dresser. She and José had to swim across a body of water to help him bust out.

What did it mean? A dream was a passionate hope or fear? The priest at the chapel in the hood taught that St. John interpreted dreams—if only she could have that spiritual knowledge. Even if she didn't yet, the vision had braced her for this trauma. The brain is an amazing thing.

"Where's the doctor? I can't hold this much longer." Gabe's eyes darted to the bass player.

The audience and band members pressed closer. The leggy female vocalist kept her distance. Gabe realized the blood-soaked flannel shirt was the one this captivating señorita had shed in the act. The singer looked at Gabe as if she distrusted her for being so close to Ramón.

Aunt Olivia broke through the crowd.

"*Vámonos*. Let's go! Remember what I said about getting in trouble?" Gabe prepared to leave. Then she saw José. She gasped as he leaped up next to her and Olivia, kneeling by Ramón's side and taking his hand.

Ramón seemed to be losing consciousness fast, but the blood flow had stopped. She felt her heart surge with hope. José leaned in.

"How did this happen?" José shook. Gabe saw his strange connection with Ramón.

Gabe raised an eyebrow.

"Back up. Help is coming." Diego, the bass guitar player, shouted to José.

"No, I won't back up. You weren't backup protection for Ramón!"

The bassist gave José a sullen look.

The janitor and students ran back from the health center without a single supply.

"You got muscle," José said to the janitor. "Let's move him away so he can breathe."

"Come on, Gabe. Let's leave." Olivia pulled at her said as the janitor and José positioned themselves to pick up Ramón which Gabe protested.

"Why can't we pick him up?" José was shouting.

"Troublemaker. You want to move him from the crime site?" Gabe stared him down. "Get chased by the law and the gangs?"

Clenching his fists, José pounded one hand into another like a boxer whose opponent had said *no más* in the second round, ending the fight early and leaving him still hungry-mad.

"Last chance, Gabe." Olivia pulled at her.

Ramón raised himself on one elbow, then fell back. He whispered, "Fika—".

45

Gabe strained to hear. "Fika or her brother?"

"I heard Fika envies you, Gabe. She doeesn't get noticed like you." José fidgeted.

Ramón looked far from being "the Provider," the man who joked about competing with pharmacies.

Olivia repeatedly clicked her phone. "Listen when I say to leave Ramón the OG."

"I can't leave him without medical help. This is what I do." Gabe's medical calling her teachers had noticed was strong in her in a crisis.

"*Hermana*, Ramón needs us."

Gabe motioned to José. "All you do is press down on the cloth, stop the blood."

"Hold on." José was shaking again.

*Could Gabe get away to join Olivia?* She smelled the smoking-gun threats, the danger of retaliation. If she didn't follow, she'd be in the center of a fiasco.

The sound of emergency sirens cried out, signaling the approach of the paramedics. She looked at Olivia one last time to see a black crow pick at the trash in the stands and then become disgruntled. It flapped its heavy wings to become airborne and circled the sky above the crowd.

*What was taking so long?*

# chapter 9

THE PARAMEDIC VAN CAREENED around the corner toward the college. Gabe watched the van pull over at the entrance of the college access road. The driver and his partner exited the vehicle to check equipment in the back.

"Whoa, gringo, where you going?" A voice boomed from behind the men.

The driver whirled around, instinctively reached for what looked like a gun he wore concealed on him, and scanned the scene. The paramedic shouldn't be carrying a gun, but lately, some medics in gang territory were resorting to packing for self-defense.

Gabe thought maybe he'd had arms training and was certified. It seemed he had parked by the grove of maple trees, as some were hired to do at events, but he should've stayed behind cover until a police car came to mark the area. He slowed until he could assess the active shooter situation. No police cars came onto the property to offer protection. Several gang members moved toward him. An ambush.

From across the grounds, the burly janitor weighed the consequences of running toward the trouble.

"You hear me? I said, where you going?" The Puma Rafa snarled, with his crew advancing on the paramedic. A paramedic walked around the side of the ambulance, so they were now seven on two.

One called Wheels, a bare-chested kid in a wheelchair, spun directly into the action.

The driver looked at Wheels in a nonthreatening manner, offering to make peace with the gang. Gabe heard EMS body armor could protect them from stabbing injuries but not much from gunshot wounds.

"Rafa, gonna let them go?" A Latin Puma in the back shouted up to the leader in front.

This mouthy Puma would be happy to let him bleed out. Ramón had said the Pumas hit her brother Sal—could she believe him?

"I won't let go," Rafa said and moved up in the driver's face.

"Yes, you will." The driver faced him. "We treat everyone. You too if needed."

The police siren sounded in the distance. "Why didn't the cops come earlier with the paramedics?" *Medics aren't safe here.*

Rafa heard the sound and relented. The driver wrestled Rafa to the ground, took a sharp object from him, and held him down.

Gabe jumped as she saw Wheels spin around gun-to-gun with the driver, motioning him to drop it.

*First rule is "Do no harm."*

The driver held fast, but the meanest Puma now signaled the homeboys. "Let him go."

Wheels put the gun away.

"Gotta go." The driver hopped into the ambulance and drove it up close to the stage. He and his partner positioned a brace and backboard behind Ramón's neck and spine.

"Family? Ride with us?"

José faltered then nudged Gabe toward the van. She felt the press of the crowd, some undoubtedly gang-affiliated, inching closer. The encroaching crowd lifted her up, pushing her against the van. To avoid being crushed, she scrambled in.

*Let me out.* She looked for help. No one responded.

*I'm my own advocate.* But the burgeoning mass blocked her way out.

From the side window of the van, she saw the driver trying to control the crowd as he walked backward toward the ambulance. The attendant seated her near Ramón who was connected to machines. Ironic she should be looking at abstract impressionist Cuban art now, not Ramón's distorted human form.

The paramedic started to work on a semiconscious Ramón as she watched, trapped in the coffin-like van.

Then, a policeman came right up to the van, opened the back doors, and peered in.

"Assess, stabilize, ascertain level of consciousness, get an IV line going—" The driver checked in with the attendant.

"How're you doing?" the medic asked.

"Pain." Ramón was mumbling.

"If you can say that, you're okay." The medic touched him.

"I feel dead," Ramón whispered. "Maybe I am dead."

Onlookers jammed against the ambulance. The policeman left the back doors half open.

"It's your emergency, not ours." The attendant snapped at an annoying spectator then seemed to bite his lip, as if they'd taken enough risks. "We wouldn't be any good for anyone if we got ourselves killed now, would we?" Gabe nodded in agreement.

The paramedic began to close the back doors, but people pressed up against the doors. Two vulture-like, black squad cars sat to the side of the quad with officers moving them away.

In one quick burst, an arm poked through the opening between the doors. An arm, a gun, and then a face masked with a bandana—determined. Ramón's body lay a few feet away from Gabe. She screamed and threw her body back away from the gun, but the gunman didn't aim for her.

A loud boom, boom, boom! and Ramón's body jerked, reacted to the pelting of lead. Gabe froze stiff from the shock of the gun blasts and the thought of a corpse next to her.

Then, a third shooter came from nowhere and popped a clean shot into the masked hitman, who fell to the ground. She couldn't believe it—the craziness. One paramedic covered Ramón's chest with a sheet, leaving his face uncovered. He got out his instruments to check for vitals. The other paramedic held out a hand to help her back out of the van. Into the frenzy.

# chapter 10

P ANIC. ABOUT A HUNDRED frightened, crazy-mad people yelled and collided. No one had expected a second attack.

Gabe couldn't stop shaking as she looked from behind the ambulance shielding her. She'd seen the gunmen. One gunman with his face covered by a bandana looked her in the eye with his finger on the trigger but didn't shoot.

More squad cars sped into the area, followed by a park ranger car and a crime scene investigation van. The cop cars parked crossways to each other, setting up an informal line that separated the crime scene from the people watching.

A young Latino officer and a redheaded one jumped out of one of the cars.

Gabe backed further away from the ambulance, although she heard a moan from inside. She tried to slink into the crowd.

The officers hadn't been there to see her help to stop Ramón's blood flow.

"Get on your knees and put your hands behind your head." The young Latino officer waved at a suspect looking for a fast way out.

"What's your name?" The older cop took out a smart-phone from his pocket. Cops with guns and smartphones froze over fifty people as possible witnesses.

Gabe looked around a-flutter.

"Lie on your stomach, hands behind your back!" The Latino cop frisked a suspect caught escaping and pulled out a handgun from inside the suspect's baggy pants.

"You got it all wrong." The homeboy's voice raised. "I carry that for back up."

The wild-eyed homeboy wore a black cap decorated with a colorful emblem of the sun god, looking similar to the emblem that Ramón once showed her on the silver-plated spoon he used to carefully measure drugs. Ramón had bragged he got it from the drug lords in Mexico.

She was drawn to the image on the hat: the brown-skinned warrior had a broad nose, huge white incisors, and a split red-and-green tongue, which stuck out as if to jeer at the world. Brilliant green ornaments nestled in burnished gold earrings made the emblem stand out even more. Light beam reflections spiraled up, combusting with the hot, dry air to explode into a leaping warrior. *Was it real or in her mind's eye?* As history said, innocent young maidens were killed as sacrifices to this Mayan sun god. Those maidens who had flaws like she had were fed to the idol as appetizers or thrown off a cliff into a pit. A voice aroused her.

"I didn't say to lie down. Get up and on your knees!" The young Latino cop helped the black-capped man struggle to his knees.

*Gabe's warrior vision disappeared.*

Close by, another homeboy watched; his dark hair was neatly combed and fastened back into a slick ponytail. He seemed savvy and better dressed than the others, wearing an oversized black shirt with white, vertical ribbons. "Not hiding anything."

"Your buddy here was hiding a .45."

Ramón's band members were sectioned off in the crime scene area with their equipment still half packed to go. Diego stared ahead with a blank look as if he were in the trance of a solo while the sexy Latina singer moved away until a cop motioned to come back.

Gabe took a last look as attendants slammed shut the van's doors and sped to the hospital. This time, they weren't moving out of the area until it was safe.

On the ground, still hopelessly swamped, police interviewed witnesses one at a time.

If she'd left with Olivia, she wouldn't be in this mess. She'd be with Rosa surveying the art gallery, or with Olivia sitting on a nice, fluffy couch, meeting some Disney personnel for a job, as her aunt had hinted.

Gabe looked over to where Olivia had exited.

"Want to run for it?" The janitor signaled her.

"Yeah." She readied to sprint. But ... she could hear the sound of a helicopter.

A pale-skinned, redheaded officer burst into view. "Everybody, put your hands over your heads."

She looked to see if the more sympathetic-looking Latino cop was close by.

"Sir, did you see who shot the man?" The redhead barked at the janitor.

"Which time?" the janitor replied.

"Good question, sir. Think you're smart?"

"No, sir. Teenagers."

"Any distinguishing characteristics? You know, specifics, scars?"

"The first one was riding an orange bicycle head down—"

"Orange bike—the most important item. But, as you know, bicycles can be painted."

Gabe got ready for a long night.

"Homegirl, maybe we can ask you some questions at the station." The Latino held out his hand to her. "Ride along with us. I'm Louis, and my partner looks as if he'd be named Red but he's Jeff." Sweat came out of Gabe's every pore. A greasy strand of hair fell across her face. She had taken a shower after the exhibition fight, but that was another life.

# chapter 11

G ABE FELT LUCKY GETTING a squad car. Then she wasn't so sure as an officer loaded others into a van. "Don't talk to each other. You got a gripe, an idea, keep it to yourself!" The officer's voiced carried over to her. Now she wished she were going with the group—with the friendly janitor and the band members. Was she separated because she had a view of the sniper?

Now it was almost as if she'd gone down for the count, and she was struggling to get to her feet. She saw a cop asking questions of José. José seemed to have a mystical calm about him, or perhaps his shock was as profound as the night their brother Sal died in the drive-by. José's real brother had been murdered, and now Ramón was critical— tragedy struck again.

Officer Jeff shouted to José about his involvement. Gabe looked back to see José herded into the van.

Her family was separated. Her aunt was safe, but she and José vulnerable. To think that only half a day had passed since her successful boxing exhibition, and only minutes had passed since Olivia was lining Gabe up for a costume designer interview. Should have known a professional design job was a fantasy. No matter how hard she chased after a new life, bad vibes came after her, as if she were a trouble magnet.

Officer Louis surprised her by politely opening the door of the black squad car with the blue lettering Gang Detail for her. The car door got caught on coarse branches from dead palm trees lining the edge of the quad. As the branches obstructed the car door from opening, the cop pulled them away carefully so as not to scratch the paint. Gabe wished the cops would've acted as gentle with her brother.

She reached out to support herself with her arms on the car door as she lowered herself carefully into the deep pit-like back seat. And Officer Jeff began to interrogate her.

"Is the victim in the ambulance your *novio*?"

"No. Why?"

"Love is a motive strong as money. People have been killed for a lot less."

*Didn't they know it?* Gabe thought of the guy who owned the pet shop on Nineteenth Street who had been shot for the thirty-seven dollars in his cash drawer.

"Your parents beat you?"

"*Mi padre* was deported."

"You in a gang fight?"

"If you call being first generation a gang."

"So, Miss First Generation, how do you explain this?" Officer Jeff pointed to her cuts and bruises on her arm and wrist.

"From boxing."

"That's an original excuse." He nodded to his partner Louis. "Says she's a boxer."

It didn't matter if they believed her or not.

Officer Jeff let out a low whistle. "Could be the lady is a tiger. If she's a boxer, better watch out." He turned to her. "Now, you may be telling a lie, but you look pretty strong, pretty and strong." His glance made her uncomfortable.

"Jeff likes boxing." Officer Louis interrupted, stating his words flatly.

*A good boxer doesn't flail at the air—she wouldn't hand out just any jabs.* Gabe played with the thin seat cushion.

"Tell us more about the shootings. You were up close."

A series of emergency calls came over the car radio but not for them.

"When you're a cop, you want activity." Sitting shotgun, Officer Jeff sighed. "The other day we had a 'crazy' on his roof. Shot at police when they tried to help him. So, one of our men had to take him down."

*Take him down? Off the roof?*

"Yeah, shot him in the leg." Jeff blabbed on. "Won't be causing any more trouble."

"Tranquilizer gun?" Gabe blurted out.

"Not trained that way. Hear the funny story about 'Your Name'?" Officer Jeff was on a tear.

"Don't. Not funny. Don't tell her that story." Driver Officer Louis spoke to warn him.

"I don't mean 'Your Name'—Gabriela."

She tensed. Gabe didn't like the way "Jeff" said her formal name.

Tight-lipped, Officer Louis drove straight ahead.

"One of the homies is stopped by police officers. They want to check for tattoos. The officer in charge asks this guy, 'Do you have any tattoos?'"

"Gabriela won't like this story."

"Then, Officer Louis, I'll tone it down. . . The dog says, 'I have 'Your Name' tattooed somewhere you won't look.' Well, the officer is offended at his disrespect. The officer thinks. 'How does he know *my* name? Does he really have *my* name tattooed on him?'"

Gabe scowled.

"The officers are angry. They think the guy is a smart mouth and handcuff him, frisk him, see he really has the tattoo 'Y-O-U-R N-A-M-E' on his rear!"

Gabe squirmed uncomfortably.

"Dog says he was the only one in the whole barrio to have this. Now there's a whole gang, and each one has this same tattoo. You know which gang?"

Gabe dropped her head so her chin touched her chest. Her long hair fell forward.

"Every barrio kid knows. You know?" Officer Jeff pumped her for information.

She could see Officer Louis's cheeks blotched red.

*What made him think he could talk like this, like he was in the men's room, and she didn't even exist?*

Officer Louis took a corner too fast, making Officer Jeff slide toward the car door.

"How do these 'public servants' get hired?" Gabe muttered aloud. She shut her eyes. She had rights, and she'd show them, but not now. Truth is she'd be better off in the streets than this hearse—the squad car, an easy target for a pig-hating psycho, a homie being initiated into a gang told to kill, or a gang affiliate after cops turning someone into a snitch. If cops knew the hits put out on them, they wouldn't take time to tell crass jokes.

She was cold, and the hard, bumpy steel of the back seat was a reminder nobody cared about her aches.

A message came in over the car radio, and Officer Louis made a quick left. "Picking up a girl for violating curfew."

The car stopped on Fig Street. She knew the dark street well. For recent shootings.

They pulled up to see a pretty young Latina wearing a midriff blouse and more makeup than she knew how to skillfully apply. "Desiree. Twelve. You're supposed to be home hugging your teddy bear by ten p.m." Officer Louis was ramped up. He asked her in Spanish: "You went to a party and came here with your homeboys?"

"No, I went with my sisters to a movie. I don't go out."

Desiree's white platform shoes, lace see-through midriff top, and flared pants gave her away—a teaser, as the party crews called them. She flashed for the hombres at the parties while the pleasers did the stripping and more. Teasers and pleasers. Gabe knew both types.

"If we knew it was Ladies' Night, we would have brought you girls a blanket for the back." Officer Jeff acted like an overgrown adolescent. "You with a gang?" he grilled Desiree.

"I don't hang with gangs."

"You don't call it that old term."

"My older sisters are home now, I swear. I stopped to text some friends."

Gabe nodded to her.

"How come cops think we're bad?" She looked at Gabe like she was her homegirl.

"You're only twelve, Desiree. You're almost home, or we'd cite you. Someday you'll understand we care and protect you." Officer Louis acted sympathetic.

"You care about me? This seat jabs." Desiree winced and frowned. "Don't tell my mom. She doesn't understand."

"You're at a crossroads in life. Maybe tonight you got lucky," Officer Louis growled. He threw a blanket into the back seat. "Maybe we're going to have a little talk with her."

"I have 'family' here." Desiree pointed at an apartment.

The car stopped in front of an A-frame with chipped paint. Desiree got out and slipped Gabe a ragged flyer for a party. "See you there?"

"I doubt it." Gabe crossed her arms.

"It'll be a rager." Desiree stepped out.

Gabe slid down low in the seat. A draft of cold night air wafted into the car. She pulled the blanket around her.

# chapter 12

THE SANTA ANA POLICE station was buzzing. Over twenty witnesses arrived for questioning, with none of them happy about it.

"Don't move," Officer Louis directed as he guided her onto a shaky metal chair. "We're saving you for last. Martha has her eyes on you." He motioned to a fleshy lady cop with streaked silver hair.

Gabe tossed her hair back and gave her a cool, defiant look. Inside she steamed. It was a big clue to separate her.

The slim, blond cop in charge of the paddy wagon paraded her group into the front of the line. She looked trim with hips pressed tightly into the uniform beige belted pants and fitted shirt. Like a boxer, she took good care of herself.

"Lean and Mean," Officer Louis whispered to Gabe. "Lean, mean, fighting machine," Coach would say. With an athlete's build, she probably worked out four or five times a week.

The big woman they called Martha was her opposite. When Martha bent over, the flesh of her stomach spilled out of her pants in large ripples.

"Let's move it," the trim cop said while herding her passengers into line in front of the interrogation desks. The cops' attentions were on the suspects and identifying the gunmen while the victim seemed forgotten. What was she caught up in?

From across the room, Ramón's band member eyed her as if he caught her looking at somebody the wrong way.

"Bad guys may be here, and we're going to kick your behinds to find out." This was Lean and Mean?

"I got plans, lady." A local vendor tried to move up in line.

"You *had* plans. Tell the truth, and we'll get you home." Martha lined them up with an almost motherly touch.

The witnesses looked more relaxed, but Gabe knew Martha was only playing good cop, bad cop. *Mind games. Trying to get us to trust her.*

In the station, investigators motioned them one at a time to the desks.

"May I call Mamacita?" No one paid Gabe attention.

Diego passed, jolting her elbow, giving her another look. "Keep your mouth shut, sister. You don't know anything."

"What are you talking about?" Gabe felt a cold, hard jab at her back. He prodded her along with an instrument that felt like a knife. How did he get that in the station? Or had he poked his finger into her back?

"If you talk, it'll come down on José."

"*Mi hermano?*"

"*Si.*" He pulled the object back in his coat. *A gun, unnoticed by the law?*

The investigator at a near table eyed them, then walked away. Gabe knew what not to do or say. Her mind set itself to erasing details. One gunman came from the South Side Longos gang, wearing a red-striped shirt. Was the other

Fika's brother? She deliberately changed facts in her mind so she wouldn't snitch on Gangstas and Pumas.

She could confront Diego to find out what he was covering up, then she could piece together the story.

When she sat back and looked at the scene, the cops looked like parrots. Quick-talking red faces and beaks, blue necks, upright posture, green bodies and ruffled feathers—curious, squeaking, mimicking the words, engaging in basic nonsense. Eyes closed, Gabe thought of birds chattering in a tropical forest. *How I'd love to be there.*

The cops narrowed it down to a few generic facts fitting a thousand young men.

What looked like an easy ID with multiple witnesses was becoming a circus of various acts all in one ring. Martha reminded her of the Fat Lady Lion Tamer with no problem throwing her weight around, even when interviewing the big janitor. She pulled out a file of photos.

"See if you spot a familiar face in here." She gave him a sloppy wink. "We have here over fifty percent of the members of any given gang."

The janitor's head was down. "I can't help you." Martha checked to see if his face showed any flash of recollection but he looked seasoned.

Gabe watched Officer Louis chat with a suspect in the main room. Clearly, he had a talent for watching things quietly—expressions, gestures, details—things others often missed. He squinted across the desk at a well-dressed affiliated *hombre,* who stared uncomfortably down at his Italian leather shoes.

"I got no reason to be here." The man fidgeted and swore under his breath.

Cool Officer Louis didn't say anything. In the lights she noticed more wrinkles on his forehead and a glint in his steel blue eyes encased in eyelids, showing crow's feet when he grimaced. His calming ways made her want to confess she felt caught between cops and gangs.

Officer Jeff stood over the suspect. "This guy knows more than he's letting on!" Then he went at him emotionally, blowing his cool.

Officer Louis glared at him to shut him up, then stared back at the suspect.

"You know Ramón."

He blinked.

"Again. You know Ramón. I know who you are. I know what you did."

The well-dressed suspect crumbled. "Let me go, man. I'll talk."

That was quick. What would her own breaking point would be? Lean and Mean called for Gabe, and she went to the desk thinking—a cop is just another person in uniform paid to do a job by the hour.

"What's your name?"

She paused as if she didn't understand.

"*Nombre.* Name." Lean and Mean pointed at her.

"Gabriela. Gabe."

"Hey, Gabe, you know the victim. Tell us about it."

"*No se,* I don't know."

"You're bilingual. Let's just go into a quiet room, and talk just the two of us."

Gabe followed Lean and Mean.

"Tell me about the first shooting."

"*No se,*" she said. It was a half-truth.

"We can legally hold you forty-eight hours." Now she had her interest.

"Mamacita—" Gabe almost bit her fingernail.

"You were a bystander—"

"*No se.*"

"You're family to a victim?"

"Not family. Only heard the shot." Gabe's shoulders slumped.

"Let's get to the point. We think you're the one."

"No gun."

Lean and Mean was lying to get her to talk. Petra had told her: cops will say or do whatever they can to get what they need. Now, here it was in her face. Somewhere she'd heard a tale of how they like to arrest young homies: for every kid up to seventeen years old they put behind bars, the government rewards them with a lot of cash.

Lean and Mean grinned, showing a gold filling.

"We'll make it easy. Immunity, protection, less time."

"I don't know anything."

"If you don't tell us, we can take away your family's legal rights for residence and send you back to your country."

# chapter 13

THE OFFICER STARED GABE down. Gabe gulped. "It's my country too. I'm first generation, and I didn't do anything." She plain didn't know her rights, and she didn't have money for a lawyer.

Where was Diego? He'd been standing over by the restrooms where he had bumped into her, whispering to the lead singer. She could feel their poison glances now.

*I know boxing, but who are the contenders here?*

"What are you holding back?"

"Nothing."

"Says here you're the one who ran up to the stage to help the victim?"

"I'm a medic."

Lean and Mean rolled her eyes. "Did gunmen shout anything or flash gang signs?"

She looked exasperated. "Get the detective in here." Lean and Mean's voice snarled over the phone.

Detective Louis opened the door, came to the table, and stared at Gabe.

Gabe lifted her eyebrows. *Detective? More than a cop.*

"Look at this like a card game—the more cards you have, the better game you can play. Would you take a look at a 'six-pack' photo line-up of Tiny Rascal Gang, TRG?"

Gabe was poker-faced. Cops were off track singling out TRG, one of the most harmless groups.

When Lean and Mean showed her six mug shots of one of Middle Town's rival TRG, careful to keep a poker face, she perhaps saw one familiar face.

"Young lady, it's an incomplete puzzle. Do you recognize anyone?" Detective Louis took over. "With puzzles, you start with the border, frame it in, set the boundaries, and then you work toward the center pieces. So here we are."

*He knows I can't snitch and point to anyone. Are cops trying to see if I flinch?*

"Hey, we know about you." Detective Louis quietly searched her face.

If someone made an identification from the mug shots, and she didn't, it may make her look like a liar. Diego and others could put the blame on her anyway.

"We know enough to hurt you." Lean and Mean attacked.

Gabe shrugged. She had to play the waiting game.

Lean and Mean called Gabe's Mamacita to come pick her up. When Mamacita arrived, Gabe knew she was on her side but sorrowful at her being detained.

"Gabriela doesn't belong here!" Mamacita shook her head.

"She belonged here." Detective Louis smiled wisely and handed her his business card. "Call me if you have any concerns or information."

Easy as that, Gabe was released.

Mamacita was quiet in the car.

Gabe wanted a hug or at least an arm around her, but she wouldn't show hurt feelings. She was frozen in the game. Not the way she wanted to act around her loyal Mamacita.

In the Ford Sedan, Gabe felt happy and strangely secure—Mamacita and her. Like she was a little girl again and she had someone who could always protect her from her fears. As if Mamacita never had any health problems, and she didn't have to be afraid of her heart ticking like a time bomb, then going off someday when Gabe needed her most.

"Long day?" Mamacita's voice softened. "Hungry?"

"Yes. Yes."

They pulled into the Taco Primo stand.

"Two enchiladas, two tacos, with rice and beans. Two ice teas."

Her favorite. She sighed. She isn't mad at me.

Mamacita told the girl at the window to keep the change. "I love you, but I'm disappointed, Gabe."

That hurt.

Mamacita pulled out the business card from the detective. "Detective Louis."

Here it comes. Gabe braced herself.

"I'm thinking you missed something ... this is one strong, friendly man with a steady job. Your homegirls should give him a call. He's a better man than those *cholos* they run with."

"He's a little serious. Aunt Olivia might like him." Gabe chuckled. Mamacita tried to make good things happen for the homegirls.

Mamacita cruised slowly home, never tipping the speedometer over twenty-five miles per hour, an enjoyable snail's crawl. Today, all the lights were green on McFadden.

# chapter 14

"**B**USINESS IS WAR," AUNT Olivia tells her customers. "Never overlook the value of the right uniform."

When it comes to fashion, Gabe's aunt Olivia had more know-how than anyone. In Olivia's favorite place, the sewing room, she designed her sophisticated fitting rooms decorated in silk for customers wearing her own designs and new imported fashions.

With the high cheekbones and sculpted good looks of a model, Olivia had been selected to merchandise a new line of European creations. Fashion-forward women around town knew of her intimate, intelligent way of fitting the silks, cottons, and linens to the figure.

Artists and actresses from Santa Ana's downtown cruising section and the uptown business district found themselves especially comfortable in Olivia's setting. In the privacy of her home, they could get even the most personal articles properly fit.

Olivia had Gabe over to pin the dresses for alterations. She always liked to invite her over when unusual guests came to the house, as she was a good bouncer if any of the customers got out of hand.

Matty, a cabaret singer who worked on Grand Avenue, slinked out into the hall in a black, fitted evening slip— catching everyone's eye.

"Marvelous," Matty smoothed the lines over almost non-existent hips. The naturally flat stomach looked smashing without the expected tender curvatures.

Dramatic black seemed especially suitable with Matty's orange hair. Doris, a thirty-year-old performance artist garbed in padded leotards and platform shoes, nodded in agreement.

"Alluring. Artistic." Rosa approved. With her arm healed, she'd been sculpting again in the downtown art studio with others of Cuban-American and Caribbean-American background.

Gabe hugged Rosa.

"Missed you at the gallery, Gabe, but all's forgiven." Rosa nodded. They both knew Ramón was half-alive in the hospital only because Gabe had saved his life.

Then Gabe admired Matty's fit, glancing sideways and trying to suppress a slightly envious smile, feeling her desire to have her body adapt to the sleek, svelte look.

"Gabe, why don't you see if we can alter this suit for Doris?" Olivia motioned to Doris who slipped the suit over the leotard: first, the jacket had to be let out in the shoulders but hung loose at the waist, and then the skirt fit nicely, showing off the legs.

Rosa searched the racks to find the right threads to match her Afro-Cuban vibe.

Gabe knelt on the floor, straight pins in her mouth, adjusting the fabric to measurements—with both she and Matty staring into the tall mirror. She pinned the jacket easily, indicating where the shoulder seams might be let out.

"How does the skirt feel, Doris?"

"Good Gabe, but it might be a bit tight."

Paying close attention, Gabe carefully smoothed the lines of the fabric over Doris's body—she feared touching too closely. Olivia helped pin the finishing touches.

"Doris, that's going to be fab-u-lous!" Olivia stated the obvious.

"Gabe." Olivia's voice was barely a whisper to Gabe. "Your shoes are like the ones *they* wear, black Vans. Look at your makeup and your hair sticking all the way up."

*Olivia should keep quiet. How could Olivia lecture with pins in her mouth?*

Kinky black hair bun sprang out as Rosa whipped around to see Olivia fuming.

"How is it running in the street, my niece, looking behind your back all the time? Hope you like daises because you're going to be pushing them up. Boyfriends tell you it's good when it's bad and bad when it's good. You can't dress like those gangbangers, or you'll stick with them." Olivia strutted away.

Rosa arched her eyebrows.

Gabe gave Olivia space because she knew she spoke from a bad experience a year back when Olivia dated a guy fresh out of jail. Her tough guy spent a lot of time asking around about a former con man.

Locals answered Olivia's man, saying he should look for the man at the market where he works. The next day, Olivia's guy shot him in revenge for snitching on him, sending him to the slammer. Olivia didn't know about his plan to use her, but she almost did jail time as an accomplice. When she spent weeks doing community service, her design business offers slowed down.

"I'll take you to some nice parties where you'll meet some sweet guys … yum, now this cotton jacket—stay away from the trouble-makers. I'll give it to you—you're the medium sample size." Olivia kept up her patter of auntie counsel.

Matty came over to ask Olivia to adjust the dress strap. The dress wasn't a misfit. It was the uneven padding Matty had in her personal areas that made the dress hike up.

Matty eyed the jacket Olivia was promising to Gabe. The shoulders were broad enough for both of their ample builds.

"That's classy. What color would you say that is?" Matty touched the fabric.

"Real red. You can have it if you like it." Gabe handed it over.

"Oh, it's not in my palate."

"Reds work with every color combination," Rosa advised. "Passionate."

Gabe nodded, but she'd learned not to ask too many questions as some had ideas about their colors. Matty, for example, wouldn't wear a garnet red color without being in the winter color category like Gabe—a strong, dramatic presence expressed by gem colors: red, violet, blue. Little chance of that with orange hair color. Matty seemed like an autumn whose coloring would be accentuated by fall colors of olive, forest green, brown, beige and orange.

"Dear niece, like Rosa, you have real potential with design—you work with fabric and colors so well. My girls like you." Olivia changed her tune.

Matty smiled, looking over at them.

"I have this friend at Disney, Gabe dear—in wardrobe," Olivia continued. "Maybe you fix yourself up, go and see him. You won't have to teach those self-defense classes for long. He'll find you costume design work for college money.

Then you can become the Latina doctor your teachers think you can be to make us proud."

Gabe half believed her. Matty gave her a wink. Gabe felt cared for, even though her aunt Olivia took the craziest times to spout her words of wisdom.

"I like teaching self-defense and doctoring."

"You have talent. Don't hang with your brother and his friends, I don't want to be seen with you if they're around. If I'm with you, they think I like those thugs. More people may end up shot or dead. Maybe me too. I'll set you up with nice guys. I'll call the man at Disney."

"You might like it, darling." Doris winked charmingly from across the room.

"Try me." Gabe fingered the silk blouse that went under the red jacket. Like Petra wears but better.

A dream from the night before flashed into her mind. Ramón and José tempted her, and she realized she didn't care at all for them. Instead, the Gabe in her dreams wanted her clothes tailored to fit out of attractive fabrics. In the dream, Gabe strolled by the coast, fresh and breezy, looking gorgeous, teeth gleaming in a huge smile, neck cocked back, hair with lowlights and highlights, shaking her lustrous, brown hair off her shoulders, infusing flecks of bronze from her hair strands out into the air like those stunning models in hair color commercials.

# chapter 15

BEFORE YOU GO OUT the door every morning, you pray, "God, I hope I don't get shot today." It's already in your mind. You stop, take a breath, check around, eyes alert. It could be nothing you did; only a gang initiate wanting to make a mark.

Gabe walked across the street to Aunt Olivia's house early in the morning to ask if she'd go with her to the boxing exhibition at the community center—that's when she saw this bird with a big head and cloudy eyes perched on top of her roof. She stared at it mean-like.

The bird was clearly an owl—its moth-light, brown feathers were streaked with white flecks that looked like snow—and when it swiveled its head around to stare at her, it gave her a look more piercing than Fika's mad dogging.

Their eyes locked, but she stared it down. This owl was wary, but it looked too tired to fly—maybe it had a big hunt the night before.

"Hey, owl, must be tough. Everybody thinks you're old and wise. But I know better. You're just as slow as anybody after a late night."

Last year, on a high school field trip to a museum, she saw a great horned owl, stuffed and stiff. The lady-guide had a badge pinned to her tight pantsuit. She said, "An owl can rotate its head all the way around in a circle. It does that because it can't see sideways—it has no peripheral vision. The owl also turns its head around to see what's behind it."

Gabe laughed just thinking of such a ridiculous sight—a pompous owl with its head spinning foolishly around ... and around ... and around.

In a fight, you've got to know what's going on behind your back or have eyes in the back of your head. That is, unless you're an owl.

She turned and went home to tell Mamacita about the owl.

Mamacita smiled at her and stopped hanging the clothes out to dry in the inside stairwell. The new Santa Ana city code said clothes couldn't be hung up outside in the fresh air to save appearances in the community. Mamacita frowned when she realized that she had not made Gabe feel guilty enough to come back home and help her.

Gabe looked the bird up for her in the cheap encyclopedia set she bought from José when he went door-to-door to raise money for the freshman class (the year before he dropped out of school). Her owl may be a burrowing owl. They like to use the abandoned nests of hawks and crows. This one was using the old crow's nest on top of Aunt Olivia's house.

"Don't tell Olivia." Mamacita raised her arms in a warning.

She shook her head "no" in agreement. With Olivia's flair for the dramatic, she would freak and screech something like: "No, you didn't see it on top of my house!" She played the role of Olivia for Mamacita, her arms flailing wildly, saying, "We will have bad luck!"

The owl was just like a tired, early-morning barfly. Petra would be sure to remind her, when the Native Americans saw an owl, it meant the spirits had come for a soul—someone was going to die or leave. That happened to Sal, and he died. Abuelita left. Then Papa left. Gabe was angry about these horrible separations. Her stomach felt all scraped up on the inside.

"My friends would say it's 'a premonition,' but I don't think that. I'm not afraid of death," Gabe whispered into the morning. She followed Olivia's advice not to dwell on Ramón.

Mamacita said the owl stopped by our neighborhood to tell us we're all going to die someday. At least, it thought to come early in the morning so we had time for a full day of living. Coach had comforted us about death. We had Sal's funeral and several burials for homies in the hood who died of ODs, drive-bys, or suicides. What worried Coach about death in the barrio was that, most of the time, the young ones made worse mistakes than the older ones, even though he tried to counsel them. Gabe remembered she and Abuelita learned about Jesus rising again after dying for man's sins: they sang hymns at church and learned about eternal life.

No, Olivia would not want to hear about the owl. Walking back across the street, Gabe saw the owl flap its wings, fly off the roof, and hit the ground with a thump.

Down the street, the eight- and nine-year-old boys from the hood hauled old, beat-up tires up to the hill and behind the trees above the busy corner. They made a game of watching and waiting for important cars to drive by, pushing the tires over the hill, rolling them dangerously wild down onto the path of the oncoming vehicles.

Cars would come to an abrupt halt, drivers screaming insults, yet they rarely saw where the tires came from since the boys had safely hidden behind the full tree branches.

Gabe peered at the boys and dog from the small window in her cubbyhole room. Young boys bent frames, knocked shocks out of alignment, and occasionally shattered a windshield if the tire popped up high enough when it hit the car. Older ones with scars inside nothing seemed to heal would collect the huge rocks, mini-boulders.

About a week ago, the first grader next door was crying loud enough so the whole neighborhood could hear he wanted to go ride bikes on homemade ramps with the kids across the street. Ernie, the neighbor's dog, barked loudly and jumped up and down. Boys made two ramps to go up one and down the other. Some little boy moved the back ramp further away than normal after his friend next door went off the first time. When he was getting ready to go down the ramp the second time, he went face-first into the sidewalk and cried. The lady across the street came running over. "Hurry, Gabe!"

Gabe gave first aid and comforted the scared kid like she'd been trained to do, and he surprised her with a hug.

When Gabe got to Olivia's house, she tripped over boxes of clothing merchandise samples she had packed up to send back to the designers. Olivia's fashion event was over, and she looked relaxed yet bored, changing channels with the remote control.

She agreed to turn off the set and come with her. Before they left, she offered her a shot of vodka and orange juice—a screwdriver—in a Styrofoam cup.

"You know I have a boxing exhibition later today." She shook her head. Olivia, and Olivia poured her a glass of water.

"Ever thought about giving up this stuff?"

"What stuff—the orange juice or the vodka?" Was Olivia joking?

77

"Neither. The Styrofoam," Gabe held up the cup. "Think about it. "Styrofoam will last longer than the human race."

"Are you trying to be witty, Gabe? Or are you lying?"

"My science teacher says it takes five hundred to a million years to break down. It won't decompose. Just breaks into pieces."

"Into pieces? Like you... in the ring?" she jested.

"Careful. Unless you want me to try out my new jab on you."

"On me? Not in a million years."

# chapter 16

GABE GRABBED HER TOWEL, ducked the fans, and ran out of the community center ring. Olivia followed. How humiliating—the exhibition match was a throw-over. An embarrassing win. She barely had to execute what she'd been practicing with Coach Al, and her male opponent seemed floored, defenseless. He'd been imported from another community boxing program and had a good reputation. Just no footwork.

The key to having the upper hand over a male contender was quick footwork and rapid, devastating delivery—left hook landing on his chin, right jab finding his nose. Her mind and body connected in the zone.

One, two, punch, one, two, punch, repeat, and quickly, it was over with the small neighborhood crowd on its feet screaming for her, "Gabe! Gabe!" She felt thrilled, in top form, the fair winner. Coach Al went to find the loser's coach. Still, a nagging worry: *Had she been sent a pushover on purpose?*

She didn't know how she found herself in a sweat again.

Bounding up the steps to Petra's office above the boxing ring, Gabe's niggling mind-swirl ran wild. She'd whispered to Olivia she didn't see Petra at the exhibition. Gabe sensed trouble. Ramón promised to stop Fika's vendetta against Petra. *Never believe it until you see it.*

Gabe couldn't see the stairs at all. A light above the stairwell was knocked out.

She nervously got her last cigarette out and then flicked it away. "Done with that," she grumbled.

Her mouth was dry and not from the boxing match. Gabe hated herself for trusting Ramón to protect Petra in exchange for the delivery of his package of contraband. She listened to her feelings (oh, how weak)—bang!—betrayed. Knees high, she bounded up the steps.

The wooden railing up to the second story didn't look quite right—heavily scratched and partially colored with what looked like blue, yellow, and red drips from a spray can. Olivia looked at Gabe as if she knew what was up ahead.

Before their eyes was a grand assault. Someone had painted huge, garish, black symbols over everything in Petra's office.

Whoever did this had tagged—not merely tagged, more like trounced on, destroyed property—evidence of certain hatred. Deep incisions covered vicious, indecent lettering and black gang symbols. Scared veins streaked over the Navajo white paint, spelling "Las Locas Latinas." She'd seen a lot of words on buildings, but never such a disrespectful violation of this boundary, neutral territory—untouchable as gangs vowed.

Was Petra hurt?

Jagged pieces of broken glass from the window above the door lay on the ground before their feet, and loose fragments clung to the open circle, probably from a large rock. The effect was crystal-like: shimmering fragments, shattered particles of glass holding the sunlight and reflecting it, forming a maze-like spider web in the sunshine.

Papers and furniture cluttered the room; obscene tagging spurted like blood on the walls. Petra, in a dazed, maddened, nervous state, searched through her desk, tossing papers, broken glass, and dirt out over her head and into the air. She pulled at the smartphone, drawing it near and shakily dialing 911. "I'd like to report a break-in—"

"You good?" Gabe asked. "Your face is white. Sit down."

"I feel green, like I'm going to lose my lunch. I hate this feeling: you want to get sick but won't." She hurried off to the tiny bathroom in the back.

Gabe followed after her and heard her flush the toilet. The door was ajar.

"I know who did it. Fika went after me, but she turned on you."

"*No importa.*"

"I thought I earned you protection."

"Counseling notes gone." Petra wasn't the only one who didn't want her secrets in Fika's hands. The drawers were spilled out, and articles tossed or thrown everywhere.

Petra opened the door of the bathroom, swabbing her face with a paper towel.

"Better?" Olivia asked and put her arm out toward Petra.

"My stomach muscles ache." Petra settled down into her chair, holding her midsection. She shivered and shook.

For sure, Petra didn't have the guts to be a boxer, only she'd never tell her that.

"*Las palabras*, the words," Olivia looked at the angry scribbling on the wall. "Insulting, offensive. The usual tagging, the expletives.

Fika is touched in the head. She'll stand puffing, yanking on a cigarette, like she's going to suck the life out of it, looking down, and tapping her feet like a raging bull."

"Reminds me of someone I once knew, Gabe—"

"Not me. Not now anyways."

"Fika's trying to stop you," Olivia said.

"Fika's off." Petra diagnosed the situation. "As long as the struggle's been with us, there's always opposition to people who want to work hard and work together to get ahead.

"Women can heal bad words with good, such as courage, freedom, forgiveness. Grandmother gave me wisdom to pass on." Petra stood.

"Petra, that's your Navajo grandmother?" Gabe looked forlorn. "Abuelita left us. All she gave me was a mind-picture of stained-glass church windows and the two of us praying together."

"That's sweet, bittersweet, Gabe. You feel abandoned." Petra's knees wavered.

"Grandmother's words are for you, that is, until you see your own abuela. I still have an image of Grandmother hiking with me in the mountains of Palomar. To this day, in the ground are buried, circular, round-shaped work areas carved by Native American women working shoulder to shoulder in an assembly line, grinding maize, corn, into tortillas. They also ground mortar for pulverizing mesquite beans, acorns, and wild oats. Side by side, they knelt at the meal trough. I remembered what she said— women working together, a place of power and healing, sweating elbow to elbow with each other, grunting with strained muscles."

"Your memory—what's to show for it?" Gabe kicked at a window shard on the ground.

"Corn tortillas and clay pots for the village. Grandmother said: 'Listen to the earth, one must do the will of the earth. Feel the clay in your hands; move as the clay wills and not as you choose. You must do the will of the clay, and only then will you have an object of true value, of power, or reverence for the Great Spirit.' Grandmother converted to Catholicism but kept the Indian ways. She said she'd always been worshipping the One God, Jesús Cristo."

Gabe rubbed her temples. "That's the name Abuelita and I prayed to together, and I felt at peace." She looked at Olivia, who sat pensively.

"If only there was somewhere broken girls could go after the barrio when the heat is on or after getting out of prison." Petra looked lost in reverie.

Gabe dropped her chin and prayed that even as she might clean up her life, the girls in the community might rise as well.

"Sounds like a homegirl heaven. We'll leave it to you, Petra." Olivia elevated the mood. They laughed tensely until their ears picked up the sound of police sirens.

"Don't count me out." Petra gathered herself up and folded her arms like a squaw. "Go, get. Come back later. My door won't be closed."

Gabe scooted out with Olivia, sirens blasting in her ears.

# chapter 17

THAT NIGHT, A LOUD knock sounded at the front door. Gabe heard Mamacita gingerly pacing.

"Police!" Official voices shouted and the pounding got louder.

Gabe had no idea where José was. She went to the door and motioned for Mamacita to move back and let her handle the door. It was Lean and Mean, with her gold filling shining in the moonlight, accompanied by her male partner.

*Where was Louis, the friendly, young bro detective?*

"You didn't tell what you knew." Lean and Mean on the attack.

Gabe's ears started to ring as if she heard a gunshot. It was one thing getting hauled down to the station, but it was another to have them come into her home where Mamacita, she, and José lived.

"We talked to the others, and your story contradicts. You know one victim and possible suspects. You assisted a known dealer."

"I'm a medic, bro—"

"Gabriela excels at medicine. She'll be a doctor." Mamacita's eyes and the corners of her mouth drooped, but she looked like a fire lit inside her.

"Mamacita, now's not the time."

"Don't bring that trouble here."

"Your girl is the trouble." Lean and Mean smirked.

"Your Louis, the detective, is not a good match for Gabe's aunt Olivia or any of the homegirls, after all."

"You're in a fantasy land, ma'am. We're not here to see if the slipper fits Cinderella."

Gabe knew Mamacita didn't get the sarcasm.

"We're not taking her to the castle. Princess Gabriela just got a free pass to Juvenile Hall." *Oh, Lean and Mean.*

Mamacita whimpered.

Gabe's head fell to her chest.

When Gabe closed the door and put her arm around her mamacita, she heard her forlornly praying: "Dear God, what has happened to our family."

Gabe's insides grated as she shuffled out.

The black-and-white stopped at the back entrance of juvie. A female officer escorted her to the incoming fish—or newcomer—entrance where she was processed. The officer lined up guys next to the girls: the regular Hispanic crews with a few Asian and Samoan bangers, as well as a few lost-looking white kids mixed in.

Hands clenched behind backs, they walked in a procession, not allowed to talk or to break the line formation. Gabe tried to read the thoughts of the girls in her group. Through whispers, she got the word that one was a third-timer and not to be messed with and another would be out in a week, so if you wanted to get word out to the outside, she was your carrier—free, if you knew her, for a price if you didn't. Still, another carrier was in the T building, the section for the worst offenders, juvenile hall's own little hell. Gabe hoped to be out in a day or two, so her spirits were bright.

A supervisor led her and others out into the yard for exercise. A counselor ran her through a battery of tests and questions. Throughout the juvie facility, Gabe worked out her studies and homework in her head. Her academic thinking broke even the tedium of mealtime and the unpopular restricted walking regime.

*Discuss Hamlet's "antic disposition." How would this change in character affect his relationships, and how does it contribute to his despair in his famous "to be or not to be" monologue?*

The question from Gabe's AP preparation essay tests jumped out at her, and she wrote in a journal for a half hour. She started to let herself into her own life.

The white noise in her head quieted down. She breathed deeply with mindfulness. She waved away the despair with happier thoughts of the community center girls, her boxing, her medical assisting, Mamacita and Luz. Despair could lead her down many avenues; like Hamlet, she considered the path to end it all but knew she could never hurt Mamacita like that.

This had everything to do with the fact that José had gone and lost it. As his kid sister, she knew José had brains and heart to spare, but he never seemed to use them together in working order. He was mad for a fight before, but after their brother Sal was taken out, José was crazed in a way that made him an unthinking slave to the gang. Sal's murder turned her kind brotherly adviser away from a saint into a guilt-ridden dark angel, errand runner for Ramón. Gabe recalled José screaming out at a supposed apparition while dreaming of a vengeful Sal: "Are you an angel or a demon?"

Even to imagine Sal as a spirit was terrible for Gabe, so she kept down her heart and swallowed the call-note of dark dreams. Sal had a wife and baby Luz when he told Ramón he was through being a gangster. When he quit, the gang thought Sal might betray them, so a gang shot caller put a hit out on him. Sal knew it might be coming because once, before he met his wife, Ramón talked him into riding with him. When he drove next to a victim's car at a light, as soon as it turned green, he drove by and—

*Someday she'd save Luz.*

More than the cramped walking to meals, Gabe dreaded the isolation.

Rain pounded on the roof of their tight cubicle, and she felt like a jungle animal in a cage. She thought back on the afternoon when she arrived in unbearable heat and wondered how the temperatures could swing so dramatically. Now all she had for warmth was a thin blanket. The cells seemed like vaults, with neither circulation nor heat.

*Focus on what you'll do when you're out of here. In the ring, Gabe rages poetry. When gloves go flying, she's a brilliant artist.*

She enjoyed inking phrases and sketches in her journal. One shooter's face started to take shape in her drawing until she almost violently erased it. Discipline thoughts.

The time seemed to pass slowly, and she could hear her heart beat rapidly from anxiety and cold. Waiting was the worst, and she kept hearing familiar-sounding voices. Her brain was tricking her into believing rescue was imminent, but instead, she could hear only the continual patter on her cell roof. At home, the rain made her feel clean. Not here. Here, the rain was another clear reminder of how trapped she was, stuck in her own head, helpless to even make a

restroom run when needed if it wasn't perfectly on sched-
ule—after meals and before breakfast.

When she got to walk outside after mealtime, she saw
the skinny green spruce trees and a patch of sky up above
and between the buildings. She had seen the sky only twice.
A girl had pointed out the group from T-building returning
from the medical station and said it was maybe the only
time they got outside that week.

She noticed the girl flipping her long brown hair and
laughing in the sunshine as if she wanted to soak in as
much as she could before returning to the quiet. Talk in
the hall was a couple of girls in T sat in a cold cell for seven
months. If a night was hard to bear, what would almost a
year be like?

*Pobrecita, poor little one. Mamacita.* Gabe couldn't
bother with the guilt of her cherished Mamacita finding
out her *peccadillos.* This was a world Mamacita was mostly
sheltered from, even though her stiff fingers ached making
tamales to save for Gabe's college money. In heaven, someday,
Mamacita would see the things she didn't like about Gabe,
but maybe there and then, she would understand.

She shook her hair out from her pillow. It had been only
a day, although the rainstorm had made it seem so much
longer, and she could hardly wait to join the chain gang
march to eats.

The girls sat eight to a table with Lorena, an inmate who
was waitressing because she had earned three points for the
day. Girls with one or two points were rewarded with some
popular tasks and early restroom passes. Gabe knew Lorena

would be discharged the next day, so she listened when the waitress nudged her to look at a new girl.

"This girl just came in today, and she says there's word on the street about you." Lorena's tone was conspiratorial.

"You a snitch? Homies are talking. Bad stuff." The new girl ranted.

"I said nothing to nobody." Gabe was adamant.

"They say you left your homeboys—and those guys are now on probation and putting a hit out on you."

"No freaking way." Gabe slammed the table.

"Can't be." Lorena leaned in closer, defending Gabe.

"Keep moving!" an attendant shouted to the waitress, who turned to help someone else.

"Nobody likes a snitch, a snake!" The newcomer hissed at Gabe. "Watch your back. Diego is talking smack about you."

"No!" Too late, Gabe turned away from the new girl.

"You are road kill." The girl spit out.

The other bed in Gabe's room at juvie still seemed tousled but empty by nightfall. She came into the room and slammed her body down on her cot. It was less than a week before her big fight and then her final exams in anatomy and physiology. Still shaking her head over what the new girl said but not naive to its implications, Gabe looked despondently around her empty room-for-two. A shimmery silver specter appeared under the other bed's covers. A rustle of the sheets. A roommate playing tricks on her?

"Hello?" Gabe's voice echoed back. "Nobody fools Gabe." Gabe ran and patted the other bed down. No one. Hmm, the bed was warm and smelled of lavender and citrus. A waft of air curled above. Air from the floor heater?

She wilted into her bed and tried to count sheep. She hadn't wanted to be one of those girls who acted tough saying they'd been to juvie, and she didn't feel so tough now.

That first night, she slept for a time like her world was calm, and then some flicker of thought would send a flinch through her muscles, and she jerked awake.

Gabe then drifted into a deep sleep. She dreamed she ran her fingers along the pieces of an old baseball puzzle in a box on the nightstand and began to assemble it. With any large puzzle, she separated common patterns into groupings and then joined pieces of one color to form the boundary, similar to Officer Louis's detection puzzle theory.

"Aha!" She squealed when she completed the solid green boundary. She remembered to follow a word or a logo, here some letters, there a giant hand. In the foreground, the wings of babies; in the background, an imposing ladder to the heavens; on her lips, the tune of Led Zeppelin's "Stairway to Heaven." Wasn't it Jacob in the scriptures who climbed up through the clouds on the stepladder to heaven? Painstaking but rewarding, the puzzle-making process gave Gabe some peace of mind. She fit piece after piece until the obvious shape or design was constructed from each section of similar parts. Section by section, the area took form, and she finished the faces outlining a mural of a chorus of angels.

# chapter 18

GABE WANTED TO ESCAPE the bad feelings rising up in her gut from her juvie stint. Clutching the flyer Desiree gave her in the cop car, she read: "Club Jupiter, Rock *en Español,* Latin Hard Rock, Best Mexican Rock Bands North of Mexico, Beautiful *Chicos y Chicas, Todos Los Domingos.* Guys and Girls, Every Sunday." Desiree's party looked like the place she could find Diego and stop his threat before it got around and she'd have everyone gunning for her.

Gabe sensed her aunt Olivia didn't want to let her go alone since shady characters could show up at Club Jupiter, but Gabe said she'd meet her aunt at another party later. Maybe José would come to the club. So fresh after the shooting, Diego with other band members released from jail would be there, as well as some bad actors. Anything could happen. Yet Gabe felt she could convince Diego not to let anyone put a hit out on her.

*Showtime.* Her stomach fluttered. She picked out a pair of frayed jeans and then put them back. Too relaxed. She dressed in her tightest black pants with slightly flared bottoms and slipped her firm arms into a tight, white cotton top that tied at the midriff above her tan, bare stomach.

Looking in the mirror, clouded over from her *mamacita's* shower, Gabe saw the face of an older teenager. Had she aged since Ramón's shooting and the near miss from the spray of bullets? She had escaped death. "When you cheat death, death sits and waits for you," she chanted at her reflection. The old saying bounced back from the mirror and hit her hard in the face like a left hook. It jarred her memory, and she felt tense from the bad vibes.

Were her self-defense students—Carina, Lupe, and the others—keeping out of trouble or did they see the action? Why was her stomach still fluttering? She bent down and reached past her panther tattoo to fasten the strap of her new white open-toed sandals. Would it work to kiss Diego firmly on the mouth and tell him how she hadn't talked to the cops—no matter how the cops made it look?

"I'd never snitch on a homie," Gabe practiced aloud to the mirror. Diego would apologize for his threat at the police station.

Mamacita poked her head into the steamy bathroom. "Very pretty, Gabe, where are you going?"

"Out for a while." Did she sound believable or would Mamacita ask again?

"You just got home. Can't you stay? What's more important than family?"

"Aunt Olivia's party at Deborah's." She winced at the half lie. Well, she thought, maybe twenty minutes of it.

"Olivia's party." Mamacita sounded appeased.

Gabe knew she'd like that. Should she feel worse for bending the truth?

If Olivia wanted Gabe to come to her party to meet her clients and Congresswoman Deborah at the Sanchez's elegant hilltop home, her clients may be cool. Though she felt sure

Olivia would want her to be sensible, to talk to some boring gringo wearing a suit. She grabbed Olivia's sample jacket out of her drawer, just in case she party-hopped.

One last check in Mamacita's mirror, and she saw in her darting eyes how thoughts of danger possessed her—in her waking and sleeping hours. She closed her eyes and, on the insides of her eyelids, saw red streaks. Then when she squeezed her eyes real tight, she could see only a wash of the color red, only like someone had mixed it with water, and for some reason she couldn't stop her tears from flowing. How much longer play acting?

Mamacita thought Gabe cried because she hated being locked up overnight at juvie. But no, she could take that. She texted her brother José to see if he'd meet up, then left for Desiree's party.

She looked down on the concrete sidewalk to see a dirty, trampled ad for the flyer party, promoting "Bad Boy Bill, Massive Sound ... 100% Bust Free," and now it didn't seem as much fun as she thought. Then, a block before Desiree's Club Jupiter, she noticed a toothless middle-aged man with a placard sporting: "I Need a Beer—And That's the Truth!" Laughing, she thought she might tell Ramón and José about him. At least the guy was honest. She had her goals and intentions. Why had those losers popped into her brain? *Let go.*

She poked open the door to Club Jupiter. The thin straps on her white sandals slipped, and she reached down to fix them, then took a deep breath, lifted her chest, and slinked into the room. Two of Ramón's homies stood near the entrance; Diego and the band members would hardly recognize her looking like a real chica. Why was José sitting close to Desiree and smoking at the bar? They waved her over and ordered her a beer. Gabe laughed at Desiree filling sugar into the saltshaker to trick a distracted José into sprinkling sugar instead of salt into his margarita. She looked askance at her brother smoking.

"Hey, man, cool?" José said to friends who walked by.

At ease in spite of the wild dancing going on in the dark section of the club, she tried not to stare, but kept stealing short looks at the pulsing, throbbing mob. The flyers were right: "Southern California's Hottest Place-Seductions!" Tonight's scene may prove the phrase meant more than the name of the headliner band.

The men were big names in the city. They ranged in age from about twenty-three to twenty-eight years old, too old for the girls. They wore baggy pants and shirts but with an elegant texture or flair—not your average street look. Some of them had their hair neatly pulled back into slick ponytails, almost Indian style, and others had buzz cuts cropped short with a goatee. The richest ones from the homes closer to L.A. or outside the area had two-toned hairstyles with thick, blond bangs layered in front of medium-brown straight locks. Why didn't their styled look attract her? She considered flirting with the more athletic-looking ones.

Was any girl in the dark place over eighteen? Free admission for girls, of course. She knew most of them from the barrio, church, and school. It had been months since she'd been hanging, especially at a place with club attire like this. Satin crop tops in unusual colors but most often black, bare midriffs, and hip rider shiny shorts—the brighter, the better. One dancer wore a shiny black leather get-up with links and loops. The loveliest girl wore her thick, dark hair up and danced smoothly in an ivory cotton halter top. Unlike the others, she left something to the imagination. Even the fleshly ones looked at her like she was precious, yet she was also lost in a pit of vipers.

Two girls in the ninth grade, fourteen-year-olds Vita and Marta, faced each other dancing on a tabletop and copied each other's moves. As the music pumped out, males and females rocked to it. She closed her eyes at the scene before her.

Vita didn't seem the type. Didn't she pull an A in algebra? Now, she was proving she knew a lot more about statistics and measurements, not to mention chemistry.

"Look at me," Marta hissed as she copied Vita's motions, twirled, and went off into her own routine, swirling her hips sweetly to the music. She didn't have any choreographed moves, and that's what seemed to charm her audience.

The men whistled.

Feeling embarrassed for her, Gabe thought to invite her to be a student in her self-defense class, but Marta looked oblivious. Would Marta even remember this night? She leaned over to whisper to a man in the snake pit.

*You'll regret that.* Gabe's stern look was for the young group. She checked around for Diego. She didn't see him. Darla, Desiree's sister, was dancing in another area.

"Darla's here too." Gabe got back to José, still with Desiree. "Darla." Gabe called and waved. Was Darla shimmying up to an available *cholo* who seemed to want to step into Ramón's shoes? With Ramón gone, homeboys may be positioning to take over as leader, and their girlfriends stood by their men.

"Gabe, homegirl." Darla looked very protective of the man and her territory.

"Desiree said to come."

"Of course, she did." She gave her a "hands-off" look before dragging the new man away.

Another visual sweep of the room told Gabe her self-defense students hadn't arrived at this one. At least so far. She took in a breath.

Gabe felt the air temperature turned colder. Chilled in her little white top, she put on the sample-size red jacket from Olivia. It may help to summon up thoughts of her aunt. Tejano, Texan-Mexican music, blared over the DJ's speakers. Desiree, José, and Gabe giggled; the Tex-Mex accents sounded so funny. She tapped her white, strappy-sandaled foot to the beat.

What was Cheep the Snitch doing here? Was the mousy homeboy named Cheep for ratting and mishandling money being snubbed as usual?

In another room off in the corner, men switched channels back and forth from soccer to boxing. She was feeling tempted to join them to watch sports when she felt a large presence come up behind her.

"Margarita, *por favor.*" It was Ramón's dog, Diego. Everything she wanted to say came to the surface unspoken: *Diego, I was loyal and shut up with the cops.* But she couldn't get a word out.

Diego looked stern.

"Uh, you know, I didn't say anything … to the cops." Her words fell flat, words that had felt perfect before. Diego must know the cops made it seem like she betrayed them.

"Gabe—" Diego fixed dead eyes on her.

Her smile slipped.

His hand reached for his waistband under his oversized shirt, where she'd seen a bulge at the police station, as if he carried.

"What's going down?" José must've caught the tension.

"*Nada*, nothing." Diego gave her a lingering stink eye.

"No?" José stared at him.

Diego stomped out the ember that had flicked from José's cigarette, giving Gabe more mad dog glances.

"*No problema.*" José turned his back to Diego and chatted nervously with Desiree. Gabe and José acted on edge.

"Gabe. Come over here." Diego looked insistent.

She slipped off her barstool to the ground. Even in high-heeled strappy sandals, when she looked up at Diego, he stood twice her height and also weight. Not a fair fight.

"Cheep the Snitch is not the only traitor, Gabe." He glared at her.

"I said nothing."

"Gabe, you snake, two homies got booked as accomplices." He tapped his waistband.

The bartender bent over and whispered something to José. José's hand holding his glass twitched, spilling drops on the counter. A spark could light up a fight.

Up front, the table dancing had reached a fast pace. She'd warned the girls.

The bartender tossed his head toward the back door for club employees only, signaling José and her to get away. José tapped her arm, and she followed. They glanced around the club to see if anyone watched as they moved toward the back. Diego stood at the front of the club, head down, talking to a homeboy. She saw Diego look up at the front entrance, thankfully not the rear exit where Gabe headed, looking over her shoulder. Fika sauntered in.

In the dark, Gabe couldn't help but peek as Fika danced up to Cheep the Snitch and led Cheep out the front way with very little persuasion. An unusual coupling. Gabe sensed a set up. Fika could kiss and kill.

Gabe and José were almost out the back door, when Diego turned to scan the club, and his head lifted. Her eyes dropped. She wouldn't give Diego the satisfaction of locking eyes, but she sensed his alertness. The hunt was on.

They ran to José's older model, borrowed car, and he struggled with the jammed lock. José pulled out a knife from his shirt and inserted the thin point into the lock mechanism. Gabe shook not having had time to go to the ladies' room before splitting. She'd have to wait.

José's engine started, and they sped into the street. They crossed the intersection and were about to turn into the alley entrance to shake a possible tail when Gabe saw Cheep and Fika. What a contrast: he short, unkept, drunk, and she teetering over him in her high heels.

José followed, the car crawling into a rival gang's territory.

"Stop. Pull over." Gabe warned José to cut the lights. He was cool, trusting Gabe's instincts. She'd seen the set up in the club, but he hadn't.

"Fika's after Cheep."

"All right." José kept the car in the shadows to avoid a trap.

Fika and Cheep strolled toward them at the end of the alley. A tinted-widow Ford entered the alley and parked up ahead of them in the vulnerable spot where their car could've been.

Gabe could see Fika nuzzling against Cheep, glancing sideways at the Ford.

Slumped down and staring ahead, Gabe wondered if Fika might charm her target before luring him to his death.

Fika stretched up to kiss Cheep.

Gabe heard the Ford gun its engine. She saw Fika jerk free of Cheep's embrace and push him into the path of the car. Cheep's brief smile faded as the Ford sped toward him.

"Stop!" Cheep threw his arms up. He faced the car full-on and ran for cover of the buildings.

"Honk, José!" Gabe envisioned the imminent horror of Cheep struck down. She prepared to tend to his broken body. While José's honking made the driver hesitate and look, Cheep plastered himself against the outer wall of a café.

The café's back door opened. A waiter in uniform with a lit cigarette stepped toward the alley. Cheep dove for the open café door, striking the waiter down as he did. Cheep and the waiter tumbled through the opening, grunting and cursing.

The Ford driver stuck his gun out the window and pointed it at the men on the floor in a tangle but didn't shoot. The Ford's passenger door opened as Fika ran toward it. Fika vaulted though the air, and the driver pulled her in.

"Hang on." José growled as he looked over his shoulder to back out of the alley with tires screeching.

# chapter 19

GABE SLID HER BODY down on the seat, slamming her knees up against the metal of the instrument panel.

Diego's words came back to her: *Know what we do to a snitch?*

Out of the alley, José wielded the car around a corner. "We lost them. For now." He motioned to Gabe, who sat upright.

"I'll call later and give the cops a tip." José kept a lookout in his rearview mirror. He went a roundabout way through the city to stay under the radar. She prayed she wasn't next. She knew if a hit was put on her, it would be tough to get a leader to call it off, even if it wasn't fair—it'd be no honor for a shot caller to take off a hit.

When José dropped Gabe off in front of the elegant Sanchez mansion at the top of Cowan Heights, he gave a whistle. Strange to hear a man—even her brother—whistle at the house and not her. She busily smoothed her wrinkled clothes. Pulling her red jacket and beer-stained crop top tight around her shoulders, she felt ready to collapse, but the beat of Mexican rock music from inside and the shimmer of the lit-up house terraced against the hillside, revived her. Waving at José, she hoped he would report anonymously to the cops.

Aunt Olivia answered the doorbell dressed in a flowing aquamarine silk pantsuit, the design Gabe helped her cut and sew. She enfolded her into the soft creases of Olivia's material, and Gabe felt as if she were touching the relaxing smoothness of silk sheets. Her hugs helped.

"Come in, Gabe." Olivia giggled happily and pulled her in. "What happened to your clothes? Here, let's see what Deborah might have in her closet."

She wondered what Deborah Sanchez, the lean and well-sculpted Latina politician, would have that she would fit into. Gabe had helped Olivia to fit her, but their tastes were radically different. If women were from Venus in the clothing category, Deborah was Venus to the core, while Gabe was from the newly discovered planet K2-229b.

"The Disney job can get us out of this mess." Olivia pulled her forward.

"Which mess?"

"Ramón's shooter. A cash reward is up."

"That hit... seems like months ago."

Olivia lifted her brows at Gabe and then ushered her through the entryway and down the hall to the immense bedroom before the guests saw her. The bedroom was immense.

Gabe caught the view from the bedroom windows on the top floor... spectacular. Open windows of the master bedroom set the stage for a 360-degree view of sparkling city lights and glamorous hillside residences. To her, it seemed like a magic, enchanted village. She had never seen anything like it.

Olivia led her into the pristine bathroom with shell-shaped sinks and a huge sunken ceramic tub complete with jacuzzi jets. Once alone in the inner chamber, Gabe pulled off her tight dirty-white top and saw her neck and chest were flushed. She let the warm water from the shell sink flow over her face and dabbed it with a plush, purple towel.

"Now try this." Olivia brought in some clothes. "I'll check back later."

Deborah had hung a dramatic, stylish black shift dress, very in-style this season, on a hook; unfitted and unbelted, it had a good chance of getting over her hips. It was an ample fit, and she looked in the mirror, imagining herself as Deborah, the newly elected politician, about to join her businessman husband in the drawing room. Deborah and her women friends founded a group to help underserved young women like her get out of at-risk situations.

Gabe's science teachers wanted to introduce her to women like Deborah who could lead her along on the path to being a doctor since her test scores and lab points indicated she could easily pursue that career. She, Mamacita, and, for that matter, Olivia all worked hard so she could someday pay college tuition. Her boxing fight might also pay off. She imagined Deborah cheering for her ringside at one of her fights. Gabe felt like a self-actualized woman around her—she could achieve her dream of being a doctor in the worst of circumstances. If she got to know Deborah, she'd see how much "at-risk" she and the ladies could tolerate.

Olivia led her into the crowd of clients and acquaintances. She immediately recognized orange-haired Matty in the sleek, black, fitted evening slip she and Olivia had created for her. Matty thanked Gabe and told her about the many compliments she'd received that evening. This time, Gabe felt she was crossing cultural lines, from dodgy gang girl to posh Latinx businesswoman. Matty waved over to Doris, who'd substituted the clever suit tailored for her with a generic jumpsuit.

"Doesn't Gabe look sophisticated!" Matty gushed to Doris.

Receiving compliments instead of threats filled Gabe with gratitude, but she felt ashamed for the horror she'd stumbled on earlier in the evening. Would Olivia care?

Olivia had said she wanted to introduce her to the executive assistants from Disney who she knew might help her find work—the men in suits and bright ties over in the corner? She'd give it a chance, but what a big leap to imagine herself sewing wardrobe costumes for Mickey Mouse and Friends.

Olivia introduced her to Deborah, who graciously said how gorgeous she looked in her dress. Deborah outdid everyone with her wavy dark hair set off against a classic ivory evening suit. She asked Gabe about her science classes and her aptitude for medicine and design. Gabe answered, totally unguarded. As each hopeful word spilled out from her heart, Gabe desired to share her goals, and a successful future was more important to her than she'd ever realized. When Deborah listened with penetrating brown eyes, Gabe could see herself as Deborah viewed her. Dr. Gabriela Alma. A doctor. A designer. A wife. It was intoxicating. Gabe felt a warm spotlight bathing all her hopes and dreams in an amber glow so that each merciful gesture lit her up from the inside.

"Have faith, Gabriela." It soothed her when Deborah said she was precious to God.

Gabe didn't want to admit it, but maybe Deborah and the women who worked in the Latinx professional network might have answers. Deborah made it clear from the way she listened Gabe could change inside and out … unfold her inner beauty. Maybe those girls at Club Jupiter or juvie weren't her homegirls now. Her scare near the alley showed her how cruel *la vida loca* could be. Could she trust Aunt Olivia and her associates? Matty had a good sense of humor, and Deborah— open, compelling, captivating. She would now think of herself as empowered Dr. Alma, in process, medical doctor. This new Gabriela knew one thing: she was seeing more than the city lights from a new vantage point this night.

At the end of the night, the men from Disney flirted and told funny stories aimed at getting Olivia and Gabe's attention. Olivia stayed close to her elbow because she knew Olivia wanted to tease them a little but didn't want Gabe to get cornered.

When the Disney execs went up to the bar for the last drink, Olivia grabbed Gabe's hand. They smiled and walked toward the door with chests lifted high, looking over their shoulders at the Disney men. The men saw the women were having fun, and their delight made Gabe curious and excited. She took a mental snapshot of that moment, what she and Olivia must look like, torsos thrust out, lean legs pumping purposefully forward—pretty women. She wondered if the men saw them as haughty, ignorant teases. Not that it mattered. Most fun of all was the women knew they made men crazy guessing what they were whispering.

"Olivia." A Disney big-shot executive shouted at her from the bar. The executive hurried across the room, his assistant close behind. "Did you say good night? Disney may have a lot more work for you, Olivia."

"Good. Do you have a position in wardrobe for Gabe?"

Gabe squirmed. Olivia may have to trade her attentions. "We might."

The executive gunned him down with a look.

"Going to freshen up my drink." The assistant returned to the bar. He looked over his shoulder and smiled coyly at Olivia.

While Olivia and the top executive traded professional niceties, Gabe noticed Olivia acted sweet without tempting, although her dress spoke for itself. The man came over and handed Gabe his card. "Call me, Gabriela. We'll set up an appointment next week." Then his voice dropped huskily to Olivia.

Olivia gave Gabe a wink.

"You can wear the black dress. Here's the matching black sweater. Keep it if you'd like." Deborah, who'd overheard the exchange, offered the outfit as Olivia and Gabe said their farewells. "I have others."

"No, thank you." Gabe felt suddenly suspicious at the offer. Was Deborah the Latinx politician, trying to expand her voting base?

"Oh, take it, Gabe. Your seventeenth birthday is coming up." Olivia nudged her.

"Then it's settled!" Deborah waved the sweater over to Gabe.

"Crazy times. Drop you off?" Olivia offered Gabe when they went back to change.

Olivia sensed Gabe's heaviness. If Gabe told her about her wild night earlier, Olivia would have to decide if she should stay close. Gabe stepped back into her clothes, Cinderella's gown turning to rags.

When Gabe saw Olivia's red Prelude she wondered if the design work paid for it.

Olivia lifted up a black rose tucked under the windshield wipers. Gabe had never seen a rose that black before. A wilted, dark blood-red. *Who would snip off a dead rose at night?*

"I like roses, but—" Olivia turned up her nose. "From one of your home dogs?"

Gabe looked around. "They don't like me."

"Whose hate list are you on?" Olivia started the engine, and the rose fell down off the hood.

In her side mirror, Gabe cringed to see the shadow of a car on a cross street. It looked like the wheels threatening Cheep the Snitch earlier.

"Make a U-turn here. Hurry. But it may be nothing."

"Yeah ... now it's gaining on us."

"Oh gosh, hurry faster." Gabe panicked as the speeding car came alongside. "It can't be ... Diego?!"

"Diego?" Olivia asked while pulling ahead.

"Who's riding shotgun? Fika! Keep steady."

"When we get out of this, Gabe—"

"Floor it!"

No matter how Olivia tried, she couldn't stay ahead. Diego and Fika were gaining.

Diego and Fika pulled alongside. Fika whirled out a gun and reached across Diego.

"Duck!"

Fika aimed to fire. As Gabe's head went down, she saw Diego grab the gun. No shot sounded out. Diego and Fika battled for control. Their car slowed.

Olivia's hands quivered on the steering wheel. "We're almost out of gas."

"Hide. Up here under the tree." Gabe looked behind and around. Not a sound.

Olivia's car was slowly chugged to a stop. She turned to Gabe with a pained face. "Diego *and* Fika?"

"My two worst enemies. Looks like they turned off back there. Diego stopped Fika from shooting."

Olivia looked anxious. "Do you hear yourself? You're in deep with them!"

"Let's get gas. I think there's a service station around the corner."

They searched the trunk for a plastic gas container. Gabe looked up to see a car coming at them. Fika was driving without Diego, like a mad woman, hair streaming out, shaking her fists against the wheel. She screeched to a halt and, with the engine still running, took a flying leap and jumped on top of Gabe. Gabe flailed at her.

# chapter 20

FIKA SCREAMED, "YOU ASKED for it!" Fika's scream sounded primitive. Gabe fought to get her off.

Fika was alone with no gun. Diego must've taken it from her. Gabe's push landed her against the car door.

Fika jumped up and down on the car door, swinging like a monkey, two legs hanging. Olivia froze.

Fika kicked and banged on both car doors.

"Get off the car!" Gabe kept balanced and gave Fika a shove. Fika recoiled from it, then came after Gabe with a fury. She grabbed at her hair, and Gabe yelped.

"You die!" Fika screeched and torpedoed her sturdy torso straight at Gabe.

Gabe implemented her best kickboxing skills against the moving target. With the palm of her hand facing out, she blocked her.

Fika sprung back, stunned. She couldn't seem to lift her own fists or legs, but she kept using her body like a cannonball.

"Gabe!" Olivia shouted, rousing herself. "I'll get help." She ran down the road.

"Olivia. No!" Gabe cried out too late. She didn't want help. Help meant cops.

A one-two punch from Gabe's right side to Fika's jaw sent her swaying. Her head went down as she staggered to Diego's car.

Gabe looked at his car. Was there any chance she still had the gun? If not the gun, maybe a knife. Fika usually carried one. Gabe couldn't afford to take a chance, so she took a running start, lifted her knees, and kicked her tightly muscular legs into Fika.

Fika reacted with a gasp as all the air seemed to go from her. She fizzled like a popped circus balloon and bent over double.

In the whole fight, Fika hadn't landed one successful punch. When Gabe started beating her up, Fika couldn't fight without her knife. Or others had always done the fighting for her.

"You're nothing." Gabe felt guilty, but only for a second. Hothead Fika was an accomplice to attempted murder and had pursued this fight to take Gabe down.

A siren sounded in the distance.

*Had Olivia called the police?*

"No, not again." *I've betrayed Mamacita's wishes for me to be a nice, normal girl again. How could I think of myself as the future Dr. Alma?*

Fika would be all right when she shook off the thrashing. She looked like a blitzed drunk. Gabe looked around to see where she could run but decided to hold her ground.

Gradually, though, the sirens faded away. "Thank God."

Gabe blinked to see Olivia hurrying to the car with a tall, distinguished-looking white man about in his fifties from one of the neighboring homes. His clothing was loose, and his hair unkempt. Olivia must have disturbed his sleep. He looked startled to see them but kept at a steady walk toward them with what looked like a gasoline can.

"Leave it to Olivia to rally a man to a cause." Gabe smiled at Olivia earning street cred. Fika sat on the curb, head in hands.

"You girls get in a little accident?" The man leaned over.

"Hit some bumps. Ran out of gas."

"Maybe we should call someone." The man assessed Gabe and Fika.

"No thanks, we're good."

He set the can down. They smiled and watched him until he was a safe distance away.

Gabe picked up the stunned Fika and hauled her like a sack of beans into Olivia's car. "A little bird named José said you envy me, Fika."

"You have it all, don't you, Gabe?" Fika swore under her breath.

"Is that what you think, Fika? We're taking you home." Gabe looked at Olivia.

"Locas territory? Let's drop her off at a hospital or the center."

"Too much attention, Olivia. We'll keep quiet."

"Fika, I'm a nobody, nobody to envy. I try and fail." Fika stirred at Gabe's words. *After all of Fika's threats, she is just a mouse and not a mad dog.*

"Gabe, she may think the teachers give you a chance they don't give her." Olivia pulled up two blocks away from Fika's house. A tagging crew was fast at work painting gang symbols on a wall at the corner. Two *chicos* scurried away as their headlights flashed on their freshly painted gang symbols. The name "Diego" had been spray-painted over Ramón's name.

Inevitable. The power struggle to replace Ramón continued while he was hospitalized. His homeboys would visit and call him OG, but behind his back, they jockeyed for power.

"Slow down." Gabe nudged Olivia as two taggers saw them approach. She wanted to give them time to see the girls weren't cops, so they wouldn't get jacked up and pistol-happy.

A man walking on the other side of the street shouted and wagged a finger at the taggers, and they fled.

Fika mumbled more words and almost woke up. Gabe took her new black sweater and tied it kerchief-style over her eyes. Fika jerked her head back, but she wasn't bad off.

As they drove within a block of Fika's house, Gabe wondered how Fika's *madre* would feel if her daughter were dropped off in a daze. If some strange *chicas* unloaded Gabe from a car, Mamacita would rant and shake her fist. Gabe didn't want Mamacita's health to go bad.

Last time Mamacita had bad shortness of breath, she went to the doctor, and he rushed her into surgery. The surgeon found out the main artery to her heart was completely blocked. She would've had a massive heart attack if other smaller arteries hadn't sprung up around the heart to carry the blood. It was a miracle, the doctors pronounced. They had only seen a heart heal itself like that in one other case. So, Mamacita had a miracle heart. Since it was a miracle heart, it had to be respected. No one was to go frightening her or putting a lot of pressure on those small, fragile, new arteries. They might bust, and then where would she be? Where would we be? Mamacita's heart beat for us all.

"Is this her crib?" Olivia quickly pulled over to the curb where Gabe pointed.

It was dark. Could they slip in? Crews partied long and hard into the night every night.

Gabe pulled a squirming Fika from the car, bringing her up the path. Her fuss caused the lights to go on at the back of the building.

Gabe put her down on the unlit porch, took back her new sweater, and busted out. As she hustled to the car, Gabe could see the Prelude, but she couldn't see Olivia. Had Olivia run away in fear? *Now what?*

When she got one foot from the car, Olivia's head bounced up from the steering wheel, and she threw the passenger door open for Gabe. Olivia's car jolted into gear and sped away.

"Homegirl. You got my respect tonight." Gabe patted her aunt's shoulder.

# chapter 21

PAPA WAS A GAMBLER, and Mamacita and Gabe paid the price. One day, he paid off a big gambling bet by giving away all of their furniture and also Gabe's favorite goldfish, Big Willie. Gabe pleaded to keep Big Willie, but Papa had hocked him.

*"No mas,* no more," said Mamacita after that incident, but she didn't kick him out. He was deported. Papa took most of the spare cash and his anger to Mexico, leaving his old clunker car behind for Mamacita.

After Papa left is when Mamacita's shortness of breath began. When the Zavalas next door left to see family in Mexico for some months, they said they'd get a message to Papa, tell him about her heart, and send help. Gabe and José glared at them. The Zavalas said no more.

Ernie, the Zavala's sometimes-fierce bulldog, was a pal of Gabe's, and they asked her to walk him regularly. Known to be a terror in the neighborhood, Ernie seemed to get along with Gabe because they had an understanding—she earned his trust by spending time getting him what he liked—green grass, Cheerios, and teething bone cookies.

Ernie wouldn't chase squirrels and rabbits like most dogs. When Gabe took him to the Santa Ana Zoo, after they saw the featured, rescued bald eagle, Ernie spotted Isaac, the ring-tailed lemur with black-and-white stripes around its long tail. He stared him down. At thirty-six, Isaac was reported to be the oldest living lemur due to his active lifestyle with his daughter.

Outside one day, Ernie confronted a bushy-tailed fox trapped in a den and barked until Gabe pulled him away. Gabe hated to think what Ernie would do if he saw one of the bobcats known to be in the area. Ernie would climb up a tree almost like a cat after a bird. Birds always found a higher tree branch or flew away, teasing him. He loved to bark at the red-tailed hawks, pink-billed gulls, and wrens, even though they flew high above him.

Ernie behaved like a maniac except with Gabe. When together, Ernie would be as gentle as a baby. One day, Candy came by, and Ernie went into a barking fit. He was the only friend Gabe wanted to see that morning, with her mind fogged up and flashing back on the night before. Ernie understood fear, and he knew affection. Candy said Ernie had bonded to Gabe, and yes, she thought, maybe that's how best to explain it.

The next morning, Gabe still felt anxious and decided to go for a walk. She hoped to rid herself of the insecurity she felt from threats. She grabbed the leash, and Ernie wiggled.

Ernie pulled ahead of her on the leash. They passed a man opening up the McFadden Market, who smiled at them. She wondered if he found them amusing: a muscular young girl and a fierce bulldog.

On the walk, Gabe prepped aloud for the Disney costuming interview. Ernie perked up an ear. "I'll tell them I've spent enough hours at Shin's garment factory I could sew a prom gown for a cheetah. And, with them, that's probably what I'll have to do."

She'd heard they'd gotten a new tech show with millennium urban combat and star fleet figures—even Latinx characters to appeal to the demographic.

Ernie lifted his head and jumped around.

"Ernie, you think I should try to get a paying gig in film studio costuming? I could update Pocahontas to look like Selena for the Tomorrowland special. Money for college."

Ernie gave her a very hard tug on the leash: time to play.

Up ahead, two teenagers dressed in red stood on the busy street corner, each holding a sign. They jumped up and down, skipping and hopping, shaking the signs sideways, back and forth, up and airborne, trying to attract drivers' attention. They looked too old to be selling lemonade. From their jerky motions, it looked to her like they might be high, but perhaps natural energy. Ernie was cautious. As they slowly neared them, she could make out the lettering on the signs: Car Wash.

"No!" Gabe had forgotten she'd volunteered to help with the fundraiser.

Junior high students smiled and shouted to one another as they hosed water at cars and into the air.

"Gabe, why aren't you helping? And who's your friend?" A junior higher pet Ernie's coat.

"Ernie, meet the crew." Gabe stifled a yawn.

Outside in the bustling community center parking lot, Ernie seemed less defensive, that is, until a girl squirted him in the nose. The bulldog sat back on his haunches with his front paws in the air and barked loudly. The girl dropped her hose and jumped out of Ernie's way, as he shook his wet fur, spraying all over Gabe.

"Tired?" Petra sounded unhappy.

"Why? What did you hear?"

"Enough. Ramón's concert. Police station. Juvie. Nightclub. Diego. Fika. If you show your face, you're target practice for hoodlums. Go for your little doggie walk. Get your head blown off and maybe your pet's too. Want to end your thoughts of a medical career?"

"All right. I give. You call the shots." She'd never seen Petra so intense before, but she realized she'd racked up a list of misdeeds.

Candy swung open a nearby car door, catching both Petra and Gabe off guard. She ran over to them, throwing her arms into the air.

"I've got an audition!" Candy broke into a tune from a current song, kicks, hand motions, and all. Candy wiggled around, poured into spandex hip, white jeans. Her white ankle boots and a hot pink crop top completed the outfit. Her hair was streaked blond and brown and colorfully braided in an ethnic look. Petra stopped, looked at the total effect, and slowly whistled.

"You look like a real rock diva," Petra affirmed Candy. "What's your audition?"

"The new *Latins in Love* telenovela, television novel special." Candy gleamed.

"I don't mean to be nosey, but aren't you forgetting a small detail—like your last name? Do they want a Candy Marshall on *Latins in Love*?"

"Oh no, I picked a stage name? They know me as Candy Alma."

"Alma?" Gabe was taken aback at the way she accented her name. "So, you think you are a part of the Almas, my family?" She held her temper back. Petra quickly escorted

Candy back to her newly washed car with gleaming hub-caps, saying everyone in the community center would be watching her show.

Candy left with a honk, a smile, and a wave.

"Looks like you've got yourself a real sister." Petra's mood seemed better.

"We'll see what kind of *hermana* she is if she shares. That is, if she gets any winnings."

"Good luck to her. After all, she's an Alma!" Petra laughed. "Use my car to take the girls to the L.A. Museum of Tolerance today? It's clean." She motioned to her Hyundai.

"Next, you'll want me to take over your payments."

"Stay out of sight a while."

A light rain started to fall, and drops splashed into puddles of soap and water. Ernie nudged Gabe.

She prodded Ernie toward the gate. "This way."

A red '55 Chevy gunned its engine and raced out of the parking lot over the large puddle of water in the driveway, splashing more water all over Ernie and Gabe. Ernie growled and lunged backward. The kids were still drying the windows on the red car when it lurched away from them with wet car windows. The girl with the chamois in her hand tried to motion to the driver inside, but the soap bubbles dripped down from the windows and windshield. Could the car washer see the driver?

Gabe caught the Hyundai keys and yanked at Ernie's leash. Ernie refused to move, growling at the loud car, and still, the driver's face could not be seen.

"We're out of here, Ernie." Gabe pulled forcefully. Ernie acted as if he wanted to attack the unseen car occupant.

"You're like a bull in a bullfight, Ernie. You charge when you see red." Gabe saw a head appear in the window. Dark hair, long from the back, then the head turned—

Ernie snarled, leaped ahead at the car. Gabe almost dropped the leash.

The long, dark hair flew away from the face to reveal the features. Diego snarled.

Gabe clutched Petra's keys. She pulled the leash away, and Ernie responded. They raced together toward the closed gate near Petra's car.

As the red car gunned its engine, its wheels spun, slipping on the deep, soapy water puddles.

Gabe and Ernie ran like two cheetahs. They leaped up at the chain fence together. Gabe's legs caught higher in the links, and she reached down to lift Ernie up over the fence.

The car charged forward.

Ernie squealed, his leash caught in a point of the fence, almost strangling him. Gabe reached for Ernie but just missed as he dangled above her from the fence top. Lumbering at a run from the boxing gym came big Coach Al.

He grabbed for Ernie's neck and freed it. Coach hauled both Ernie and Gabe over the fence while he stayed below. Gabe wrestled the car open with the key and tumbled in with Ernie in her lap, while Coach stood hands on hips facing the racing Chevy. The red Chevy charged straight at him. Coach cut away to the left quicker than she'd ever seen him move, and Diego's Chevy plowed into the fence.

Wheels squealing, Diego backed up to try to follow them out the other exit, but Gabe had a good jump on him. In the rearview mirror, she saw Diego's tire go flat as he pulled over to the side of the road. Coach was still running after him. What an hombre, Coach. He'd juked Diego good.

# chapter 22

GABE SAW A HINT of a rainbow after the slight shower, but now it rained more steadily. Gabe and the students on the field trip cruised in Petra's car at about sixty-five miles per hour in the fast lane.

"Bamba, bamba, bamba, bamba ..."

On the road, Gabe felt good as she screamed out the words at top volume. She headed for high times with girl-friends, even if it was at some high-brow cultural museum.

They rocked and rolled to the beat, driving on the 55 to the 405 headed into L.A.—Gabe and her junior high community center girls Carina, Lupe, and others.

"Turn it down." Lupe shouted over the loud music. "I want to tell you what went down. Don was getting friendly with me. Then his sister had a party, and she didn't invite me. Well, I showed up anyway."

"Cool." Carina said to the song. "That's the way I like it, uh-huh, uh-huh."

"You know what I wore?" Lupe's voice mounted.

"Tell me, girlfriend, your blue shirt?"

"Shut up, Carina! So, Don. . ." She lowered her voice. "Now I can't say this too loud."

Gabe laughed and looked over her shoulder at Lupe as she whispered in the back seat. Gabe enjoyed hearing someone else trying to hide a secret for a change.

"Okay, ladies, enough. You all know what 'tolerance' is?" Gabe took charge.

"How much beer and drugs your body can stand, Gabe?" Lupe joked.

"I hope you're kidding. You're in for an education."

Security was tight at the door to the Museum of Tolerance. Gabe walked through the metal detector doorway, and the sound went off. A female attendant frisked her with an instrument while the girls smirked at her. She flinched as the woman ran the electronic baton over waist, breasts, and arms. The beeper went off at her silver bracelet, piercing the air and making heads turn. A diverse spectrum of people waited in crowded lines. Vivian, the silver-haired tour guide, said she was Jewish and her son-in-law was Hispanic. Gabe saw the girls' heads bob.

Vivian steered them over to a section with Hispanic heritage: "In the 1940s, many signs in the Southwest said—"

"'We serve *whites*. No Spanish or Mexicans.'" Carina read the sign with snark and then pretend-kicked it in the breadbasket. Her spit was flying. "Move that sign. It offends me." The girls murmured insults.

"It's historical." Vivian sought Gabe's whereabouts. "Our exhibit honoring Hispanics and Latinx has been here years."

"You can't say you only serve whites. Mooove it." Carina repeated. "I'm gonna kick some you know what!" The girls joined in with Carina's murmured insults.

"The only tush gonna get kicked is yours. The sign is from the 1940s!" Gabe held Carina back. "We can all fill out comment cards at the end."

"If she's not gonna move it, I'm gonna make her. I'll write on those cards."

"Fair enough." Gabe elbowed Carina.

"Look!" Vivian waved them along.

Lupe leaned in to read the text of the Mendez v. Westminster case exhibit. *Para Todos los Niños*—for all children—Fighting Segregation in California. That's better!"

"They closed what were called 'Mexican schools.'"

"Vivian can't talk like that." Lupe's red face showed embarrassment.

"Telling it like it was back then. Latino families aimed to end school segregation through the courts."

"Think we have it better now?"

"Somewhat, and we need to honor our history." Gabe led her group into a room with an authentic three-tier bunk bed from the concentration camps of Nazi Germany. Twenty-four men had slept on that bed, eight on each level. They must have been thin, Gabe surmised, and by the photos you could tell they seemed close to death. Vivian said the girls could touch the wood.

"It feels so real."

"Lupe, that's because it is." Gabe paused, humbled.

Vivian stood with deep respect.

One by one, the girls touched the bed and shivered. This connection with the concentration camp horror felt surreal to Gabe. "Thought you'd seen it all?"

They stood silent.

In another section, Gabe and the girls walked into a space with two doorways. One said "Able-bodied" and the other said "Children and Others." The girls looked awhile, then Lupe darted ahead, and the other girls followed behind, all choosing to walk through the arch that said "Children and Others." Gabe got choked up when she followed behind them, feeling sympathetic for those who lived then in Nazi Germany, as choosing "Children and Others" meant certain death.

"Death either way. Whatever they chose, the end would have eventually been the same." Vivian pointed the way into the model of the extermination area where the Germans gassed prisoners. She asked them to sit down on a ledge made of rocks and showed actual film footage from the Holocaust. They sat elbow to elbow.

One scene projected on the walls showed a hospital where people tossed out all the sick from upper-story windows onto army trucks waiting below to cart off and dispose of the bodies.

Lupe gasped.

Gabe knew she and the girls looked skeptical at first, not wanting to believe what they saw on the film—a crowd of relatives lined up outside the hospital. The girls stood speechless as babies only a couple of days old were tossed from five stories high to certain death on impact with the truck beds below.

Gabe rocked back. Carina sniffled.

One woman interviewed on the film said her day-old niece was in that particular hospital, and she saw her plummet down to her death then be whisked off by Hitler's trucks for cremation.

Now Carina couldn't hold back and wiped teary eyes with her shirt sleeve. Other girls fought back tears. They had walked through the archway for the children. Room after room they trudged until they were emotionally exhausted.

Lupe thanked Vivian, and the others followed.

Petra had asked Gabe to lead a discussion on "tolerance" when they finally left the claustrophobic quarters of the museum, but it took a while to get adjusted to reality, and she didn't want to tread on anyone's feelings. They stopped at a drive-through to get burgers and fries courtesy of the center.

Her life was bleak in some ways. Fika and Diego were conspiring against her while Ramón lay in the hospital. She wondered what darkness Carina, Lupe, and others would have to face in their real worlds.

They got back in the car, slowly cruising back down the highway, but this time, the radio had less volume, and they were quiet.

"What hit you the most?" Gabe looked each in the face.

Everyone squirmed.

"Forget it. It's just something Petra made me ask—"

"The children." Carina broke through.

"The babies that died." Lupe shook her head.

"Yeah." Carina choked up.

chapter 23

THEIR CAR FLEW TOWARD the barrio like a homesick angel. The girls looked pensively out at the rainfall.
After waves of sadness about the Holocaust hit Gabe, anger
gripped her. She sped some and almost hydroplaned on the
wet freeway.

When they exited the off-ramp in Santa Ana, the rain
clouds lifted but still hovered overhead. Carina jabbered
about her plans to hang out with Party Crew 2 that night.

Denial. Gabe assessed the girl's emotions.

"Chill, girlfriends." Lupe told them about Anita and her
boyfriend, who went into seizures from some crystal meth
they bought. "I haven't heard from her."

"Gabe, do the dealers care?" Carina finished her burger
and folded the wrapper.

"Those people are dead, Carina." Gabe took a breath.
"Only their bodies just don't know it yet."

"Yeah. Try to have some fun, and even your own people
hook you in."

"Like the Jews in World War II, Carina. Maybe not as
bad." Lupe chewed on the last of her fries.

When Gabe turned the corner to the community center, the Márquez's grocery store awning, newly scarred with graffiti, told her a tagging crew had been there recently.

"Look." Lupe pointed to the street graffiti. "Nazis were here."

The girls laughed stiffly.

"Barrio or ghetto—what's the difference?" Carina commented.

"Not much." Lupe's voice held a note of bitterness.

"If you're dead, you're dead." Lupe frowned.

Gabe inserted herself: "Petra wants us all to stay out of trouble with gangs and not get in the family way too early. Girlfriends—thirteen, fourteen years old—have babies already."

"Keep those men off me." Carina laughed at two men standing on the sidewalk, staring at them. Carina flashed a smile at Gabe. "I had fun with you today."

Gabe beamed, "Thanks. "We're all friends, partners, after today."

Carina leaned towards her. "Could you drop me off up here at the corner?"

"I would. Only you know the rules. Everybody leaves the center together and comes back to the center together." Gabe felt like a heavy.

"There's something I have to do. Please."

"Sorry."

"You want to be a doctor. You care about my life?"

"Of course, I do. Carina, we'll talk."

"Okay." Carina's smile looked forced.

"We're friends. I just can't go over the line. Wish I could." Gabe tapped her right hand as if she were wearing her Everlast glove.

"Teach us more boxing moves, Gabe?" A shy student broke the ice.

"You got it."

A note was taped to Petra's desk at the community center when Gabe dropped off keys saying Petra was in a planning meeting. She was going to help the children sew for a party and parade. She scribbled in a few costume design changes from her sketches. Then she called Olivia on her smartphone.

"Olivia, this may sound funny, but do you remember studying World War II?"

"Since when do you care about history? I thought all you wanted to know about was science and the world's champion lightweight."

"Already know that. Tell me something I don't know."

"Is Coach Al there? He should know."

"Coach isn't that old. Al!" Gabe screamed off the phone into the gym. "Al! You live during the Second World War?"

"How old do you think I am?!" Coach bellowed from the ring.

"Olivia, thanks, I just about started World War III. You spar like you're almost that old, don't you, Coach?"

"You want to see a perfect cross jab?" Coach had comebacks.

"Good to have you in my corner, Coach."

"Didn't say nothing about being in your corner."

"Darn, love the guy." Gabe muttered, and Coach turned his chin slightly.

Gabe doodled a design and asked Olivia about the Disney interview.

"All right, you're first on the Disney interview list at five p.m. for a costume designer, second level, great pay."

"I'm there." Gabe drew a ray gun in a jack-o'-lantern's tummy pack. Finishing with flair, she moved the paper to see another note from Petra.

"Catch this, Olivia. Petra left me a note: 'Ramón's getting out today and wants to see you right away. I'm coming with.'"

"Me too, Gabe. And, I'll prep you for your interview."

"From the Nazis to Ramón and the Mouseketeers in one day. I'll need some tips. Somehow, I don't think I'm meant to be in a fairy tale castle with cartoon cut-out characters living happily ever after." Gabe sighed.

That night, Gabe scribbled in her smartphone notes about "the fleeting innocence that made the community center junior high girls seem as vulnerable as the persecuted groups. Oppressors."

"Impressions of the Holocaust." She pondered then wrote: "Lethal showers of gas and the mass executions left me bleak and questioning about the depraved nature of human beings. I wanted to talk to someone who lived during that time to ask if they knew what was going on. If they did, why didn't they do anything to stop the killing?!"

*Why didn't they stop the killing?*

*Why didn't we?*

People lost. Gabe's journal opened the door to remembering brother Sal's murder. Family lost—first, their father gone, then Abuelita Grandma, who some said had run away to South America. When Sal's wife picked up and left Santa Ana, more than distance complicated Gabe's plans of seeing her niece, little Luz. *What could she do?*

# chapter 24

PETRA AND OLIVIA WAITED with Gabe outside Ramón's room at the community hospital.

Just think, Gabe, you'll work at a medical center like this someday."

Petra nudged Gabe. "Stay strong. Even when Ramón is weak, he's a controller."

"Some men are just plain disastrous, but the women are happy he's awake."

Ramón had his back to them and turned around slowly. His face mesmerized Gabe. It was framed by lush, dark-brown hair, newly washed, long, and smelling like musk and tobacco. His brown eyes flashed at them, his mouth opened to a broad, glamorous grin, and his voice deeply resonated with a lounge singer's sexuality, "Gabriela."

She took a quick breath. Was this the man who was near death? This was more than a miracle of modern medicine—it was sorcery.

Ramón bent his head and cocked it to the side while looking up at her with his eyes, a motion of humility and vulnerability.

"I've missed you, Gabe. You were a great doctor taking care of me."

"It really was awful— … uh, nothing." She shifted her weight to her right foot. "No, really, the shooting was awful and very frightening."

"I like the way you and José show me respect. That type of loyalty is *familia*, family. We stand by each other. It's all part of the struggle that's always with our race. Americanos."

"How long did you rehearse the speech?"

"To prove it, I have something José will like to reward him."

She imagined Ramón's head swell up and float away, like a black character balloon. She jumped at the apparition on the ceiling and circling its way down. Maybe it was the lies, the decay personified. She trusted her sixth sense.

"You're no good for José."

"I know what he'd like. A nurse like mine," Ramón leered at his nurse.

"You're rude. If I do anything for you, it's on the condition to *never* see José or me again. We're free."

The moment Gabe said it, she regretted it. The surreal black character balloon bounced on her head.

"Good, it's done!" Ramón grinned. "Meet me at José's storage place where I keep my guitar and motorbike. Sign to get in, your name is on the card."

Gabe shoved the door open and rushed for her friends in the waiting room. She escaped into the busy corridor. The vision of the magic black balloon of a character head—the Aztec warrior or a Disney character—urged her on. She didn't want the men or the spectral balloon to follow her. Petra and Olivia were rushing out, having heard her escape. Gabe swept her friends out of the waiting room and the hospital.

"Ramón in a hospital gown." Petra snickered.

"Ramón reminds me of the man in the blue bathrobe," Olivia said as they drove.

"When I was fourteen, my sister and my brother and I came to this country from Mexico, led by a smuggler." Olivia's eyes looked dreamy. "I met a gorgeous young man of about twenty who, with an older woman, ran a way station for those escaping to El Norte. He came out of a hut in a blue bathrobe—with curly hair and winsome voice, as handsome and charming as an actor. The man cried in private with us. He hated his life. I was only fourteen, or else I would have stolen the man away from the woman."

"He was so sad, telling us he left Mexico when he was our age. He spoke to us about the promise of the new country, but he knew no English … and he worked for money to send to his two children, still in Mexico."

"The woman cooked for us and offered us rooms to stay in and wash up. I remember she was tall, attractive, and well-kept, but certainly thirty or forty years older."

"Ramón is a dark black spirit, not a guy in the blue robe. He asked me to help him reward José. I'll do it fast and then it's over."

"Why you, Gabe? You have so much good ahead." Petra pressed her to think.

"Not if I'm in someone's clutches, Petra. I want out."

"How is José in this?"

"I'll find out, Olivia."

"Gabe, our Latina detective?" Petra kidded.

"Fight fair, Petra." Gabe took her Aunt Olivia's hand.

# chapter 25

THE MEN ON THE Disney interview committee for the design position wore identical blue Oxford shirts and khaki pants. Gabe was startled thinking of the comparison between the young men she knew and these working men. They stood uniformly as Gabe walked in and seated herself in the candidates' workstation in front of the room, which contained the high-tech computer setup equipped with an overhead screen.

Gabe fingered a ringlet of her brown hair, curled it up with the perspiration from her neck as wetting gel, then released it as it sprung out of the tight loop, relaxing into a wave. She looked coyly out of the corner of her eye with her head tilted fetchingly at the committee.

For the practical impromptu design, the Disney vice president nodded to the Mac on Gabe's desk and motioned for her to warm up on the keyboard.

Gabe scooted down the borrowed tight, trendy skirt she wore with the red jacket from Olivia while she began to tap on the keys. She saw her swirls and squiggles appear on the overhead projector screen.

"Your characters are a group of rockers, a rock band, landing on the earth for the first time to educate humans about a new universal, musical language." The Ivy League–looking VP acted cool administering the practical.

The VP displayed the fabric for the practical exam: silver foil, gold, chrome, and metal shells for masks and other splendid, shaking, shining materials.

"We want edgy," he said. Gabe nodded, already in sync. The feminine organism on the mannequin looked like an exotic planetary counterpoint to a classic *Star Wars* character holding an electric lead guitar. Next to her, a masculine-looking alien body gripped a saxophone-like brass instrument in his tentacle.

Gabe's mind flashed to an old horror movie she'd seen: *Revenge of the Space Turtles*. She created a flashy, molted-green, reptile-skin space suit to look as if the female half crawled, half walked off the spaceship. She sketched the first layer of skin into the computer—first with broad strokes and then with fine lines. She added feathers in muted shades of green, black, gray, and beige with charcoals like a chameleon's camouflaged color signaling.

After another fifteen minutes of innovative computerized designs, Gabe turned around, looked at the panel members smiling at the overhead, and couldn't help but giggle. The VP grinned broadly.

The second interviewer stroked his chin. "Brilliant, who would guess?"

"I'm more surprised than anyone." Another interviewer joined in.

"Ingenious. This display, along with her scientific test scores, may give her the job. Remarkable combination of scores, art, and science." The vice president stared at the peacock feathers. "Gabe, what do you call this strange creation?"

"It's a civilization where the males like to show their colors and females are plain Jane, much like the peacock." Gabe explained showing her vibrant shades—each contrasting the other, so a dynamic fan of feathers screamed from the alien male.

"This gives a new direction for the whole show, a strain of the indigenous species combined with its habitat." The vice president nodded.

"It's a slapdash sketch. I can do more."

"Charming, Gabe. How much do you want to make?"

"Your move." Gabe countered him.

He motioned her over. She leaned over close. He whispered a sum.

"Could be." Gabe's heart pounded, but she tried to be nonchalant. She suppressed a smile.

The three men nodded and whispered to each other.

*Will I measure up as a professional? I'm really a nobody. This puts me so far away from my homies. . . On the other hand, could I use or manipulate them?*

"A negotiator." The leader misread her reticence. "Your recommendations from Olivia and Mr. Shin were tops."

"Well, then." Gabe stood up.

"This works for us." The men in turn, shook her hand.

Later that night, an evening drizzle moistened the air and gently pattered on Gabe's head and shoulders already glistening with sweat from teaching self-defense and kickboxing. She liked the rain. It made her moody and thoughtful.

"Why do the girls like kickboxing so much but are fearful about punching with boxing gloves?" She spoke aloud to no one in particular. "Boxing gives me an extra sense of self-reliance. And so does money for school—the creative work offer seems outrageous!"

"Gabe, got a minute?" A voice called out through the drizzling rain. Lupe, her hair soaked and stringy, waved to her from the street lamp. "I need to talk to you. Not about me. It's Carina. She's messed up pretty bad."

"Lupe, *Que paso*, what happened?"

"It's what's going down. On a bet, she took bad dope after school."

"Where is she now?"

"St. Joe's Hospital, critical care unit."

Gabe frowned. Second floor. Same floor as Ramón.

"Aye, Carina." Gabe intuited Carina's struggles. "I like my girls to stay clean. Talk to Petra. I listened to her, and soon I have good-paying work. Lupe, you will too."

"Don't know. When I wake up now, every morning since Carina crashed seems like a bad dream."

"Don't beat yourself up, Lupe. I hope one morning she'll be okay. One morning, real soon."

As Gabe grappled with the computer card entrance to Century Storage, it had a familiar feel from the time she and José stored his motorcycle there a couple of years past. Feeling happy after visiting an improved Carina at St. Joseph's and avoiding Ramón's hospital room, she went to meet José in storage as part of Ramón's deal. She dismissed a somber feeling about José's construction projects stacked up in storage.

The man said to sign the card, and of course, her name was with José's on it, and she might ask him if that made her somewhat legally responsible for the unit—but surely not signing at age sixteen. The Century Storage office manager bent over the computer and looked nice in a disheveled sort of way. Mounted television camera monitors showed photos of the storage sections as well as the clientele in the office. Fairly complete coverage.

"We got bought out by a big chain, and I'm having to work in our small computer system with theirs."

"I always forget the gate code." How long ago had she been there?

The sweet, older man wrote the combination number on the back of the card.

Gabe breezed by him toward the door. "Thanks, hope your computer work goes okay."

"Yeah, so do I. Twenty-five years here and never a paperwork mess like this."

The storage unit she and José had signed for two years before was close enough to walk to without having to drive a car up to it. Tall fences were at the perimeters, so the area lay free of vagrants. José had decided to get a large unit for Gabe's sewing machine and fabrics as well as his motorcycle. Didn't José understand when Gabe moved her sewing machine to the community center, the unit was only his?

The door was part way open. She heard a scuttering noise but didn't see anyone.

"José, is that you?"

She nudged open the door to see a trunk case. An unhealthy odor came out.

Backing up, her shoulder knocked into one of the built-in shelves by the doorway. The top of the trunk suitcase flew open, and a pungent, chemical smell emitted from it. She turned and ran out the door, her brown ponytail flying.

"What are you doing here?"

Diego. Not José. He tailed her? Or, was he the one who'd been inside the unit before she got there?

Diego grabbed his throat as the fumes mounted. He scurried after Gabe. She looked back to see Diego shut the door. He flashed a driver's license at her. Even from a distance, she saw of course, José's photo, her brother's driver's license. Diego dropped the license, and Gabe looked back. It wasn't a good idea to return. Yet she ran back for the license to keep José out of trouble. She went a safe distance from the fumes seeping out from under the door but not from Diego. He gained on her despite her fitness.

The alarm went off in the office.

She looked toward the front gate, and the manager rushed out, waving his arms.

"What's going on?" He ran toward Gabe and Diego. Gabe slipped and dropped the license. Diego saw her gimp and ducked behind a huge trash bin.

"Where is he?" The manager surveyed the scene. She prayed he wouldn't see José's license. The manager ran toward the storage shed and then stopped dead once he got a whiff. He spotted Diego trying to climb out of the area and yelled.

Gabe mounted the fence too. She had one foot on the first toehold. For once, Diego and Gabe were headed in the same direction. Not a good idea. Shivers hit her neck. Diego continued over the fence, but Gabe stopped.

Gabe sprinted toward the manager.

"Let's move!" He waved her to the front office, where the manager called the police.

"The man you were with—where did he go?" the manager asked.

"I'm not with him," she replied, waving her hands. "He tailed me. He's dangerous."

"Police are on the way. They'll find that José."

"What, José?" Gabe flinched when she heard José's name. "The bad man is Diego. José is my brother. He's not here—he didn't do anything."

The manager looked at Gabe in disbelief. "This isn't the first storage unit to be used as a meth lab. Rich men, poor men, it doesn't matter. Cooking up chemicals pays well."

"Pays who well?"

"Don't act naïve. I saw the way José ... Diego—whoever—dressed: cap, baggy pants. He's affiliated. Walk like a duck, talk like a duck, dress like a duck—you're probably a duck."

"I'm no sitting duck. I was set up. Jose too." Gabe was talking with her hands when the police flung open the door and three patrolmen entered.

"We're calling in the hazmat force. Let's get you out. The place might blow."

The policeman led Gabe by the elbow out to the street and leaned her up against the patrol car. He made quick calls.

Gabe kicked herself once for being there and twice for leaving behind José's license.

The hazmat team arrived wearing strange white spacesuit-like contraptions like she'd drawn from her imagination. The men took cautious loping strides toward the storage units, almost as if they were landing on a new planet.

# chapter 27

MEN IN CAMOUFLAGE SPACESUIT uniforms with shields of green-and-brown jungle patterns prowled through the units, spraying a white fluid that dissipated the chemical fumes. Onlookers whispered while other pros gingerly picked through the debris in the storage unit.

A man in a jacket with the word *Police* loudly printed on the back directed the activity. A van with the lettering *Sheriff,* the bomb squad vehicle, flung its doors open wide to reveal large metal tanks, most likely the holders for the bombs to defuse them.

Out came a robot—a walking, computer-driven bomb sensor—jolting toward the unit. Even if it looked cute, its system might go haywire from the fumes or an explosion.

Frontline police waved ahead at the fumes seeping like a blanket of fog soup over the storage units. A serious woman in a blazer cordoned off the street with long tape. A patrol car stopped in front of the tape, and the woman sectioned off an area where another patrol car positioned itself. Gabe leaned against it. Gawking onlookers stopped cars to ask about the mess.

"Help. Hazmat. Danger." Gabe texted Petra. But José must know about the use of the storage area. She fought back the tears, springing from fumes and disappointment.

"Where are you?" Petra texted back.

Television camera crews arrived in vans with rooftop television antennas electronically jetting up about thirty feet high. A newscaster positioned himself in front of the camera. A hip-looking balding man, attired in an olive shirt with an ID tag hanging from his neck, held his camera while two cameramen followed behind, hoisting a tall, spider-legged tripod. Cameramen flanked each other, shoulder to shoulder, pointing cameras like cannons.

Paramedics' vehicles flashed lights. One ladder truck positioned itself beside the other, and firemen communicated between the two vehicles. Despite the urgency, one fireman brought coffee to another in a white Styrofoam cup.

"No matter what happened, there would be coffee." Gabe chuckled. "One big money day for emergency task forces." She spoke to herself. Still, how was she so cynical?

Helicopters circled the scene, forming a strange shape. A nearby school was on alert and frantic parents came to pick up their kids in carpool lines. Across the street, employees evacuated offices to find themselves stuck. Their cars were in an area roped off by tape.

A policeman radioed that the local airport had rerouted flights just in case the explosives reached the flight path. One reporter came after Gabe but a policeman shoved her in the back seat of the squad car.

Gabe could see the cameraman rush to get exclusive interviews with the perturbed manager while the police tried to hold him back. When the officer tried to soothe the manager, Gabe slid out of the car and jogged over to where she saw José's license. Gabe faced the robot and waved her arms to distract it from picking the license up.

"Obstructing a police crime area. Exit the scene." The robot moved ahead bleeping.

"Is that you talking, Tinman?"

"Identify yourself. I sense an unidentified ambulatory human, not in my memory bank. Height five-feet-eight, weight one thirty."

"Um, smart aleck, weight one twenty-nine." When Gabe chided it, the robot's buttons flashed a code.

A flash came from the robot. "You can't float around my picture of me." Gabe threw her sweater over the lens.

"I have two lenses."

"Sorry, little robot fella, but I'll have to disable you." Gabe gave a swift kick to its appendage, and its camera mechanism sagged uselessly.

The robot turned backward with the finder fixed on the license. It teetered toward it slightly off balance, giving Gabe an opening to dash by it.

"You're a great fighter for a circuit board... my toughest foe this year!" Gabe tucked José's tell-tale license into her shoe. She looked back to see the robot rebound.

Two new policemen entered the scene, tight-faced, aggressively coming for Gabe. Gabe began to panic. Each escape route was blocked off by police vehicles. Behind her, the storage area fence made a timely exit impossible.

One policeman turned his head. Gabe saw it was Petra calling to him. He waited for her to run to him. Garbed in a black wool pants suit, both Petra's timing and her taste were impeccable.

"Gabe is one of mine. It's okay." Petra was always a friend, but standing up for Gabe now showed her depth.

The policeman waved down a squad car and motioned to them.

"I'm responsible for Gabe." Petra got in the car with her.

"This is different."

"How, Gabe?"

"Someone on *my* side for once."

"Come on. You think I'd let you mess up that job offer for pre-med funds?"

Gabe half smiled. Everything was all right. Then, just as quickly, all wrong. Their squad car was stopped and blocked. Officers approached the vehicle, and from the window of the car, Petra and Gabe could see the suited officers fighting chemicals.

"We need to get this car out." The driver spoke up.

"Not yet. It's not checked out." An officer held up his hand.

"Yes, it is. If you don't let us by, I'll personally escort these ladies out on foot."

Gabe smiled at Petra. She liked their driver's style.

"Okay, proceed." The officer waved them on.

# chapter 28

GABE PICKED UP THE dirty cigarette packs on the sidewalk outside the community center, deep knee bending, using the work detail as physical exercise. She was in intense training, and she'd accepted the decision from the county court judge to give her twenty hours of community service for her involvement in the storage unit debacle, although her brother was deemed legally responsible and arrested. On work duty, she could get a look at the center from all aspects—trash pickup, tutoring, activities, sports, families, business, and proposed changes.

Lupe came over to hang out with Gabe while Gabe worked early before school.

"Homegirls want the center to offer more self-defense and exercise. Can't it be a place where we can discuss choices, dating, pregnancy, drugs? You know, so we don't slip, like Carina." Lupe brainstormed as Gabe swept out the entryway. "Girls need a place they can call their own." Gabe listened, pausing to lean on her broom handle. "We're ready now for a real boxing class."

"With boxing gloves, Lupe?"

"*Si.* Taught by the California girl's boxing champion, Gabe the Attacker, The Dark Destroyer. Soon to be Doctor of Light."

Gabe laughed. "We'll talk to Petra. Gotta run."

"We're rooting for you, Gabe!"

Although happier than she'd been in a long time, Gabe felt about 80 percent mentally and physically ready for the state teenage boxing championships and knew the massive amount of work she had cut out for herself.

She placed the broom inside the utility closet and jogged to her cubby to get sweats on. She stretched down to touch her toes. As her muscles lengthened and loosened up, she thought about the grand force in the universe and how she would like to get to know the all-powerful spirit of goodness and majesty. She envisioned herself in the ring going for Devona the Demon's vulnerable left side and knocking her out in the state finals.

*Could she discipline herself to develop a strong mind and spirit?*

"I'm a lean-and-mean fighting machine." Gabe chanted the mantra as she ran up McFadden in the crisp early morning. Noisy car and truck traffic pounded. Homeless loitered. Used condoms and dirty needles lay spilled in the gutters. The lost night people had left before dawn, and school children would walk this way. A lone bluebird sat on a branch of a bare eucalyptus tree.

She stood in front of the hundred-year-old Ebell Club managed by the historical society of Santa Ana and remembered acting on its theatre stage in a community drama outreach to at-risk kids, including José, Rosa, and Fika.

Latch-key children walked from home to school to tutoring after school at the Grace Community Center. Some of the kids who came to the center after school told stories of jewelry being snatched, lunch money stolen, and gang invitations forced on students of all ages. "People watch you walking, they give you creepy, weird looks," a sixth-grade boy had confessed to Gabe while hanging out after school.

"Good morning." Gabe smiled at a couple of adults wearing orange vests and carrying cell phones. They smiled back.

Unifying parents, police, and school officials in the neighborhood, a new "safe corridors" program aimed to see children get home from school without interference from thugs. Volunteers within a two-block radius inspired residents to open their homes—to be identified outside by a flag. Officials looked out for unsavory-looking characters. *Would it help youth, or was money just thrown at the problem? Would tough guys conspire against do-gooders?*

Gabe pantomimed, punching the bag as she jogged—a left jab, a right hook, and a left crossover, feet moving.

Gabe stopped her run at the railroad tracks near Main and Chestnut to look at the new camera sensor aimed to take pictures of cars and people coming close to the railroad tracks. Not even warning signals and safety arms could stop those determined to cross tracks when the engine approached. What was it about the lure of a train's whistle? It drew people to race it, even knowing they could get sucked into the vacuum created by the train's speed and thrown underneath the wheels.

The simple gift shop on the next block appeared pristine and proper, but everyone knew, if you ask the right questions in the back of the shop, you could score some illegal *medicina*, drugs smuggled from Mexico—no questions asked, the price was right.

The awakening city gave Gabe a raw sense of the raw day-to-day. A visit to the Artist's Village would pick up her spirits. Maybe Rosa would greet her with her new, angular, Afro-Cuban sculpture pieces and some black tea. They could peruse a few blocks of bohemian craft shops, cafés, and bistros together. Or, an escape room.

"Rosa, R U at the studio later?" Gabe sent a quick text.

"Tomorrow." Gabe read Rosa's text.

Gabe gave Rosa a thumbs up. She ran several fast-paced miles, and then Gabe doubled back and headed for the center to shower before school. A new hotline and more programs for girls, a fresh sense of purpose was on her mind. She imagined a hotline office bustling with activity and with excited volunteers learning how to refer callers to agencies offering sensible solutions.

Gabe liked the success that the Disney job offered, but why did she feel guilty? Working with the homies in her spare time may be a way to give back. Disney didn't know she'd come up the part-time ranks in the sweatshops, working elbow to elbow with women in warehouses, garnering indecent pay because work was offloaded outside the country. Gabe felt humble for openings coming her way. She felt a light breeze stir her hair. Grateful, grateful to say the least.

# chapter 29

TURNING THE CORNER WITH her sights on the center, Gabe picked up speed and burst into a sprint. She felt fast and sure enough ready to take that Demon Devona ten rounds in the state championships if she had to.

Abruptly she slammed into an unseen person around the corner. She caught her breath and stepped back, recognizing the face.

"Gabe." Diego purred and stood to greet her. "Out for a jog?"

Gabe's breath came in spurts.

"Want you to meet Vince." He pointed to a tall young man with him.

Gabe warily sidestepped Diego but glanced at Vince.

Buzz cut, tan face, Vince looked like a nine-to-five-er with a tech-edge. He plucked away on his iPad while moving forward. She thought, "Bet he stepped out of a chauffeured shiny black SUV with twenty-four-inch wheels." Sure enough. Across the street, she saw the driver of the car leaning against the tinted glass back window, chewing gum and flipping through smartphone messages with one wary eye on Vince.

Vince had a rep. In the barrio, people said he was a cold, hard-hearted mover and promoter. It was rumored he had a tech degree from one of the Cal State universities, but he could make more money out on the streets than in a tech job. It was said that he passed every class on sheer intimidation, yet once, when his computer science professor threatened to give him a D, the lecturer was found dead the next day in his home office. Crushed. Under a pile including a Mac, modem, speakers, and metal bookshelves. Word of Vince's specialty in "tech-executions" quickly spread, and he became the savvy, connecting link between the blue-collar barrio gangsters and the white-collar world cybercriminals who got their shirts and money laundered weekly.

Vince stepped uncomfortably close. "I've heard you're a real good fighter, for a girl. Have we got the match-up for you!" Vince snarled menacingly, without a trace of nervousness, while cleaning his teeth with a toothpick.

"Oh, do you?" She tried to smile sweetly, but she sensed some sort of setup.

"Professional. In all respects." Vince pulled out the toothpick.

"Thanks, but I'm training for the state championships." She moved to go.

"Of course. This won't interfere with your fight." He clicked on a calendar on his iPad. "This weekend. State finals and your school finals are next month."

"Next week!" Gabe corrected him as she walked.

"Wait, Gabe. It's worth your while." He pushed Diego back and tried to catch up to Gabe. Vince carried his screen, and Gabe pivoted to side-step him and continue her run.

"Got to finish my route." She moved away.

Vince's attention returned just in time, and he reacted swiftly with a right hook, swinging his iPad out at her like a boxing glove out in front of her nose.

Reacting instinctively, she ducked her head, lowered her body, and put up her fists—a skillful move, and she almost escaped contact, but the handheld device smacked the top of Gabe's head with a sharp thud. She winced with hurt then felt a surge of rage. The cut would bleed, but the blood from the cut would not show for a few seconds because of her thick, brown hair. But Gabe shook it off and instead tried to attack them with humor.

"This is what's called an introduction to the newest device?" Her hand soothed her smarting head.

"This girl can move! Let's give her a chance to use her talent. It'll work for us all."

"Never speak to José again, and we'll talk!"

"It's the fight of your dreams." Vince the promoter. "Only three hours of your time. L.A. Saturday."

"No can do. Olivia and I have a big design gig, then state boxing finals—"

"Olivia can come, and there'll be something in it for her too."

"We don't care about the money, Vince."

"An easy twenty-five grand if you win, ten if you lose. Two grand for Olivia, your, say, 'manager' either way." He did some figuring. "It's a win-win for all."

"I need college money. But I want freedom."

"I can get you freedom. You'd be surprised at how much pull I have."

"You don't have pull for where I want pull, Vince."

"Where's that? You'd be surprised where I have pull."

"Heaven? I want José out of this evil gang. I'm aiming *up*, no going back."

Diego stepped toward Gabe. "Your brother is not very popular right now, with the law and the gang. He's crossing the shot callers so he's expendable. Hey, Fika just brought Ramón home from the hospital." The men looked to see if Gabe registered hurt.

"They're a good match." Gabe smiled.

"What's your play, girl star?" Vince moved forward aggressively.

"Let José out of your clutches, and I'll fight."

"Agreed, super girl Gabe."

Diego leaned his ear to Vince. "No one else will do?"

"I want *her*. She's so hot she makes steam look cool."

"Deal." Vince looked at his device and walked to his car with Diego slinking after him.

"Tell them you have an appointment to get your face made up ... ah, broken."

"Ouch." Gabe winced as Olivia delivered her callous comeback when asked how to ditch the Disney orientation for the fight.

"Yes, ouch! You expect me to sit there and enjoy you getting beat up when you could work an honest job? You'll be a doctor if you can pay for school. You need someone to pound some sense into you!" Olivia turned her neck to see if Coach had arrived at the center boxing ring.

"It's our ticket out. José free, and some college funds for me."

"What makes you think José wants to go free?"

"He doesn't. But he doesn't know how close he is to getting taken out. I fight, and it's a professional version of getting jumped out."

"What about championships?"

"I don't want to blow my chances there and disappoint Coach."

"Of course. And you think you got a deal with Vince? Those people don't know what a fair deal is." Olivia shook her finger.

"It's a week before the state finals." Coach walked in slowly.

Gabe hoped he didn't hear much of the conversation.

"Blow your chances? Sounds like you're going for a 'Puncher's Choice'—a knockout blow—but the odds are against it."

"I can do it. I'll fight to be free. Olivia, come with me!"

"If I come—" Olivia hesitated.

"You be there, Coach?"

"Take a hand, Gabe, rather than a fist." Coach handed her the red gloves as she pranced into the practice ring. "That's the move. Now give it a little shimmy ... and turn it into a jab." Coach quietly stalked around the outer perimeter of the ring as Gabe mimed her footwork in the match. "Think 'Eye of the Tiger'.'"

"*Vámonos*, let's go, chica." Olivia cheered.

Gabe stepped up the momentum with a vigorous one-two punch.

"That's it. Think your rival's a pussycat, and you're a tiger." Coach directed Gabe. "She's in your territory. Make her your prey."

Gabe tried not to smile or to let anything break her concentration. *If Coach is anything, he's a great big pussycat even though he growls a lot—a pussycat or a big California bear.*

"You're better than most men I've worked with." Coach looked sincere. "But Vince is not one to mess with. He's got some mean front men behind the scenes at these dodgy fights. He's even into some kinky video, closed-circuit TV, audiences pay to see ultimate fighting-plus stuff."

"Bottom line?"

"Funky. He may take more than he'll give, Gabe."

The phone rang. Coach turned to pick it up and whispered gruffly while wiping the sweat off his brow. "Have the doctor call me." He hung up and shook his head.

"Everything okay?"

"Gabe, my son's condition is critical."

"Your son?" Petra entered the gym.

"He still hasn't come to from the surgery. Ex-wife won't let me in the room."

Gabe leaned against the ropes. "Wow. What's his condition? Was it your son who stopped a fight?"

"Coach is too humble to say his son's a hero. His son stepped in between two disputing parents at our gym." Petra read them in. "Kept them from killing each other. One landed a blow to his son's head. Internal bleeding. He's in ICU."

"Now there's a champion. Hope the bleeding stops soon."

"Gabe, nothing's worth getting your body totally worked over." Coach sighed.

"You can't see him?" Olivia frowned.

"Nah. Can't always protect the people you care about."

"What if we could get some money for his medical bills?" Petra offered.

"The fight." Gabe pounded her glove.

Al looked unsure. "Uh. Take care of yourself, Gabe. I been hit so many times I wanted to write on my gold robe, *La Piñata de Dios*, God's piñata bag."

Petra and Olivia winced, while Gabe looked at him curious.

"You know, when I was fighting at the Olympic Auditorium, I had a mean, monster-like opponent who had bitten his latest opponent's neck and caused nerve damage. And when I was in the room getting taped up for the event, he came down the hall, swearing at me, talking bad things about my mother, bad things that made me boil inside. I couldn't sit still. I just got up from the table and beat him up right there and then."

Gabe gave him a fist bump.

"It only took a minute to turn him into a bloody mess. That's all the fight there was that night—right there in the therapy room. Sadly, spectators' ticket prices were refunded, and I was suspended from boxing for some peak years."

"People said you were great and could've been greater." Petra tapped his arm. "But Gabe—"

Al practiced holding Gabe's hands up in the air while he hummed the *Rocky* theme in his gravelly, low-pitched voice. "*Ta da da da, ta da da da* ... rising high now."

"Coach. I'm going to win just so I don't have to hear you sing that awful song off-tune ever again."

# chapter 30

GABE MANAGED NOT TO flip Vince off, but she came very close to doing it. She wanted to give him the finger in front of "the suits" or choke him until his neck turned purple, not just on account of the iPad assault. He'd promised her a limo. Gabe was looking forward to taunting him while riding in the limo. In her imagination, her skirt would hike up when she leaned over to accept the sparkling champagne Vince poured for her, and she would distract him with a glimpse of her shapely thigh. Instead of the exclusive limo he promised her, Vince rolled into the community center in a lopsided retired bus with three tires and what looked like only a hubcap. Gabe and Olivia stood at the corner of McFadden—they were uninformed and unimpressed with their cheap transportation. Petra had previous commitments.

Olivia looked shocked over the bus being full of chattering young ladies arranging their clothing, hair, and makeup. Gabe had told her friends it was an exclusive invitation. Now she was seeing the real Vince: fast and cheap, all the way a promoter, if not a trafficker. Although she shuddered at what the setup for the match would be like, she was excited that the prize money might be something to give Coach for his son.

"You're going through with this?"

"Vince will pay, Olivia."

"Money up front? No?" Olivia lowered her eyes and sighed.

"Welcome, Gabe. Ladies." Vince observed Olivia's defiant confidence and style as she took one look back at Gabe before mounting the steps of the bus.

"This is some limo." Olivia climbed over a Selena-look-alike applying charcoal eye makeup and robin egg blue, and sat down as Vince waved them to come to the two seats he was saving at the rear of the bus.

"We have some openings in the prefight beauty contest, Olivia."

"This 'lady' is above you, mister." Vince left them and skulked at the front of the bus.

Gabe burst out laughing.

As Olivia squeezed in, she said, "Vince is a class act, wouldn't you say?"

Gabe and Olivia huddled together in a rickety row. The sound of thunder rumbled at close range. Rain splatted against the loosely sealed windows and made them grasp their jackets tighter.

"Well, so much for the celebrity treatment." Olivia leaned forward to hear Vince shouting on his mobile.

"Pack as many high rollers into the boxes as you can. Remember: lots of booze and you know what else." Vince started rock 'n' rolling.

"Keep your eye on the prize money purpose, Gabe—Coach's son's medical bills and your pre-med funds." Gabe nodded to Olivia.

"Hi, I'm Lucia." The petite, dyed blonde turned around in the seat in front of them. "Vince is the kind of guy who gives a girl a break. You'll see."

"Hi, Lucia. Your name reminds me of my niece named *Luz*, for 'light.'"

A flash could be seen crackling through the dirty bus windows.

"Look, lightning always makes me shiver." Lucia pulled her sweater close.

Gabe melted back into her seat stitched of half cloth, half stuffing, sliding down low so as to cover her eyes from the Cyclopean whirlwinds. Storm fell. The winds blew across the traffic lanes, forcefully ripping out shrubs at the side of the highway. For the next twenty minutes, the rains poured unrelentingly. Wind tipped over small trees. The strongest ones still held by the roots swayed back and forth, bending with and submitting to the elements, with the stiff ones resisting, while the tumultuous wind currents were snapping and breaking.

"Ay, yi yi!" a tall brunette screamed and clenched tighter to her crucifix.

"Why doesn't it stop?" Lucia whined to Gabe.

One girl rocked back and forth, supporting her makeup case in front of her as if it could stop the attack of nature.

"This little light of mine, I'm gonna let it shine." Lucia began to hum and then sang the words. One after another, the girls joined in the chorus.

"A gospel swamp was here years ago, at the Santa Ana riverbed, Costa Mesa." Gabe pointed out the city freeway sign. "Abuelita said preachers found wetlands islands and set up tents."

"For singing?" Lucia asked.

"Singing and maybe shouting. I don't know! One preacher held meetings at his or some neighbor's house where people would gather. 'Swamp angels,' they named worshippers, as I remember her telling."

"Amazing you remember this from Abuelita."

"In the 1800s," Gabe whispered, turning back to Olivia.

"Swamp angels are calling!" Lucia sang out. Her body swayed as the girls' voices swelled. Cecelia jumped up to join her and soon the whole busload of young women stood. Pounding feet, clapping hands, and jumping crazily on the rickety seats, they giggled and threw tissues, socks, leggings, and T-shirts.

Soon, the bus was full of clothing piles. Caught up in the dance, half clothed, hands over ears, the girls sang out every time the thunder clapped. One girl gushed: "Who has a smartphone? A camera?"

Lucia shrugged to the girl. "Who would want to see pictures of us?"

"What do you mean? Who wouldn't?" Olivia elbowed Gabe.

"My sweater is halfway across the bus. Look at me." A girl stood up and twirled.

"Yeah, they'd look at you, 'swamp angel'!" Lucia started to film. "Let's put the pictures on YouTube! A gospel swamp website for young women who want to enter beauty contests to see how we do it. Backstage makeup, hair, costumes, you know, how a girl does it, how we dress."

"Yes, undress. Good for marketing." An evil edge tainted Vince's voice.

"Undress? Explain the process? Let the camera follow us around like this—"

Lucia moved her video around.

"Go, girl. *Mucho amor.* Love you so much." Vince threw her a kiss.

"Why do you wear such short earrings?" Lucia fingered the brunette Selena look-alike's earring.

"I don't know. Maybe so you don't tear them off me!"

"Put it all online. We'll make some profit." Vince stirred them up.

"Show them ... how to make it look good ... make it <u>real</u> good." A pop star look-alike sang, not leaning out into the aisles.

"Oh yeah!" Lucia looked fearless.

"This is good." Vince stuck his nose in more. "Film of the girls dressing and undressing on the bus. We'll be interviewing you girls who want more talent work."

"Petra would find a way to help these girls." Olivia was incensed.

"I think I'm sick. Open a window." Gabe moaned.

A window opened, and the air rushed in—a blast blew hail at all the girls.

"Hurry up, close it, I'm freezing. How will I fight after all this?" Gabe coughed back the phlegm. "Huh? You tell me how I can fight."

"Like you always do, my niece. Like you're pure, mad, raving, out of your mind!"

Vince swung a lacy T-shirt around his little finger up high in the air.

Lucia giggled.

Gabe coughed again. "Olivia?"

"We're in over our heads, Gabe, but we won't let Vince know."

# chapter 31

THE CROWD MOVED AS a whole organism, slithering, snakelike, and filtering into the foaming arena cesspool. Gabe trembled like a captive to the exotic sights of people of every gender, androgynous and alternative, gathered around ringside waiting for the promised prefight parade and festivities.

Her nostrils filled with odors similar to the foods that she'd smelled late nights at the Asian sector's outdoor festivals they'd cooked for the ghosts of their ancestors. Row after row of dark-street-corridor smells would waft up—aromas of broiled pork barbequed on a skewer and meats cooked in rich, fatty oils.

The crowd, only some of them women, were some of the most amazing creatures she'd ever seen, garbed in less fabric than would befit Jane of the jungle, and many looked like a combination of wild cheetah, leopard, lynx, or tiger—a human jungle, and a steamy one at that. Unsurprised at the mix, Gabe saw a seemingly perfectly sculpted blond runway model in demure spandex tights and a pink floral top. The model stuck her tongue out at the Master of Ceremonies, who took the stage.

Stuffed like a penguin into a tuxedo over a starched shirt, complete with tails, the MC looked uncomfortable, and his announcements came in corny, banal sound bites. An actor, who had been told to memorize his cue cards only seconds before, huffed and spit out clichés. The audience hooted at his ineptness until the parade of contestants was preempted by a beauty contest of the women Gabe had traveled with.

Gabe surveyed the room. Did Vince hook up the entertainment and illegal flash-fight events to live satellite cables? Why did select groups pay to go into virtual and in-person rooms to watch someone live get thrashed in a stagey, cat-type fight to the end? Girl fighters couldn't stop until one was down. She gulped. This didn't fit with her medical ethics. Was this Gabe's fight category? Nah. And, she's never the one down. Up close and personal, cameras streamed reactions of friends, beauty contestants, and spectators. Vince moved around, seeking out his high-paying connections.

Vince's Asian affiliates scurried around in the background. A cross-fire of glances erupted between the two rival Asian groups, who feuded in Westminster. Multimedia cameras caught a prefight catfight. When an Asian gang leader talked to Diego, Gabe listened from behind a booth. Did he say he wanted to do a trade, sell electronics black market through his network, get back at the Westminster gang, and blockade the group's business with Vince's help? Or were they traffickers? Were the fights only a cover?

Vince left the gangster and pulled Olivia forward to the front row, where she tripped over a cord attached to another hidden camera. His hand strayed to her back. Olivia flinched. Gabe jumped, responding to her aunt's movement.

"Don't touch me." Olivia lectured him. "That's not to be filmed."

"Business networking." Vince was insistent.

"Is this how this is going down?" Gabe saw the cameras manned by rough, unshaven men in black jumpsuits with reflective stripes. A greasy-looking man sat at a soundboard, manipulating volume and closing camera angles.

An Asian wrestler did deep knee bends and breathed deeply at a woman wearing a zebra-striped skirt. She echoed back with a hip swivel on a light-enhanced hula hoop. Black-and-white zigzags funneled into a tornado-like strobe light with a fluorescent searchlight effect.

"What's that flashy hula hoop like?" Gabe came close to the woman.

"It's a heavier hoop. Fun. How about finding yourself a costume?" She pointed out some garish-looking garb.

Gabe's face fell, and Olivia's eyes widened.

Vince nudged Gabe. "Come on. Don't tell me you've never seen any of this before."

"Bring it, sister!" The hula hooper yowled.

"The group paying Vince to watch off-site." Olivia nudged Gabe as they looked at a secreted sound booth set. "I've even heard cops set up and tear down for these groups, and then everything looks normal hours later."

"Good thing Petra didn't come. She wouldn't like me here!" Gabe flushed.

"It's not how I roll." Olivia groaned. "You're making college money and helping Coach's son, right? Otherwise, I'll split. I don't want a cent of manager money."

As Vince signaled Gabe to get in the ring for the main event, canopy curtains over the ring came down to reveal a chain fence around a striped surface with all the gates padlocked. Vince yanked Gabe by the arm, threw her through the gate, and locked it. Gabe looked at her opponent, who was already in the opposite corner. A monstrous creature almost twice her size gave a guttural roar and raised its arms. The crowd screamed back at it.

Shocked, Gabe gazed at the gigantic metallic image, lit up by flashing spotlights and strobes. Gabe sighted the Kevlar costume, which absorbed blows, and a metal left arm. *What am I up against? A cyborg? Was it the dark warrior image at the festival?* She tried to keep composed, assessing the embodiment of cybernetics, body parts enhanced by computer technology. Gabe stared at Olivia, who got on her phone.

*The creature looked like one of Gabe's designs!*

It charged toward Gabe first. Gabe stepped aside and let it run through and past her into the chain mail of the cage. The cage rattled, and the crowd roared more. The creature then flung itself at Gabe and landed an unexpected blow to her right torso. Gabe grasped her shoulder. The crowd hushed, all of a sudden realizing this was a woman against not another woman in costume but a being made of artificial composites.

Gabe's shock halted her pain. Pure spectacle.

"Scumbag Vince." She wheezed. Gabe's balance and quick movements kept her dancing as the creature's metallic arms struck out one blow after another. If she could keep away from the armor and let it wear itself out.

Another series of blows and Gabe was on her back. The crowd was on her side, screaming, but she couldn't get back up. She looked for a way out. Was this ultimate—a fight to the finish?! Another shock. She drilled in mentally to win to save her life.

At the fence, she saw a fuzzy, familiar face with a strained look—Coach! He glared at her furiously, hands held high in a time-out sign. He wanted her out *now*!

*The only way out is to win*. Coach's concern inspired her. She struggled to her feet, and the crowd gasped.

Al shook his head as Gabe went back into action with a strong right and then a left hook, which just glanced off her rival.

Against the odds, Gabe started to get up on top of the artificial adversary—leaping, kicking, then fading back. She set her sights on winning for Al's son and her college fund.

The opponent played dirty, grabbing at Gabe from all angles and then whipping around its metal arm to sting Gabe from the side. Stunned and winded, she turned to look where Coach popped up. He was gone! Her head started to spin. She staggered, fell to her knees, and tried to get up. The crowd screamed for blood. She struggled and got upright.

Gabe boxed legit, the only way she knew how. Yet she'd have to try different tactics. She quickly jabbed the cyborg's artificial obliques. Then she backed up. It looked confused. She gave a sweeping kick to the opponent's legs; it lost its balance. She swept out a clever kick, and it wobbled. Another kick and the monstrosity stumbled over. It hit the deck with a clatter. She jumped on it. *Here's my chance!* As she kept jumping, it tried to punch up and out with the metal arm. She heard a ding. *What was off?* The giant danced with exploding arm wires and then thudded to the floor.

A girl referee in pink counted a quick ten from outside the cage. The creature lay motionless, gasping. Gabe raised gloved hands above her head in victory!

Olivia looked as if she half-fainted in relief. Coach was nowhere to be seen. Gabe saw Vince and Diego's deflated scowls.

Through the air rang the sound of whistles and speakers.

"Hands up! Everybody!" The policemen gave commands. Uniformed men searched the crowd, probably looking for

Vince and Diego, the fight promoters. Police proceeded to shut the event down. They took everyone, even the beauty contest entrants, whimpering and shivering in their skimpy outfits, not at all like 'swamp angels' anymore. Still locked inside the cage, Gabe complied, putting her hands in the air. The form—human, hybrid, or composite—with a costume of machinery components lay oddly crumpled up.

Coach ran up with Petra behind him. Petra helped to direct the police toward the promoters. Vince stayed with his business face on, as if he could talk himself out of anything, while Diego scurried away. Coach ran down to the cage, ripped open a hole in a weak area of the wire, and helped Gabe out. He offered his arm to her and threw a fighter's robe over her. The two ducked until warning shouts stopped and police made arrests. The police lifted up the creature and seemed to have trouble transporting what looked like a huge man inside the metallic creature costume.

"Some fair woman-to-woman fight." Gabe became more alert.

Vince and his paid henchmen looked at Gabe and Coach with hatred. "I'll get you!" Vince sneered as he was taken away.

Gabe looked around. Diego wasn't there.

"You'll never be safe!" Vince screeched, while Coach and fighter ran out of the area. Gabe threw her arms around Coach and sobbed for a few seconds. Petra came up to hold her and Olivia while Gabe's body shook.

"I tried to win for your son."

"No matter, Gabe. This kind of fight you don't want to win."

"I'll take you and Olivia home. We'll sort it out later."

"Diego will put a hit out on me, Petra. I'm a target."

"Yeah, there's that. But Vince will be gone for a while." Leave it to Coach to accentuate the positive.

"What do you say to someone who has a hit put out on her?" Gabe turned to Petra as the solemn group walked out of the makeshift fight venue.

"*Paso a paso*, one step at a time."

# PART II
## CARTAGENA, COLOMBIA

*When one has faith the odds of good things happening become short rather than long.*
—David Baldacci

# chapter 32

*HOMEGIRL, I HEAR YOUR prayer.*
It came in the still quiet. The whisper. Gabe didn't move.
Was this the living spirit she'd prayed to?

She found her way to Petra's office the next morning, feeling as if she were gliding, and once again sat down on the familiar worn couch to share. Gabe reminded Petra about her students excelling in self-defense class. She shivered as she spoke about the certain hit put out on her by Diego and Ramón. Ramón and Fika were back together. José was sure to be arrested.

"I need to get out of here fast. Coach won't let me fight in the championships, too much exposure." Gabe pounded her fists inside her sweatshirt pockets.

"Looks like you need to make a change."

"After my anatomy final, I'm clear, but I don't have anyone I can stay with." Gabe shifted her weight. "Mamacita is looking for a place."

Petra peered at the calendar above her desk.

"The women's network may help. Can you get your shots and an expedited passport?

Maybe it's time to find your *abuela*." Petra pointed to her bulletin board map where a small country in South America was circled—Colombia.

"Colombia? Abuelita is Colombian but lived in other places. She became a US citizen, and later she disappeared."

"Your family hasn't heard from her, Gabe?"

"No. She left."

Petra texted and waited. "They have an opening for a clinic assistant and self-defense instructor. New Day: Women, Cartagena, Colombia. Flights paid. Sounds perfect."

"Sounds like me."

"Congressman Deborah and her charity friends are in this networking group. And ..." Petra lifted her eyebrow.

"And what?"

"Your *abuela* may want you to be part of her life."

"Abuelita can't be in this group. I think she's alone, away from family, off the grid."

"Time will tell. Anyway, Deborah and this group, New Day: Women, they'll support you. They're admired by women's networks internationally."

"I'm not sure."

"How would it look on your resume: clinic assistant to an indigenous doctor?"

"My life's in jeopardy here. Now I'm supposed to sprout wings?"

"Free airline flights."

"I'll have to put on my oxygen mask first."

"Care for yourself before you fix others. You're my off-kilter fly girl!" Petra laughed and gave her a hug.

Takeoff gave her a new sense of freedom as the wheels lifted and the plane carried her into parts unknown. Although Gabe had seen the modern complexities of the John Wayne airport before through naive eyes—ticket machines, long lines, baggage conveyors, personal scanners, boarding bridge this was her first experience with an international flight, air turbulence, and a rocky descent. Seven hours later, still steadying herself from the flight, Gabe clasped her instructions and entered the Rafael Núñez International Airport in Cartagena, Colombia. After she disembarked, Gabe followed signs in familiar Spanish. She prepared to meet another Hispanic culture, one very much its own entity. The local girls who'd be in her self-defense class spoke English and Spanish, and she was excited to meet them. She ruminated over Petra's counsel to get more pre-med practice.

Gabe hunted for the woman who would take her to the humanitarian base. A Latina with a tanned and wrinkled face in a greenish serape appliqued cloth waved at her, introduced herself as Teresa, and guided Gabe out.

"I'm part tour guide and part jeep driver." Teresa changed jerky gears. "Although I enjoy the touring part, it's just a hobby." Gabe climbed into the military-looking olive-green and khaki-beige camouflage jeep, matching Teresa's outfit, all looking very out of place at the sophisticated airport. Gabe prepared herself to meet Colombia.

"Mysterious South American coast." Gabe had a lilt in her voice.

"You bet!" Teresa exclaimed. "We love it."

A half hour later, Teresa pattered on about the uneven village streets with ancient black and brown stones paving the way to the astounding Cathedral of Cartagena de Indias in Colombia. "Stone by stone, this is the most beautiful site I've ever seen."

"It's the first cathedral outside of my hometown I've ever seen."

"The height and grandeur of the spires!" Teresa said. "Whereas in California, Gabe, most churches were built very recently, here, the architecture dates back to 1577. Spires rise up into the sky as if to reach to a place far beyond possibility!"

"Heaven." Gabe scrunched her face at Teresa, then stuck her head out the window.

"Carvings on the outside here reflect ancient saints and columns from the colonial era, a strange mix altogether here. Main portal, cornices, tower, and dome were added later."

"People are lined up two across to get in." The scene took Gabe by surprise.

"Two abreast they walk through the heavy wooden doors during pilgrimage."

Gabe noted Teresa was prone to pontificating.

"Penitents and tourists, the paupers and the well-heeled alike gather to enter the mystical edifice."

"I'll take things up with you soon." Gabe whispered up into the air as a continuation of her hometown prayer to God in the breeze.

"Pardon me for hearing, but this country does have a way of bringing people in touch with their spiritual lives."

"I see light everywhere, but what's too shiny may not be true."

Teresa nodded thoughtfully. "You'll get to know Dr. Martinez and maybe his wife. Good people. I think you'll like working in the med clinic."

They drove into a rural forested area on the way to the humanitarian base, New Day: Women. A protective cover of lush vegetation on both sides flanked the long and winding roads. Gabe grinned, feeling more enthusiasm than she'd felt in a long time. Teresa chatted about the facility and its mission to rescue and equip young women. A squawking of colorful birds made Gabe jump so her head almost hit the ceiling of the jeep, and she let out a shriek back at them.

Teresa smiled at her and spread her free arm, acting like a bird. "Almost two thousand species of birds fly here. This is also home to the teensy poisonous Colombian dart frog. Try not to step on one." Teresa laughed. "Actually, it's not funny. The skin emits a toxin. It hospitalized my friend for a month."

Sweat beads sprung out on Gabe's forehead, and her heart pounded.

"Of course, we gear up when we go off the grid to protect ourselves from the inch-long bullet ants, which can paralyze humans, and the huge, hairy pink-toed tarantulas."

"I'll be on the grid then. I don't do monster ants, and I like tarantulas behind glass."

"Used to the roads already? You seem relaxed. It usually takes newcomers a while."

Jostled by a ditch, Gabe reached for the overhead hand grip.

Teresa's hands held steady on the wheel. She maneuvered the jeep past several pathways, more often than not taking the roads less traveled.

"Quite a remarkable maze we're in."

"We like only *invited* guests. These roads would really slow down anyone else."

"Are we in the rainforest?"

"You'd know if we were. Wild parts are the rainforest entrance, but here is mainly farmland."

Disguised by overgrowth at some bends, the switchbacks appeared to come to an end many times before the jeep burst through. The right forks led to a facility about the size of three football fields or twenty times as big as Gabe's Grace Community Center. A few outdoor areas looked like gardens and recreation fields.

New Day: Women looked formidable.

At the entrance stood three burly young men and one woman with automatic rifles. They wore camouflage shirts, pants, and vests holding ammo rounds. Gabe tensed to see this display of force popping out of the natural habitat, although Teresa looked relaxed. Gabe had thought she'd left guns behind. The guards looked inside the vehicle and scrupulously checked the trunk. As a unit, they tipped their hats to her. One burly guard, a little older than Gabe, gave her a wide white-teeth smile. She smiled back curious.

"Roberto. He's in charge of the specialists." Teresa's voice went up as if she admired him. Gabe looked around one hundred eighty degrees. The tops of the walls of the entire compound were composed of irregular, broken glass to ward off intruders. "You'll like Jessie." Teresa pointed to the strong woman guard about in her forties.

"I hope Petra was right about this being a not-to-miss opportunity. I may miss home."

"Think your neighborhood was home, sweet home? From what I hear, they have a hit out on you." Teresa cast wary eyes on Gabe.

"Never said home was homey. I'm happy to be where I can teach self-defense and work in the medical clinic. Maybe do art or design."

"We offer a wide range of activities."

"Oh?" Gabe stopped to see if Teresa would say more.

Instead, Teresa handed Gabe a note that read "Get settled. Your first assignment is to meet the Cartagena mayor's Honorary Citizen of the Year at the dignitary ceremony. Prepare to leave at 18:00 for the historic Castillo San Felipe de Barajas."

"Who's this from?"

"You'll find out when you get there. I'm your wheels," said Teresa. "Oh, and put on your best threads."

"A donated black dress and sweater. Homegirl's finest." Gabe gave a big smile.

"Absolutely." Teresa bantered back. "That's more dressed up than we usually get."

"Oh, I like this place already." Gabe jumped out of the jeep, relieved when her feet hit the solid dirt road.

chapter **33**

"THE CASTILLO WAS NAMED in honor of Spain's
Phillip IV and Governor Pedro Zapata, and it was
the greatest fortress ever built by the Spaniards in any of
their colonies." Teresa rattled on. "It's another one of the
reasons I'm crazy about Cartagena. By day, the castle looks
tourist-friendly, with its fresh green lawns and an unfurled
flag. By night, it looks like a treacherous compound holding
an enchantment, as it did in historical times, over the city's
enemies and even its own citizens."

"Treacherous, you say?" Gabe pulled her black sweater
close over her dress.

"At the time. See the terreplein, the horizontal top of a
rampart where cannons are placed and protected by a para-
pet? What great battles must have been fought here against
seafaring marauders challenging the city! It's austere and
well preserved, the most formidable defensive complex of
Spanish military architecture ever."

"A castle's a castle. Really not on my radar."

"Pirate ships shot cannonballs and even hit a nunnery.
What once was a holy convent is now a top tier hotel and

restaurant with authentic tile, lush greenery, exotic flowers. Original balconies, arches."

"The pirates must've had really bad aim to disturb prayers."

"In the US, you celebrate the explorers, but they were the real pirates."

*Does she think I skipped school?*

"Well, here's something you may not know about the castle. Underground tunnels form an enigmatic, complex system of tunnels with inner chambers able to be exploded in the case of overhead attackers."

"Serious backup."

"Indeed. I've studied them."

"You said 'enigmatic.' I'm in AP English, but I don't get how tunnels are enigmatic."

"Difficult to understand, mysterious. If you study defense systems—"

"You have?"

"I have. This historic castle fortress was quite ingenious. An engineering feat. Also, in the seventeenth century, the Plaza de los Coches, close by here in the Old Town, contained a world slave market. Courtyards housed a bustling slave trade for Europeans bringing enslaved people from Africa and some islands. Brutal."

"Hope that was then and this is now."

"One would hope, but slavery still exists in many forms." Teresa sighed.

"Enigmatic."

"Many people escaped the slave market in Palenque. In fact, a population of five thousand was able to keep their tribal language as they hid in San Basilio de Palenque about fifty kilometers north."

"How'd they escape?"

"Braided money and maps with directions in their hair."

"Can I get my hair braided?" Gabe gave her snark.

"Maybe."

"Can you let me off? I can see El Castillo from here."

"No. The city can be … dangerous."

"I can take care of myself. It's only a couple of minutes."

Teresa paused. "Off with you."

Near the castle outskirts at dusk, people walked briskly past Gabe, most at a steady pace, in the sultry evening air.

"Gorgeous." Gabe admired a woman who swished by in a dress of bright Caribbean yellow, blue, and red. Many women were attired in bold primary colors, and the men wore jeans and leather.

As the sun set and light turned to dark, the crowd thinned. Gabe walked closer to the castle. Shadows played against the walls, forming eerie shapes. *Was that a Colombian artilleryman or the ghost of a captured sea marauder?* Gabe mused about Teresa's appreciation of the castle's presence. In her mind's eye, she could see artillerymen positioning, taking in the seascape from the wall, rotating their heavy cannons, aiming at sea pirates as well as foreign navies. She imagined what the underground tunnels must be like and marveled at the creative vision of Spanish architects. The night was still, and she felt calm. In Deborah's black dress and sweater, she haunted the nightscape.

Despite Gabe's slight jet lag, her Santa Ana street-sense picked up. Her mind sensed two shady characters clinging to the walls of the monument. With a whiff of night breeze, she took in the human scents and shapes, probably in dark clothing. A black half shadow fell across the cathedral walls and disappeared. Was it a bike or a car? At the same time, an unwelcome feeling hit her gut. At home, the Santa Ana streets would burst into gang activity if soldiers were hiding from their prey, but this milieu was distinctly different. Gabe felt goosebumps on her arms.

Flashes of crinkled leather in jacket form and dark shocks of hair appeared, and hyena-hysterical laughs poured into the night. Tracking a new breed of predator prowling city streets, Gabe felt unsure she could keep her footing. Now, she clearly viewed two thugs with the home advantage. She held her breath and waited, silently shifting her weight ever so slightly from foot to foot, compact, ready to spring as if she were in a boxing ring.

*Who'll make the first move?* She would posture as long as needed. She got her bearings, calculated the lights at the ceremony at approximately a hundred yards away. She could sprint there in several seconds.

Gabe figured the predators were still checking her out. They waited. She kept up her quiet boxer's patter. "This is what my homies can do." Coach had said this to her, and she could almost hear him approve of her careful footwork from many countries away.

She'd handle this at home differently than she would here. Back home, someone would directly confront her with the question, "Where are you from?" Here, she didn't know what to expect, but she anticipated they would act like common criminals given their first opportunity. She was right.

The larger of the two men lunged, and Gabe reacted with instinctual readiness, fists up and feet readying. The large man moved back. She considered her response. First, Gabe thought, she could move forward and kick him. Next, she could take him by surprise and hit him with a left hook. Third, she could run. *Run now!* Her brain screamed.

Gabe ran two blocks to where lights from flashing cameras shone on the castle wall. Over her shoulder, she saw the threat had dissipated. The moonlit scene absorbed the men with only a kick of their tennis shoes flashing in the reflections of car lights. She shuddered at the confrontation averted. She looked at her hands, shaking slightly, knowing she was fortunate her foes hesitated.

A loudspeaker blared.

She felt more nervous to meet the mayor's honorary Citizen of the Year than facing opposition in foreign streets. Lights beckoned her to come forward to the crowded ceremony area. In the middle of the flashbulbs and photographers, a man in a suit shook hands with a white-haired woman in an exquisitely woven, purple floral-patterned dress and shawl. The scene seemed familiar yet odd. Gabe took a second.

The celebrated woman in front of her, founder of the Cartagena branch of New Day: Women, broke free of the crowd and rushed toward her, arms outstretched. Gabe took a step back, thinking she'd blocked the way of wherever this woman was headed.

"Gabriela, *m'nieta*, my granddaughter!" The white-haired woman greeted her warmly.

Gabriela? How long since Gabe had heard her formal name aloud? Not since the police station? And what else did this matriarch call her? The woman approaching Gabe looked familiar.

"How was your trip, Gabriela?"

"Good." Gabe awoke into recognition. *Could it be her?* Gabe stiffened. She turned away.

The woman stretched out her arms to Gabe, pulling her back, enfolding her into a love and security that Gabe sensed even after so many years and miles. Her face nestled up to clean hair and a fragrant neck. Gabe now understood this was the woman she'd loved as a child. Yet, Gabe didn't feel cozy seeing her. Mounting feelings of abandonment overshadowed any delight.

"It's me. Your abuelita. Micah to others."

Gabe felt a whirl of conflicting emotions.

"I hope you're feeling welcome and finding your way around."

Gabe nodded nervously, trying to release her tension. She'd already rebelled against their rules by almost engaging in a street fight where she was not supposed to be walking.

"These are my helpers: Teresa, who you've met, and Jessie." Gabe recognized Jessie as one of the toned compound guards about Abuelita's age. Jessie looked at her sideways as she tied her long, dark hair back with a colorful cord. Gabe noticed Jessie's Anglo features.

"This award would never have come to me without their help. The New Day: Women activities, teams, and efforts are all coordinated by our leaders. We've worked together for years." Micah's eyes circled around the group and landed on Teresa. "Gabriela, you'll train with Teresa."

"All right." Gabe smiled. She nodded to the aides.

"I'll be seeing you." Teresa chuckled.

"You'll meet others, Gabriela. They are also honored citizens." Abuelita spoke in a low voice. "They don't want their identity exposed in public. There's more to this than you see here. It's not quite as it may seem."

Gabe stepped back.

A gentle rain started to fall, and the woman identifying herself as Abuelita looked tenderly at her granddaughter.

Gabe felt the pain of the silent years. She'd ached to feel the love of Abuelita since childhood, but it wasn't what she'd expected. It was a different type of heartache than unrequited love, more like lovesickness for her long-lost ancestor, combined with the metallic feeling that life wasn't always kind.

"I run New Day: Women."

"Abue-Abuelita," Gabe stuttered, taken aback. "I'm here to teach and work in the med clinic. I'm not sure I can work with you here."

"*Sí, se puede.*" Abuelita's words rolled easily off her tongue. "Yes, you can." It sounded like Abuelita must say this to all her workers.

"Our taxi is here." Abuelita walked to where Jessie drove the base's van.

Gabe followed, sensing the light drizzle. In the back seat of the van, she tried to hold it all in, and then took the offensive. "How can you be so smooth?"

"What do you mean?"

"You abandoned us." Gabe fired out the words.

"I had to leave."

"Mamacita misses you. José misses you. We spent years and years without you. We'll never get the time back."

"I'm just realizing it, seeing how you've grown."

"Why did you leave?"

"I had reasons." Abuelita tossed the shawl corner over her shoulder.

"Cruel ones?"

"Reasons, whether or not you think they're good enough."

"You left to become honorary Citizen of the Year?" Gabe hung her head.

"Now I see what it looks like to you. I'm sorry."

"That's all?"

"I hear you. I'm here now." Abuelita moved in on Gabe's sadness.

"I'm here too, thousands of miles from home. Here for myself, not for you."

"The point is to get you helping the indigenous doctor and teaching self-defense to the girls. I had some of your same struggles, Gabe. I'll tell you why I left. Later."

"We need you. Needed you. I have a hit out on me. And José, your grandson, has been arrested. He got in with bad men."

"Sí, *pobrecita*, my poor little girl. Petra told me about it."

"Petra?" Jetlag seemed to be making Gabe groggy.

"Now rest. It's late."

Gabe's head fell back against the headrest. "Abuelita, I'm tired. Though I *will* find out why you left and why you asked me to come." Gabe's eyes felt heavy.

"I hope I can tell you, *m'nieta*." Abuelita hummed, and Gabe sensed her close through her smell and touch. When the van arrived at the base, her abuelita reached up, closed her shawl coat against the cold wind rising, and swung her legs down to the ground, where she stood to her full height.

"Go on. I'll see her to her room." Abuelita waved a royal wave, as if she were a parade queen, and directed Jessie to drive ahead to the compound garage. Then she walked to the dorms with her granddaughter's head resting on her shoulder.

chapter **34**

STARK YET SOLID, THE Cartagena gym wasn't too much of a disappointment for Gabe. In fact, she liked its gritty, no-nonsense setup: basic boxing ring, punching bags, mat for self-defense classes—all minus any frills. She whiffed the air and, wearing her trusty gloves, worked on footwork. A short, solid-looking girl about fourteen gave her a pretty grin. Her expresso, brownish eyes matched her hair. "You our new self-defense teacher and med clinic assistant? I'm Julia."

"Yeah, I'm Gabe."

"Maybe you could've come a little sooner."

"Oh, did I get the time wrong? I'm down for class tomorrow after med clinic."

Julia dropped her head, and Gabe tilted her head to listen.

"My friend María is gone."

"I'm so sorry." Gabe could tell Julia was trying to be strong, but she seemed delicate somehow. Unlike most of the homegirls back home. Teachable.

"Want to chill or talk more?" Gabe opened her arms.

"With all respect, I don't think you'd understand."

"I can try."

"They won't like it if I chase you away with a sad story."

"I'm not going anywhere. Are you headed home, Julia? Mind if I join you?"

"No, uh, I'll be all right."

Gabe knew that type of hesitation. It was the same in Colombia or California, and it sounded like trouble. "Hey, I need to get another mile or two of cardio in tonight. I like the adventure of running in the city." She stepped along with Julia into the night.

Julia called Teresa for the New Day: Women van, and after a few minutes wait in the balmy night air, the three rode into town.

"If these mean streets could talk." Julia recounted to Gabe stories of vulnerable girls followed, targeted, picked up, kidnapped, trafficked.

"Cartels prowl. Sometimes, local families receive ransom notes. Families of tourists in hotels are watched from the moment they arrive at the airport. The tourist father may receive a note at the hotel saying pay a ransom, or his family will die."

"Did that happen to María?"

"María was taken after walking back from the compound by some men. Her family is not rich, but her mother brings home a good paycheck working at the design shop. They want her to pay cash, or they'll kill María. She's not to give the ransom note to the police."

Gabe's voice dropped to a whisper. "Does María's mother live near you?"

"Yes, but her mother won't talk to anyone."

"New Day tries to find girls like María?"

"New Day is ingenious. It has proven informants, technology, and know-how," Julia lowered her voice. "Teresa and Jessie work under the radar. Micah helps a lot of young women. It's her passion."

"I see."

"You don't really see. I can tell."

"Don't know anything about her system. I haven't seen Abuelita—Micah—since I was a child."

"She wants us to be safe here, to learn life skills and self-defense. Someday, we'll help endangered women in other countries. Well, that's my barrio." Julia pointed down the path leading to a small condo with a rust-colored tile roof. "I think Mamá's home."

"Good."

"Do you want to come in? Teresa, you too? She makes the best *tacos de hongos.*"

"Tacos with mushrooms."

"With cilantro-lime rice. Cures all ills. What do you say, clinic assistant Gabe and Teresa?"

"I'll wait here." Teresa peered out warily at the neighborhood.

Gabe nodded and got out after Julia. "Thanks, Teresa." She stepped beside her on the broken concrete. Then she edged her shoulder into Julia, stopping her. "Let's see María's mother first."

"We can try, but she's lost trust. Is there this much danger where you're from?"

"Santa Ana streets are carved up into over forty zones, one gang in each selling drugs. Imagine walking the city blocks to get food, knowing you're on a rival's turf. Is it territorial here?"

"On our street." Julia lifted her chin toward a scruffy-looking teen as they walked.

"You know him?"

"He's around afternoons."

"Back home, dealers 'own' their street corners. Shootings come out of nowhere. Even if you said or did nothing, a bad leader can order a killing just to initiate a new member."

"Senseless." Julia shook her head.

Gabe and Julia looked out into the bustling street. Gabe eyed a large group of men under the trees.

"Almost there." Julia pointed ahead.

"Back home, tough guys ask you, 'Where you from?' You'd better quickly flash their sign, or you might get shot or shanked."

"Shanked? What's that, Gabe?"

"Uh, knifed, but I'm too quick for that." Gabe noted gray clouds gathering in the semi-dark. "Once, three crosstown gangsters stopped me crossing into their territory and asked me where I was from. I prayed hard. One said he saw me box. Another said it couldn't be me. 'How could this girl in a hoodie be a boxer?'"

"Yeah!" Julia giggled nervously.

"While they argued over it, I turned and ran through a dark alley. One ran after me but didn't catch me. I heard him yelling, 'Boxer, I'll get you!'"

"Alert and on your toes!"

"You can prevent attacks by being alert, and you girls need to walk home in groups."

Julia scowled. "When you grow up here, you think it will never happen to you."

"No one does. How long does the rescue system take?"

"I heard they were stuck on María's case." Julia pointed toward a blue house with some chipped paint and an amber porch light beaming. "María's."

Gabe knocked on the door. Julia shouted for María's mother. No answer. She motioned for Julia to come around to the back door.

"It's me, Julia!" Julia bellowed with Gabe's prodding.

A curtain rustled, and a woman peered out.

"Can I come in? I'll be quick." Julia spoke close to the door.

Gabe and Julia waited a couple of minutes. Julia motioned to abandon the idea, but a tired-looking woman opened the door a crack to let Julia into the back sitting room.

"Julia? Careful. Who's this?"

"A friend."

"Were you followed? My María! I can't believe this happened."

"This is Gabe. She's trustworthy. Gabe, this is María's mother, Señora Alvarado." Julia hugged the woman as she collapsed in her arms and choked back sobs.

"Do you have word of my María? It's been two weeks." She motioned toward two chairs with quilted seats.

"Gabe is our defense teacher and clinic assistant. Gabe, Señora Alvarado."

*"Mucho gusto."*

"Thank you. So sad." Gabe noticed a half-open copy of Gabriel García Márquez's *Love in the Time of Cholera* on the side table. "Márquez writes deeply of love and loss."

"Yes." Maria's mother wiped her nose with the sleeve of her cotton dress. "He is true."

"New Day is trying to locate María," Julia offered. "Can you give us more details?" Gabe could see Julia was uncomfortable pressing. Señora Alvarado shook her head.

"Who are these men?" Gabe pointed to a photo of María with serious-looking, leather-clad men.

"One is our guard, our police."

"I haven't heard María talk about him." Julia looked curious.

"He's a new acquaintance."

Gabe raised her eyebrow. "Mind if I snap a photo?"

"The note said no authorities."

"I miss María so much." Julia teared up. "We're praying for her."

A loud knock came from the front door.

"*Buenas noches*. It's Father Alfredo."

"Oh, Father, can you come back tomorrow?" Señora Alvarado shouted.

"How are you doing, my dear?"

"I'm not feeling well."

"We know. I have the police here so you can give them details."

Gabe saw the woman freeze. "No police!" Señora Alvarado was almost crying. "Tell them to go away!"

"One says he's a friend of your daughter."

"What should I do?" Señora Alvarado implored Gabe and Julia.

"Say you're sick." Gabe let out a hushed warning. "Maybe they're not on your side.

"They seem too insistent."

Father Alfredo pled from outside the door.

"Police! We just want a word. We know you're scared. We can help." The men's voices sounded more menacing than helpful. Gabe heard them pushing hard at the door. It would've swung wide open if it wasn't deadbolted.

Señora Alvarado gasped. "Wait. How do they know María's gone? I didn't tell."

"Her friends are sworn to secrecy," Julia added.

"Police. We're here to help. Open up!"

Gabe shook her head.

"Not today, Father." María's mother straightened up to her full height.

"All right, gentlemen. Let's leave her in peace." Father Alfredo conceded.

Gabe heard footsteps but wasn't sure if some were coming around to the back. The women kept silent. Minutes later the sounds abated.

"Leave you in peace? Those men are aggressive." Gabe felt chills.

"Maybe the police threatened Father Alfredo." Julia's face scrunched up.

Gabe took the mother's hand. "Who's behind all this?"

Gabe and Julia gave Señora Alvarado admonitions to stay inside and their assurance Abuelita would find her other lodgings if necessary. When they saw she was settled, they tiptoed toward Julia's home, looking in all directions.

"Well, this is my home." Julia pointed down the path. "Tacos, after all the fuss?'

"Delicious, but next time. Walk in a group now, Julia. Or with your boyfriend."

"You know I have a boyfriend?" Gabe pointed to Julia's ring finger.

Gabe asked Teresa if she could go into Old Town, and Teresa drove her while questioning her about every detail of what occurred at the Sanchez home. Then, to blow off some steam, Gabe put in two miles of cardio, keeping close to the well-lit establishments downtown. She ran through streets where locals and tourists spilled out of painted doors into the traffic lanes, and she assessed the area as a nightclub row. She tilted her head back to see a thirty-five-foot mural, color-splashed art of an Afro-Colombian woman.

Gabe stuck her head into an outdoor café. "Smells good. What's the street art?"

"Hey, yeah. Prisma Afro by Vertigo, one street art crew. Want to sit and eat?" The young owner stood, hands on hips.

Gabe shook her head. "No, thanks. Out running."

"You're not from here? Make sure you see the Getsemani neighborhood old quarter at dusk. More street art on Butterfly and Umbrella Streets."

"Sure thing." Gabe took in murals, workplaces, and historical sites. Arching over the street, she saw a display of the Colombian flag of yellow, blue, and red with a bird in the center. She didn't have the name of the hotel, but she searched for the one with a room named after the Colombian sculptor and painter Botero and the home of novelist Gabriel García Márquez but took some wrong turns. These streets contained dark areas like those at home—character on the outside, but who knew what could crawl out? Feeling a little tingle, Gabe dismissed her fear and threw her hair back. Teresa was en route to pick her up. Gabe wanted to get ready for the next day's medical clinic and self-defense class. She pranced boxer-like as if she could hold her own in these sketchy venues.

"Where, oh where, would anyone hold María?" It unsettled Gabe to think of the kidnapped girl, perhaps others, and maybe corrupt police. What type of place was this? Enticing, she decided. "Colombia, you're taking hold of me. You're a mysterious mother," she whispered through panting breath. Her insides rumbled as if a challenge was looming on the horizon, and she sent a text to her ride.

A bird with a flaming headdress flew over the castle and squawked out a challenge to all Colombian creatures. Never mind the evil human kidnappers. The natural world still held its beauty. While waiting, she googled to read about Colombia's river with up to seven colors and remembered Márquez's writings of his steam journeys down the Magdalena River and "magical" riverside towns. Yet those manatees and iguanas held nothing over the Amazon River's terrifying creatures like the crocodile-like black caiman, green anaconda, and the legendary vampire candiru known to violate humans in a most gruesome way. She shuddered and scrolled, preferring to read about Colombia's one thousand musical rhythms.

She gazed at the foliage surrounding the castle and watched a creature jumping from tree to tree. A large tree frog—or a monkey?! The starry sky lit up with species of colorful birds cavorting here and there. Sounds of salsa wafted up from nightclubs. Shadows of lovers kissing against barricades centuries-old filled the breach.

"No doubt this is a magical land." Gabe lifted her hands to the sky.

# chapter 35

THE CLINIC DOOR OPENED with a smack, and Dr. Martínez looked up. Pastor Pérez, a kind-looking, fiftyish-looking man in a rumpled denim shirt carried a young girl of five or six whimpering in pain, and the men lifted her onto the table. The patient's faded green pants and tattered cotton shirt told Gabe she lived near or in the jungle.

"Pastor?" Dr. Martínez acted as if they were friendly.

"Cami stepped on a piece of glass, doctor."

"You've not had a good day, Cami?"

The girl winced.

"Gabe, get the injection for me." He whispered his instructions.

"A bit of a trip to get here, huh?" He cleaned the area and injected it while Gabe scrutinized the jagged glass hanging from Cami's foot.

"Cami, can you feel anything in your foot?"

"Yes. A little."

"Okay," he told Gabe. "This looks easy, but sometimes it can get away from you." He motioned to Gabe to come closer, and she touched Cami's arm.

"How about now?" Gabe made a sweet face.

"No." Cami looked cute anyway.

"Good. You're numb. It probably doesn't seem so right now, but you're going to be fine," the doctor consoled her. "Cami, where'd you get this bad boy?"

"Playing in the dirt." Cami whimpered.

"Lots of broken bottles. Rebels celebrating. It's a real mess." Pastor Pérez groaned.

"Oh? What's happening?"

"The general of the rebels is nervous. He thinks someone may betray him even though his group scored a success, though no one will tell if it was in terms of human life. The general is in a panic looking for anything suspicious or some interference."

Gabe's eyes widened. Abuelita had told her the general assented to her comings and goings because she never reported the rebel activities unless they tried to harm her girls. In this way, Abuelita had access to the interior area miles inland from Cartagena when New Day: Women needed it.

"Any kidnapped, trafficked girls?" Gabe saw Dr. Martínez flinch at her question. "María, for one."

"I'm sorry. I heard about her disappearance, and I'll keep my eyes open."

"Her mother and friends are worried about her."

"Pastor Pérez works with families in the interior, Gabe. Then he leads Bible study here." Doctor Martínez stepped back. "Well, Cami, looks like this is repairable."

"I'm happy." She grinned at the doctor.

"The glass is coming out. We'll flush the area and start you on some antibiotics." He turned to the pastor. "Up to date on her tetanus shot?"

"No such resources." The pastor lowered his head.

"Well, we can take care of that too. No more playing in the dirty areas."

"I'll be more careful, Doctor."

"You're a tough girl, Cami. You deserve a reward." Gabe reached behind her back. "Oh, but too bad you don't like candy."

"Yes, I do."

"Then you're in luck today. First, hold still."

The doctor fingered and administered the tetanus shot Gabe had prepared. Gabe watched the shot go smoothly without a hitch. She rustled plastic bags on the counter.

Cami grinned when Gabe gave her the candy.

"Gummy bears!" The girl stuffed one into her mouth.

"We need to hurry back if she's ready." The pastor fidgeted. "I can only leave the jungle so long."

"Come whenever you can." The doctor looked the pastor in the eyes.

Gabe handed them two lunch bags filled with water bottles and sandwiches.

"Gabe, you're an angel. Doctor, what can I do to show our thanks?"

"Continue to lead Bible study in town and here."

"As long as I'm able." Pastor Pérez shook hands with the doctor and clasped Gabe's hand. Carmi waved to Gabe, and the door rattled shut behind them.

"Gotta fix that door."

"Cami's name reminds me of a self-defense student back home named Carina, and her health."

"Anything you want to talk about?"

"No doctor, but thanks."

"Homesick, or do you like working with medicine here?"

"Not homesick. Love it."

"You've caught the bug, Gabe."

"It's the only bug I want to catch."

"Stay healthy. It's much worse for those in the interior. Glass, rocks, lack of medicine. Malaria, sicknesses. Bad bugs."

Gabe shuddered.

"Speaking of which, my wife and I can show you some beautiful bugs on our annual hike, not to the interior but to the rainforests."

"Is that what indigenous plant exploration is about? Bugs? Hiking? Gear? What about the clinic?"

"Your abuelita Micah and Jessie can sub in while we're gone. It's worthwhile. Ask my wife. She loves going for marmalade bushes, pekea nut trees, encenillos, Flor de Mayo orchids, *palma de cera*, banana passionfruit, peach palm." Dr. Pérez put away medicines while Gabe scrubbed the table. "Herbs, pineapple sage, lemon thyme, purple basil, wild mint, wild oregano, sawtooth coriander, Melissa, verbena, marigold, nasturtium—"

"*Híjole!* What gear do I need to get?"

"You have some time. Tall boots."

"Tall boots? Like for freshwater fishing?"

"No."

"What for? Snakes in the grass, doctor? Or chunks of glass in the dirt? Green anaconda, giant centipede, electric eel?" Gabe stammered, "I'll get the boots!"

The doctor lowered his eyes and turned away.

# chapter 36

"*NO MÁS*, NO MORE violence against women. Learn to defend yourselves!" Gabe coached the handpicked self-defense participants. "You can be in trouble early on, fight your way back, and turn the tables."

Her Cartagena crew of young women had potential, like the girls in Santa Ana, for their grit and willingness to get scrappy in a fight. The ten women ranged from age thirteen to twenty-seven.

Julia put in a respectable session with the boxing bag and in the ring. As Gabe directed the class, Teresa chimed in, and she could throw down against the dummy. The younger women were equally fit and feisty.

"We're bringing women's voices together, speaking out against the abuse of power. Teresa joins us today."

"Disreputable men are kidnapping our girls. Let's get equipped." Teresa spoke like a drill sergeant.

The women looked around at Gabe. Some looked disheartened. *Are they thinking of their friend María?*

"I promise to make this class worthwhile." Gabe tried to gain trust. "Anyone who's on a shaming trip needs to let go of thinking she's not worth anything."

"We women have to defeat the macho thinking of this culture, defend ourselves, promote change." Teresa preached out.

*Teresa's tone was bossy though.*

"Thank you, Teresa. My brother José and I went to community center sessions, trying to work through his issues." Gabe let her hair down in front of them. "We learned first to make sure you, the individual, is not a source of violence. Then to protect yourself from others who may be acting in violent ways toward you."

"Explain." Isabel shook her curly hair. Gabe noticed a defiant streak in her similar to her students back home.

"Say an addict in recovery or a criminal trying to change behavior distances himself or herself from the feeling underneath their actions. The feeling has to be explored to find the reason for it, or if it's not dealt with, the perpetrator will feel resentment and strike again."

"So, is this what doctors treat?"

"Some doctors do. How do you get to the source of your pain? You've been jumped, attacked, abandoned, used." Gabe's eyes bored into them.

"What do you do to change?" Julia asked the question Gabe was hoping someone would ask.

"Grab a broom." Teresa trumpeted. "Here, we'll give you repetitive work. Basic tasks are part of recovery."

Gabe gave Teresa a sour look behind her back. The girls snickered.

"You'll find doing something helpful every day brings positive changes." Teresa winked some.

"Training begins. Now, the open-hand strike." Gabe took control. "First, always have a good stance. It promotes stability when you're defending yourself and, if necessary, fighting back." Gabe demonstrated, feet shoulder width apart.

"If necessary?"

"Isabel, it's not about winning a fight. It's about doing just enough to get away."

"You're saying, don't be stupid." Isabel put her hands on her hips.

"I didn't say exactly that word, but you're right. Your mind is your best weapon. You want to avoid, prevent, de-escalate, defend, fight—and then run!"

"Run? Don't tell us you run away." Julia looked baffled.

"Of course, I do."

"I can't quite picture you running, Gabe."

"Picture it then. It's your first and best option."

Julia looked at the ground.

"That being said—the open-hand strike. Use the heel of the hand to target the attacker's face, front and back of neck, eyes," Gabe said. "Striking the eyes will seriously disturb them."

She watched as the girls mimed her motions. "Keep your elbow in front of your ribs. Don't pull your arm back, or you'll send a warning to the attacker."

Gabe set them up in teams of three. Two battled while the other critiqued their moves, and then they rotated counterclockwise.

"Does this strike work as well as kicking them in the ... you know?" one student queried between gasped breaths.

"The groin kick, yes, we'll get to that. I used to teach that first, but then, students didn't understand. First, self-defense is about prevention and awareness—not going to dodgy places and waving your smartphone around."

The girls giggled.

Gabe and Teresa traded glances.

"Anticipate well. Fight hard." Gabe explained how a woman may be forcibly knocked over if she tries to kick an attacker in the groin from too far away, as the assailant can simply grab the heel of her foot before it strikes.

"See, at close range, you can target his knees and take him out. If you're a medium distance away, you can strike at the guy's toes or shoelaces."

Practicing in groups and trying out the groin kick, the young women snickered and groaned.

"It looks so simple in the visual." Julia tilted her head and gave Gabe a silly look.

Gabe smiled, pleased most of the participants maintained their balance. "Hey, you're not bad. You have grit."

"No kidding." One tall twenty-something groaned.

"No hombre would want to mess with you." A young teen encouraged her with a touch. Gabe gave a supportive clap.

"We fight for our lives and lives of others. That's why." Teresa was full of vinegar. "And, after you learn here, Micah, Gabe's *abuelita*, says some of you may be sent to teach life skill at New Day satellites in Panama, Guatemala, Costa Rica, Nicaragua."

"Count me in." Julia held up a gloved hand.

"And me." An older teen reached up to tap her gloves.

Gabe twirled around joyfully.

"Hey, we're all in!" All the women rushed together, forming a giant huddle.

"Go to art room, ladies. Don't act all wound up for Teresa." Gabe followed and poked her head into the art room as her self-defense students filed in, still kicking, jumping, and laughing.

"Energetic? That's how I like my art students."

"You got it, Teresa." Gabe surveyed Teresa's setup of easels, paints, carvings, plaster shapes as well as pottery and sculpture wheels.

"Do you like art?" Teresa quizzed Gabe.

"Some."

"I know you have other talents. But here's a charcoal. See what you can do." Teresa pointed to examples of student work. Gabe noticed these drawings were largely of human faces and not always the best-looking ones. The cruel facial lines seemed to depict dangerous Colombians and white males. *Their subconscious thoughts of abductors, traffickers?*

Seeing the art made her wonder what Rosa would be working on at the studio back home. She sent a text to Rosa about the art class and read the reply: "Courage. In bold colors, shapes."

"You roar." Gabe texted back. She felt joyful to stay close even these many miles away.

"Your bro is in jail." Rosa's text continued. Gabe steeled herself.

"Ready?" Teresa's question reminded Gabe she was far away from home. No, Gabe wasn't ready. Her eyes clouded. What could she do for her brother here? She shaded in the face of a homegirl on the white paper. The eyes were the most difficult. She wanted to show wariness and youthfulness, and she kept at it for several minutes.

Teresa bent over Gabe's work. "I think I see where you're going with this. I like it. Maybe more dark shading at the corner of her eye. Who's your model?"

"A composite of the girls back home and here, but maybe, oh, Julia. She has that sense of loss."

"Yes." Teresa whispered back as she turned to a student's work.

Gabe glanced over to the youngest girls in the corner, constructing small craft cardboard houses with window openings containing miniature paintings and narrative text. "Love this. May I?"

One of the girls nodded, and Gabe inspected the houses more closely.

"Outstanding. Such careful work. And did anyone else help?"

They nodded and pointed to Julia.

"Julia, your tiny paintings."

Julia turned forward slightly to return their appreciative glances.

"I like what the younger girls did with the miniatures." Julia offered the compliment.

Gabe liked Julia's self-deprecating manner. How often did she see a girl give a younger girl her props? Very smooth. Julia's larger work leaned against the wall as if an afterthought.

"What's this?" Gabe bored her eyes into the painting.

"The Colombian coastline."

"Stunning. You've used almost all seven colors of the water. What inspired it?"

"My father took my mother on a walk near the beach before he—" She jumped at a loud noise.

Gabe's head swiveled. The students looked up, and Teresa looked straight ahead, beyond the room, in the direction of the compound entrance.

Gabe reached out to touch Julia's shoulder, concerned. "What was that?"

Teresa raised her eyebrows at Gabe and stood protectively close to the students.

Gabe hesitated. She saw the girls turn back to their artwork. "Teresa, is it okay?"

"Okay." Teresa looked stalwart.

"Julia, talk later?" Gabe waited for Julia to nod then glanced at her smartwatch. "If you're set here, I have to get back to the clinic. Dr. Martínez is downtown, so I'm up. I love seeing this creative talent. Keep hearts open and feet kicking, girls!"

"Clinic assistant Alma, I'd say I'd be seeing you, but not where you're going." Isabel got a kick out of being sassy.

"Med clinic." A girl squirmed.

"Shots. Check-ups. Ouch! We'd like *not* to see you there."

The girls gave Gabe sour looks.

"You'll appreciate medical care when you need it." Gabe pointed her finger at them half in fun.

Teresa pulled Gabe aside. "I'll check what's going on with Jessie and the others out front at the guard post. We haven't had trouble for some time, but you never know."

Gabe's eyes widened. "You want me to stay with your class?"

"No, they're busy. You have work." Teresa turned to go.

# chapter 37

A S GABE PORED OVER the infirmary training manu-
als, she zeroed in on the drastic cases she hoped she'd
never see but was preparing for just in case: broken legs
with infections, gunshot wounds in vital areas, new virus
combinations. Several cases of flu, colds, and scraped knees,
in addition to a broken ankle, a nonpoisonous snakebite, and
a serious infection, kept her active.

She loved talking to each person who came in and getting to know this lush new land through their eyes. With
her hidden in the compound, others felt safe to reveal their
physical and emotional hurts. They saw her gruffness as
the same defense they had when they came to the healing
center. Their defenses gradually broke down with Gabe's
healing help. Teaching self-defense was exhilarating and a
necessity, but doctoring gave her deeper rewards.

A patient mentor for weeks, Dr. Martínez had thor-
oughly walked her through several treatment procedures.
Well-respected and popular with the locals, Martínez was
called to handle house calls in the city, which often left Gabe
alone. However, she didn't mind the quiet time, which let

her own soul heal and nurtured her love of medicine. She found simple joy in healing. Dr. Martínez called it a gift and a calling, as her teachers had before him.

Gabe cleaned tools and equipment so Dr. Martínez would see a pristine office when he returned. Hearing a racket, she raised her head as the door smacked open.

"Clear a table!" One of the male guards shouted as he carried a man over his shoulder, limp, head down, arm dangling from the guard's back, bleeding lightly from the torso. Gabe recognized the injured man as Roberto, the gate guard who'd smiled at her, his wavy, dark-brown hair now blotted with blood.

Gabe told the guard to hold the arm up and press lightly to stop the blood. She went into action, darting for tools and medicines—similar to moving in the boxing ring—followed by a calm bedside manner, diagnosing the situation. With the guard's help, she pulled up Roberto's sleeve to examine his bleeding arm. The gunshots had all wounded him superficially, although they caused a vast amount of bleeding.

Gabe kept the arm lifted and used clinic bandages on the wound. Roberto cheerfully winced.

"I've got this, but I'll locate Dr. Martínez to ask him to check." Gabe assured the guards and tapped on her smartphone.

Gabe thought about her training and decided a bullet had narrowly missed maiming Roberto more seriously. How daunting to have a near-shooting crisis and a frightening situation causing it here within her first several weeks.

"Bleeds like crazy, huh? A fairly superficial wound, but we don't want it to get infected, Roberto. It looks like you're going to make it." Gabe smiled at him. "You're stuck with us."

"Not going to flat line?"

"No, far from it. You, my friend, are going to be well."

"Beginner's luck?"

"Pretty much. Dr. Martínez deserves credit. His instruction, plus a wing and a prayer."

"He's a good man."

"Fortunate for me and you. Just need to make sure an infection doesn't lead to a serious fever."

Roberto grunted as she applied medication, wrapped the arm wound, and tested the area. She boiled water and dropped in some spear-shaped leaves.

"You have all these women around you, Roberto? What's your story? How long have you been here?" Gabe waited for his reply while she adjusted the machines to take his vitals and prepared to administer a shot to stop infection and pain.

"Ah, I've been here a few years. Before this, I guarded a compound in Tanzania for a year with a friend who ran security. When Micah heard about me through my mother, she offered me work."

"Much different?"

"In Africa, the tribes fear shaming for being weak if they lose power. Rebel armies like to make a show of strength. Sometimes, they raid the compounds, the private schools, and take the girls into the jungle."

"Rebel armies?"

"They never came into our compound. In others, less guarded, they came in trucks with machine guns. Loaded the girls in, kicking and screaming."

"Hateful!"

"Hateful, yes, and tragic. Our compound here was more fortunate. It was protected."

"Is it always this violent at the gate?"

"Not so much. Bad men sense opposition here."

"Bad men? Opposition?"

"Bad men. Cartels. One and the same. Never seen them shooting at the gate before dusk … they must fear … us." He puffed short of breath at the shot. "Did you hear the noise at the front gate, Gabe?"

"The loud bangs. I was in with Teresa's class, and she seemed troubled."

"Indeed. Sorry to ruin your introduction to Cartagena."

"I already had a short run-in with some shady characters near the Cartagena Castle." Immediately Gabe regretted letting Roberto know about her encounter.

"You been introducing yourself around?" Roberto chuckled, but it seemed forced. He shifted on the table.

Gabe moved her gaze discreetly. She hoped he wouldn't find out about the men who nearly accosted her near the Castillo.

"Ready? Let me see your thigh." Gabe brought over the boiled tea leaves to administer aid.

"Really? We've just met." Roberto smiled. "That looks native."

"Reduces your fever." Gabe applied the leaves to his skin.

"I've heard. Rare."

"From hours away in the *páramos*. Dr. Martínez and his wife led me there along with some of the children and healers, all in our mud jackets and rainboots."

"Looking for trouble? Did you find it?"

"We survived. Maybe we'll see black caiman and the candiru another time."

Roberto gasped. "The candiru, toothpick fish, is horrible, worse than any bad men. Did Dr. Martinez tell you what the candiru does to humans?"

"He didn't have to. I do medical research. It burrows into the urethra."

"Let's not talk about that anymore." Roberto grimaced.

"Blood pressure mounting?" Gabe kidded. "These plants lower blood pressure, calm your upset stomach, cure stomach tumors, soothe arthritis. And heal your mosquito bites too," she said, gesturing. "I make a rub boiling—"

"Let me guess—boiling tree frogs?"

"No. Tree bark! I throw the blows and then help heal the wounds."

"I'll have to come back." Roberto's face shone. A healthy rose color now replaced his ashen gray.

Gabe's glow showed she found him pleasant. "How's the guarding work?"

"You see us. We rotate standing guard with automatics, as you saw. Sometimes, a wild animal wanders close to the compound; sometimes, the wild animal is human. More than three men today. One went away squealing."

"Wounded?"

"Shot in the leg, superficial, not critical. Usually, that's all it takes. He limped away with the others. They won't come back any time soon."

"How do they get here?"

"Foreign sedans."

"Our cameras?"

"Yeah, we saw them coming. We'll give their plates to authorities."

"Are the authorities legit?"

"Most of the ones Micah works with. Others, not so much. The uniform may not always be the sign of honesty here."

Gabe liked his directness, plus the tenderness in his eyes hit her weak spots. "Abuelita told you about me, but how did a tough guy get to New Day: Women?"

"Not so fast. I really don't know your story."

"You'll have to wait. I'm in charge here. For you, Roberto, I prescribe talk-healing."

"Talk-healing? Are you a shrink or a poet?"

"Not a poet, but I love your native son novelist Márquez."

"As I do, Gabe." Roberto emphasized her name. "*Love in the Time of Cholera* or *One Hundred Years of Solitude?*"

"Love it all."

"Colombia's spirit informs his magic realism."

"You're a scholar."

"Stop that. Just getting an online bachelor's and more later."

"How'd you end up here, Roberto?" She rolled her Rs for effect.

Roberto laughed. "Well, my mother met your abuela at a women's group."

"Your mother was at Pastor Pérez's prayer group while you were at target practice?"

"Maybe." Roberto's grin grew wider.

"Always a good guy with an Uzi?"

"Fighting some pretty strong demons. That was me. Alcohol, tough crowd, pressures. Losing my dad knocked some sense into me. Now I'm a believer. Pastor Pérez comes around, and we talk about spiritual things."

"Sorry about your father." Gabe could sense his pain and touched his good arm. "I haven't ever heard a man talk about finding a good life, except for maybe Coach Al."

"Your boxing? Word travels fast around here."

"Yes." She gave him another shot with a needle. "You have strong pain tolerance."

"Think so?"

"Of course, you're my first." Gabe stared at him.

"My first too—gunshot, that is."

"Yeah." Gabe giggled. "You're pretty cool."

"At least you've seen other gunshot wounds?"

"Ah, yes, I have at that." Gabe's mind jumped to the past concert shooting trauma, but she willed it back to the present. "This is the first I've treated as an official medic."

"Sometimes the Spirit in the Sky uses pain to get to me. I want to get out of suffering, but that's how He gets me to lean on Him. And you?"

Gabe deflected. "Helping remove the pain is my job, and I love it." She clammed up several seconds.

"Not talking? Uncomfortable when I talk about Spirit?"

"Some. You remind me of my friend Petra. And church with Abuelita long ago."

Roberto nodded. "You see, I'm at the end of myself without Him—Him being God. The Bible says something like, 'God loved the world and sent His only son, so if we believe in Him, we'll have everlasting life,' that's from John 3:16."

She parried his comment. "You ever learn to box?"

"I have at that."

"Let's spar some in the ring when you're better, unless it's too much for you," Gabe kidded. She checked his sutures, remembering Dr. Martínez would check up on her.

"I'd get in the ring now," Roberto said, "only I wouldn't want to take out New Day: Women's best medic, clinic assistant."

"It's *only* clinic assistant."

Roberto let out a hearty laugh.

Gabe liked the sound. "You laugh like Coach, a good man, protective and noble." She took a breath. Roberto was creating some stir in her. She saw him as front gunman against the cartel's guerrillas here and a former guard in Tanzania. *I might think of him when I close my eyes to sleep while he stands watch at the gate.*

"You were chasing a championship?" Roberto relaxed and let his eyes close.

*A manly man! More honorable than others. And, a muscular body.*

"Maybe we can work out." Gabe bit her tongue. How would he take that? He seemed to understand her. *Slow down, homegirl. This isn't your home.* What if she left Colombia soon? And what if Roberto may face more danger than he implied?

Dr. Martínez gently opened the clinic door. "You wanted me to inspect your work?"

"Yes, please do." She handed him the charts.

Dr. Martínez checked specifics. "The patient looks alive."

"Yes, he's very lively."

"Compresses, bandaging look good." Dr. Martínez squinted at the chart. "Medications?"

"She really knocked me for a loop," Roberto kidded.

"His inflammation came down with the poultice on the arm."

"Good. I see here you have a slight headache. Colombian folk medicine says Himalayan yew leaf rub on your forehead will help with that. All medications and procedures look fine to me. Gabe, you have more than medical skills. You have instinct applying native plants."

"Thank you, Doctor."

"Can I get up now?"

"Not so fast, Roberto. We want to show our appreciation. I heard you battled strong firepower at the gate, taking a hit to keep the other guards and everyone here safe."

"Happy to hear all are safe. Doctor, you arrived here without incident?"

"It was a close call. My van turned into the foliage to avoid the fleeing intruders."

"Good timing, Doc. Maybe you could help identify the cars."

"Anything you need. Stay, and let's heal the headache."

Gabe nodded in agreement. She reheated the water.

"I'm humbled. I'd do it all again, especially for such expert medical care." Roberto settled back on the table as Gabe tended to his forehead as Dr. Martínez directed.

"Hope you feel the same with both of us doing some final checks." Gabe continued the rub and watched Dr. Martínez look him over.

"Willing victim." Roberto closed and opened his eyes.

"We'll fix you a *pepito* and some *té*." Dr. Martínez hearted up the iron skillet and set water to boil in a tea kettle.

"A steak sandwich and some tea for our guest." Gabe nodded at Roberto with a pinch of grace. "And, Colombian *polorovsa* sugar cookies?"

"I'm honored."

*This man is sweet.* Gabe applied more warm leaves to Roberto's forehead with care to ease his headache. When she served him a sandwich and cookies, the corners of her mouth turned up, but she dropped her head to hide her interest.

# chapter 38

"**Y**OU THINK YOU KNOW what you're doing around town." Teresa had on her guide's hat. "You run by the art district, clubs, and castle. But this you haven't seen."

"No, but I've been in the neighborhood. Julia and her mother live not far from here."

"Looks can fool you from the outside." Teresa led Gabe onto an odd-looking garden path of rectangular brown pavers with dense plants flowering red with full, drooping blooms as sentinels and layered lines of white tea lights overhead. Massive trees saluted high above on both sides, and high arched walkways ran to terracotta-painted buildings.

Gabe noticed evergreen umbrellas poised over tables for outdoor casual dining. Ahead, steps on a raised surface led to a circular concrete fountain base.

"In 1607, this was a convent. It housed the nuns of the Order of the Poor Clara. This order was founded in 1212 by Clara Portinari, who came to the city to do missionary work funded by alms and donations."

"Were they nuns with medical training?" Gabe tried to get Teresa to smile.

"At least some training to work with the people. Think of that, a donated piece of land and 2,500 pesos allowed them to build a convent by the same master builder who designed the Cathedral of Santa Catalina de Alejandra in the Plaza de la Proclamación."

"Looks more linear than the Cathedral of the Incarnation you pointed out my first day."

"See its high and closed walls, its square shape, Gabe? Its halls and main floor connect naturally with the central courtyard."

"Almost a maze."

"Almost. The nuns sold bread and cookies to survive, but the main door was always closed except to a few visiting nuns. They sold their goods to city folk through a lathe, a crude rotating surface they also used for shaping wood."

"Teresa, what did the nuns do inside?"

"Mass, communion, confession, work for the community."

Gabe stared at patrons, looking for a patio seat to have lunch.

"I heard you read works by Márquez?"

"Of course. I was just telling Roberto *Love in the Time of Cholera* is my favorite work. I'm Gabriela. I may even be named after Gabriel Márquez, or Gabriela Mistral, Nobel prize-winning woman poet."

"And you all may be named after sweet angel Gabriel blowing his horn. You'll love this then. As a young reporter, Gabo—Gabito, they call him—went to convent exhumations here and saw a skull with twenty-two-meter-long copper hair coming out of the crypt. It inspired him to write *Of Love and Other Demons.*

"Gothic."

"Gabito then bought a lot next to the convent to build his home. He had a fascination with the houses of Cartagena and how dead they seemed. He said though the houses changed shape, their owners passed through life without too much noise."

"Creepy stuff, Teresa."

"There's more. Back then, pirate ships sat off the coast and shot cannonballs into the city. You saw El Castillo's cannon mounts. This convent turned hotel is where, centuries ago, one pirate ship's cannonball landed!"

Gabe whistled. "The convent seems way past the castle."

"One lucky shot at just the right angle damaged the convent. Today, the convent is the Legend Santa Clara hotel and restaurant."

"History according to Teresa?"

"Legend. Come see."

Gabe peered down some of the halls coming off the center like the spokes of a wheel. "I see what you mean about corridors connecting."

"In October of 1995, the restored doors opened to world-famous celebrities and politicians, including artist Fernando Botero. Now, a hotel suite is designed as a tribute to him."

"Oh, here's where it is! I've been looking for Botero's hotel. His depictions of large human figures make me laugh."

"Yeah, they do. From Medellín, Colombia. His work is exaggerated and comic."

"Powerful, like Gabito's writing, but in its own quirky way."

"Jungle animals, tourists, or worse." Teresa gestured to a group of sweaty-haired American and European men. They were dressed in shirts of island flowers, shorts, and flip-flops and pulled into a tight circle, laughing and drinking with some locals.

"You say worse?"

"Man. A worse predator than our feared wild cat." Teresa pulled up the collar of her shirt. A neckerchief also hid her face in the dim lighting, and her hair was drawn back with a clip. "I think they're traffickers, so they may recognize me from earlier encounters. They don't know you, and let's keep it that way for you or anyone from New Day: Women."

Gabe quickly turned away. "Could this be about Julia's friend María?"

"Don't know. It'd be arrogant for her kidnappers to go out in public. But here, it could happen—businessmen cut deals of many kinds."

"Bad men doing trafficking deals?"

"Wait, Gabe. Let's not attract attention. I like to listen and let the nature of the beast soak in. What's the saying? Knowing your enemy is half the battle."

"Another round?" The man's laugh sounded hyena-like.

The sound reminded Gabe of someone. *The shady men I saw near El Castillo?*

Teresa held Gabe off with a glance, and they listened to the group.

"Everyone stays until we get what we want." The man jotted down a plan on his napkin. "No one dares stop us again."

"I'll drink to that." A short man, with a belly protruding from his camo t-shirt, sloshed his drink on the table. "I've seen some fine women walking about."

"With boyfriends?"

"You think I ask if a woman I like has a boyfriend? I just target her, and that's it." A strident man puffed his chest up proudly.

*That voice. The policeman at María's mother's door?*

"Traffickers. Loud, greasy bores." Teresa's voice was at whisper level.

"Did they say someone stopped them?"

"Roberto and the gate guards? Go now."

Gabe drew her hair in front of her face. She saw Teresa on alert as the short braggart got up and gave Teresa a long, hard look.

Teresa broke his gaze, smiling at Gabe.

"Gotta go." The short braggart walked toward them and then made a sharp turn to go to the men's restroom. He paused, staring at Gabe's frame.

"Hurry back!" The 'policeman' cried out from the table. "We need to go over this again. Especially you."

The short, fat man grunted and continued ambling to the men's room while Gabe and Teresa ducked into another corridor of the renovated cloister.

"If I had to, I could handle them." Gabe raised her brow as if to question Teresa.

"Not now. Micah wants your hands clean and fit for New Day: Women operations. Medicine and teaching. No fighting here."

"How I'd love to tackle those beasts."

"They're not out in the open often."

"Why now?"

"I'm not sure. Traffickers meeting with new money in town?"

"Let me at least take on the short one." Gabe shadow-boxed for a beat. Her figure, backlit by Santa Clara's lamps, cast a beautiful but eerie silhouette on the convent corridor wall.

Sounds of tennis shoes coming toward them tapped along the hallway.

"Move!" Teresa led Gabe down another corridor. Footsteps echoed right behind them.

"I know you!" The same man sputtered only ten yards away.

*Did he take a shortcut?*

Teresa and Gabe ran through one turn after another in the maze of hallways. They hid behind a stone crevice partition, their deep breaths returning to normal as the minutes passed.

"The glutton's gone back." Teresa took a breath.

"We were so close to him. I trained to fight. I tell students to run, but I had him."

"Duly impressed. No fighting, Gabe, except to save a life."

I wasn't raised in a convent, you know."

"But, honey, you're in one now!"

Gabe chuckled. "You know how to get out of here?"

"Think it's a coincidence we found this hiding spot? I know an exit just up ahead."

They slipped out into the streets and backed up against a wall mural of a Colombian female jazz singer. None of the bad men in sight.

"Whew, Saint Teresa! Too long in a convent is no fun. I've been meaning to ask. Is Roberto interested in you? I see you talking."

"Roberto's a fine man, as good as they come. But look at me, Gabe. I'm older."

"Not so I noticed, Teresa."

"Well, I am. Not quite Micah's age. Roberto's studying to be a college teacher, and he likes to discuss history and books with me."

"You got a degree, Teresa?"

"Alternative institution community college degree, history, and engineering."

"Specialized work. Now, you're saying Roberto is single. He's nice ... and funny."

"Not to mention studly. Very eligible as far as I know. But I thought you're a fighter, not a lover." Teresa jostled her.

"Colombia makes me feel things I never felt before." Gabe took a quick breath.

"There's something in the air in Colombia, Gabe."

"I feel safe with Roberto guarding us."

"Good." Teresa pointed to the light coming from outside. "Let's get back."

chapter **39**

"GREAT WORK, ESPECIALLY ON how to get out of chains and the eye jab. You deserve a reward, so Julia will show you some of the *folklórico* dances she learned in Mexico, dances of the people." Gabe welcomed Julia up to the front of the class with her.

"For our footwork?" Isabel pattered her feet.

"*Sí.*"

Julia hummed a bar. "You have to point your toes, use big sweeping arms, high leg kicks, exaggerated movements. It's a folk dance, so you swirl your large black skirt. Wave your white peasant blouse sleeves. Don't be shy."

"These dances are very popular where I'm from in California, especially on Mexican Independence Day and at the county fair." Gabe twirled.

"The fair?" A tall woman dancer stopped.

"We have one with amusement park rides and competitions for best food, biggest or best farm animals, and *folklórico* dancing."

"You've been there?"

Gabe nodded to Isabel. "Julia grew up with these dances created by indigenous people in México."

"I learned these dances in grade school when we went to México for my father's work before his company brought him back here." Julia threw several colorful sombreros out into the group. *"El Jarabe Tapatío,* the Mexican Hat Dance, is the national dance of México. Some say indigenous people created it. Others say Spanish invaders. Whichever, it expresses the life and spirit of our people."

"Share." A younger girl took a few sombreros back from an older girl.

"It's usually performed by a man and woman, so we'll split up into couples to practice. We start by dancing around the sombrero on the floor." Julia grabbed Gabe's arm, and they demonstrated.

Sounds of a mariachi band lifted from Julia's smartphone, and the students were off, following her instructions, some girls pretending to lift full skirts with ruffled hems, while others with hands on hips role-played male partners. Dancers darted in and out, creating a few moves of their own, and Julia laughed at their choreography. At the music's end, most collapsed on the floor, panting and laughing.

"Watch out, or I'll have you do the Dance of the Old Men, *la Danza de los Viejitos.*"

"Are you saying we dance like old men?"

"A couple of you do. See here." Julia bent over as if she relied on a cane. "Dancers acting like old men stomp hard on the floor against spirits, a symbol of ensuring the survival of people."

"Do the old men really dance?"

"Some old men love to dance! But dancers of any age copy the old men's movements. Girls dress up in suits with hats and walking sticks. It's mostly stomping. Stomp, stomp, stomp!" Her words were all it took for the girls to stomp on the floor, acting like old men with backaches, bending over canes. Gabe lifted her head when she heard a whimper from the happy group.

"*Mi abuelo* danced that dance. He moved to Colombia as a young man. My mother told me all about it." A preteen's voice quivered, and the stomping paused.

"Isn't that a *happy* memory?" Gabe searched the preteen's face, concerned for her mental health.

A few girls leaned in.

"No. A cartel accused him of handing their information to the government. *Mi abuelo* wouldn't tell anything, but I heard they made him stand in a river with people they suspected of betraying them. They stood in the water overnight, and when no one confessed in the morning, the cartel shot them all." She related this through tears, her head drooping.

Gabe put her arm around the girl whose head hung low.

"*Mi abuela* lived, or I wouldn't be here. My mother was in her tummy."

Julia winced, and the others quieted.

"My father was kidnapped when we came to Cartagena on business." Julia swept her hair back as she shared. "Men ambushed him. Someone knocked on the hotel room door, and when we opened it, they took him. He didn't do anything wrong. Maybe they were after jewelry or what was in his wallet. My mother hopes they don't force him to do anything illegal."

"I hope they don't hurt him."

A few girls pulled in closer to hear Julia.

"You wonder why I live with my mother downtown. We only have each other now. Well, there's my sometimes boyfriend. We hope my father returns."

"Julia, I'm sorry. I didn't know." Gabe touched her shoulder.

"I should've been smarter when I was with María." Julia looked even more downcast. "I might've known something was wrong when a handsome, older teenage guy we'd never met before walked her home. When he asked her about herself, her face lit up. She liked him."

"He listened to her?" The preteen looked curious.

"He said he was her friend. We're her friends, but she kept to herself."

"María was thirteen, so young she couldn't see the guy's attention, building trust, making an emotional connection was just a hired man targeting her." Julia kicked a sombrero for emphasis.

"Grooming vulnerable kids." Gabe made sure every girl heard her. "If he sent a text to meet her, and she sent a text back, that could've sealed their bond."

"How can we tell if it's a predator or just a normal guy, Gabe?" Isabel seemed confused.

"A tip-off is when someone loads on the flattery, gives gifts, pulls you away from your friends or activities, requests indecent photos—"

"Blackmailing and shaming. But we can't think every curious boy is bad, can we, Gabe?"

"No, Julia." Gabe cleared her voice. "But María may be in the hands of traffickers. You can use the three signs to identify con men. Fraud. Force. Coercion. They misrepresent themselves, target underage kids, and cause trauma for their own gain."

"Micah has a rescue system." Julia spoke in weak voice.

"Don't be glum. We have hope." Isabel sighed in sympathy.

*How many others have been taken?*

"Until we can rescue the lost, I think we need to celebrate our lives." Gabe grinned with confidence.

Julie gave a braver smile. "*Sí, sí.*"

"Can anyone show me some club dance moves?" Gabe swayed her hips. "I've heard of the bachata."

"Yeah, bachata. Dance away heartbreak, bitterness, sadness, cheating, loss." Isabel crooned. Some of the girls in their late teens copied the swaying hip motion. "Bachata blows off steam. Traditional or urban with salsa and tango."

"Of course, I know it and can teach you!" Julia stepped and tapped.

The girls lined up to learn.

"Tap on four and eight. Side to side. Forward and back."

The girls tapped their feet to her count.

"Keep your legs under your butt. That's it. Don't raise your knees up high. Here, keep the hands above the waist."

Gabe guessed most had seen varieties of the dance, so they were quick studies. "Did you girls learn at the local clubs, family parties, community parties? I'm way behind." She found herself needing practice.

Students added turns, hip moves, and arm styles.

"Thanks, Julia. I can see I have my homework cut out for me."

"You're welcome, Gabe. Just like you give us homework. The class caught on well!"

Gabe stood with her hands on her hips. "We can practice more at the end of next class, sexy dancers."

Gabe sighed. Isabel was distracted on her smartphone.

Gabe sent a text to Petra back home: "Progress?" She added a smiling face, hoping to get back an encouraging word.

# chapter 40

A BUELITA HELPED DRESS GABE'S hair. She ground flaxseeds, wet it on the hair, then made curls from the curling end of a stick.

"Is this a special occasion, Abuelita?"

"Practicing for when there is one. It's nice to get grand-daughter time."

"Native hair design?"

"It's a custom. Colombia unlocks her mysteries gradually. You'll see."

Gabe touched her hair.

"You look pretty. Walk and talk?" Abuelita touched Gabe's arm as she handed her *mango con chile.* Gabe fell into Abuelita's pace with her long stride, strolling out to the garden.

Abuelita bent to pick at the root vegetables. "Our garden is a precious showcase of tenderness. The girls have spent time cultivating this quiet, nurturing spot."

"Carnations. Lilies. Those I know."

"Here's more. A jade plant, hydrangeas, chrysanthemum. It's too bad we can't grow the *cattleya* orchid, our national flower from the moist lowlands and Andean cloud forests.

You saw some when Dr. and Mrs. Martínez took you close to the rainforests?"

"Yes. Healing plants and all. Can't wait to go there again." Gabe fingered the jade plant's healthy leaves.

"Combining indigenous healing with modern medicine you'll be an invaluable doctor. Do you enjoy gardening?"

"I've tried it some. A garden back home was one straggly wildflower pushing up through the cracks in concrete. I'd rather be in nature."

"Tough growing up in the streets?"

"Street urchin that I am."

"Tell me."

"You sound like I was *living* in the streets. We have a place. Mamacita provides for us and I love her."

"We both do."

"Strawberries are doing well." Abuelita pointed to the leafy greens with a dash of red poking out. "Plant these watermelon seeds?"

Gabe took the spade and seeds from Abuelita and let the moist earth crumble in her hands. She smiled when the seeds tumbled into the mixture.

"You work well with living things."

"Plants don't talk back."

"I know how hard this must be, away from your Mamacita and José."

"Yes, about Mamacita. José, not so much."

"I admire what you're doing in your medicine and self-defense. I'm sure Mamacita is proud. Petra tells me they're doing well at home. Any news?"

Mamacita counsels with Petra, who's teaching my self-defense class, and worried about little Luz growing up without her father. Olivia is dating Officer Louis, the kind detective (Mamacita saw that coming!) Rosa says José is in trouble."

"*Travieso.*"

"More than mischievous. Like a weed ruining good plants. He wasn't a bad seed before. He's getting choked out by terrible thorns."

"This work got you away from a bad crew."

"Yes, but family comes first."

"I miss the family." Abuelita sighed. "Gabriela, your mission is medical. Learn about this compound we've created to protect and restore vulnerable women. You've seen New Day: Women activities and operation. By now you must have some idea of the rescue system."

"Not really. The system won you accolades from the mayor. So why haven't you found María yet?"

"Her case is pending."

"What needs to be done?"

Abuelita looked at the garden. "Traffickers remind me of plant shoots choked by weeds or seeds fallen to hard, bad ground." Footsteps could be heard coming to the garden, and the women rose to meet Roberto.

"Bad ground? Hope it's not me you're talking about."

"Of course not, Roberto. We're forever in your debt for guarding the compound."

"How's your injury healing?" Gabe checked his arm. "As to be expected. Good, but sore?"

"My arm is under your spell."

"It's medicine, not magic."

"We have video of the raid." Abuelita got down to business. "Jessie's sources say one car was owned, or formerly owned, by a rebel in the interior. Tell us, Roberto. Gabe can hear." Gabe fixed her eyes on Roberto.

"Are you sure, Micah? Rebels in the interior rarely bother guards at the compound front. Pastor Pérez says the rebels haven't been much on the move, although the rebel general in the jungle is looking for any disloyal members."

Gabe lit up, listening to Roberto report.

"Something's off." Gabe's abuelita Micah tapped her foot.

"Agreed Micah. It certainly may be. My sources say a lot of money has come into the city."

"Big financers. Were the compound raiders jungle rebels, slick cartel members? Or both?"

"We're thinking local cartels and maybe money men by the looks of it. Not rebels."

"Does cartel influence now extend into the interior?" Micah leaned forward.

"Our guards recognized some cars and men as cartel. Even Dr. Martínez weighed in. They all said cartel, Micah. Although it could be a rebel in the interior gave up his car and services, in exchange for money and power to bow to the rebel general. I'll check the video."

"New Day girls who live outside with their families and other people need extra protection. Roberto, we'll impose some limits on them coming in and out of the compound. Double up shifts with your guards at the gates. Thank you." Abuelita swept up her skirt.

"The guards are ready. Good gardening, ladies." He moved to leave, but Gabe's abuelita left first. Roberto paused and smiled at Gabe.

Gabe observed Roberto making a noble effort to hold his arm strong until he thought no one was looking. Then he dropped it to his side.

"We can give you a shot to help. Come into the clinic on a break?"

"Of course."

"I have a stake in that arm, you know."

"Now don't get your temper up." Roberto raised his arm, and in his hand were a few fresh, white carnations, which he presented to her. You're my skilled medic, and I appreciate you for a lot of reasons."

"Why, you clipped some stems from the garden?"

"For a lady."

*A gentleman. What to say to him?*

"Very thoughtful. Thank you." Gabe looked doubtful but reached out for the flowers, and as she did a huge grin spread across her face. She touched his arm.

He bowed to her.

# chapter 41

GABE PUT THE FLOWERS down safely on a counter. "Julia?" Gabe spoke louder. "Julia?" She took roll in self-defense class. "Anyone seen Julia? Maybe I missed her … a little scattered here."

"Who's seen Julia?"

Several girls looked at her with blank faces.

"Ah, Julia's mother—" Isabel whispered too low for Gabe to hear.

Oblivious, Gabe started class. "I'm counting on every student to be here to work in pairs. We've worked on some defense procedures and dummy drills. Now you'll pair up for one on one, mano a mano."

All the girls were in attendance except Julia. Last session, she and some girls had stayed after class, and Gabe had given them every spare detail of defense instruction she could think of: what to do in just about any situation with a thief, rapist, terrorist, arsonist, or gangster. She counted on the after-class group to lead other self-defense classes.

They started with stretches and blocking punches. Then, they practiced the kick to the groin. Julia still had not arrived, and the class members looked listless while they kicked and took turns checking their phones.

The door opened, and every head turned when a worker entered to deliver a message to Gabe. She read it and frowned. She folded the note as the girls watched her expectantly.

Gabe shrugged her shoulders. "You'll find out anyway. Julia's mother says she didn't come home last night. You knew something, Isabel?"

"Her mother got a threatening call. A man said to get money."

"And she doesn't want us to talk to the police? Why didn't you report that? Who saw her last?" Gabe rattled off questions to the girls who glanced at each other.

"Your walking group walked home together?" Gabe asked the tall girl.

"Um, well. Julia was alone for a few blocks." The tall girl stammered.

"Isabel, what happened to your walking group? I heard from Abuelita and Roberto you girls in the village were to be guarded."

"I, well, I got a call from my boyfriend and met up with him after Teresa dropped all of us off. Julia walked toward her home. Maybe she met her boyfriend."

"Did you see anyone, strangers?"

"No, my mom sent me a text." Isabel blushed.

"What? Your mom? Really?" An older girl acted suspicious.

"All right, it was Carlos." Isabel looked as if she may cry.

"You both ditched your group?" Gabe's face heated up.

Both students looked chagrined. So did Gabe. Gabe had asked Teresa to drive her out to the city some nights alone so she could run a few miles. She went out alone and told the others *not* to do that. Feelings crashed down on her like they crashed down on Julia's friends.

Gabe repeated the first rule, and the girls hung their heads. "Stay alert! Stay alert! Don't feel bad. Now, you tell me. This is your home. Who are the people who got to her, and what do they want?"

"These men want cash. Cash for their crystal meth." Isabel looked guilty, revealing local secrets.

"Where might they take her? Who knows where? What am I missing?" Gabe spilled out.

"Only one woman might know. Our white-haired one. Micah, Michaela." The tall student whimpered.

"María disappeared, and now Julia. She was just here last night. If we could only go back to yesterday!" Isabel wailed. Others girls sniffled.

The door flew open, and all eyes looked hopefully for Julia.

It wasn't Julia. It was Micah, Gabe's abuelita, and she took command.

"Ladies, let's work together to find Julia. Listen to these instructions. If you saw her anytime in the last twenty-four hours, or you're a member of her walking group, go over to Teresa at the desk."

A few of Gabe's best self-defense students reported to Teresa.

"If you saw anything suspicious or have any other helpful information, report to Jessie at the back of the room. Rescue committee, meet with me up front and prepare to receive assignments." Several girls hurried to talk to Jessie.

"We walked together as far as the stoplight on Villa Rosa Boulevard." A girl in Teresa's group pulled herself together to report to the twenty-four group. "I got a text from Carlos. Why did I get distracted? Julia just nodded and left on her own."

"What about you, Isabel?" Teresa was now the firm rescue commander.

No response.

"Both of you girls deserted your friend?!" Teresa fumed. Then she started interviewing them about their observations when they last saw Julia. "Did Julia get a text? How was she acting? Was the street well-lit? Did you see any suspicious people or vehicles?"

Gabe observed the team's efficiency. Abuelita was on the phone coordinating, calling in backup, outlining the tasks with her associates and the girls.

"So, this is what she does." Gabe talked to Isabel, and they closely watched Gabe's abuelita.

Within the next few minutes, Roberto and other guards arrived, along with some men Gabe had seen on the property. Ernesto taught sustainable gardening, and the other man taught fabric design, a class Gabe had once joined. Abuelita wrote on her notepad while handing out smartphones to Teresa, Jessie, Roberto, and the others.

Isabel brushed Gabe's sleeve. "How do you like Micah's assassins, I mean assistants?"

"Would the mayor honor her if he knew?"

"Oh Gabe, he knows. You can be sure! This is why she was honored!"

Gabe stepped closer to the rescue team.

"Follow along. We may need your medical skills, Gabe." Abuelita tossed Gabe a smartphone. "I've mapped Julia's mother's apartment, current cartel activity, and the whereabouts of the most recent chatter off phones of prominent predators in the area." She pointed out the grid of possible areas where Julia might be. Gabe's jaw almost dropped.

"Based on hits we're getting from local informants and our own intelligence, we have three areas she may be: a coastal neighborhood, the city's nightclub row, and the rural interior. Not ruling out any new indicator we may obtain." Micah stood as tall as possible.

Gabe could see the three primary colors lighting up each zone on the smartphone's map.

"Each team is a color. Your team color is on your phone. Teresa leads blue. Jessie green. I'll take the yellow group to the interior."

Gabe's blue stripe indicated her abuelita had grouped her with Teresa and Roberto. The blue team's schematic presented a search of the village inhabited by the indigenous population near the coastal mangrove canals.

Jessie compiled all the information and prepared to hack into the local police cameras at all targeted vantage points while spearheading the green group leaving for the nightclub row downtown.

Abuelita's team headed into the rural Colombian interior where Pastor Pérez lived, farthest away from the compound.

Gabe followed Teresa and Roberto as they jogged to the jeep at the back of the property. Roberto climbed in shotgun, looking like he'd done it many times before, with Teresa firmly in command. "Did you input all the contacts?"

"Got it." Roberto nodded.

"We're fortunate to have an assignment that's out in the open. The dark nightclub row will be teeming with party-goers, and the interior will be—"

"What about my Abuelita in the interior?"

"Gabe, the interior is thick with brush, foliage, and shacks. Hiding places are available for a low price. Her team will have hundreds of square miles to cover."

Gabe gulped. She jumped in the jeep back seat and noticed a closed bin in between the two front seats. She'd had a few hours gun training at the center and recognized the bin. *Guns. From flowers to guns.*

# chapter 42

THE THREE BLUE-TEAM RESCUERS focused on the changing hits, indicating incoming information updates from primarily Jessie on their smartphones. These communications increased in quantity while they drove out on the semi-rainforest trails, into the northernmost point of the city, and toward the village of indigenous people.

"A girl of Julia's description has been sighted blending in with a tourist group in the La Boquilla village area," Teresa read Jessie's text aloud. "Afro-Caribbean indigenous people live there in huts with spare furnishings. Locals often gather to watch the rare TVs on the street." Teresa's expertise came into play as she narrated.

"We'll kayak through the mangrove canals, like the tourists, to get to the huts on the island. A number of them house people who work for tour groups. Some of the locals also engage in illegal activities to make ends meet, even though most would never get involved."

"This seems like a world away." A forty-minute drive and Gabe's eyes filled with sights of villages in existence for generations.

"It is. To earn money, island kids will pull down natural coconuts with huge shells. They whack away at the husks with machetes and serve the tourists coconut drinks from the shell. Some of them get very close to hacking their hands off. With even a slight slip, the kid could cut off at least a finger or hit an artery. But the young locals can't let their families go hungry."

"Would Julia be on the island?"

"We'll check there if we don't find her on the peninsula."

"Teresa has worked to make many friends in the region."

"Yes, but it's not work, Roberto, I enjoy them too."

"She brings them fresh vegetables and tutors the children when she can get away from New Day. She knows as much about this area as anyone, and they respect her."

"Thanks for the kudos. If Julia is here, our sources will give her up. We'll find her."

Mangrove canals formed from the tangles of tree roots entwined in knots inside the almost 200 square mile coastal lagoon of Ciénaga de La Virgen. In the poorest parts of Cartagena, city developers built five-star hotels and luxury apartments next to wooden huts of local communities. Fishermen worked there along with a few greeters for eco-tourists. Snowy egrets, white ibis, kingfishers, cormorants, and the occasional green parrot could be found beyond the walled city and across the mangrove forests.

At the bend of a river stood several business shacks with solid roofs grouped together. Appearing vastly different from the average grass dwelling, these huts had a businesslike presence. In contrast, at most huts where people still lived, clothes hung outside to dry and windows were boarded up though people lived in most. The team viewed a few homes with open doorways and chairs cluttering the deck. Men, women, and children gathered to enjoy the ocean air wafting in.

Gabe smiled as Teresa sped over unpaved roads of the coastal La Boquilla village making it seem easy, typical of the way she could make the jeep fly in an emergency.

"Look and listen," Teresa said to Gabe. "Maybe someday you can take charge, that is, if you choose to be more than a temporary resident at New Day: Women, maybe become Dr. Alma."

Seeing her abuelita as director of New Day continued to amaze Gabe as she remembered her only from childhood. She didn't feel good about her abuelita still not taking the time to tell her why she'd left Mamacita, José, and Gabe behind to reside in Colombia. But Abuelita had promised to share her reasons.

As if sensing Gabe's mood, Teresa turned toward her. "Neither Micah nor anyone else has had a spare moment for anything other than searching for the missing girls. It's been weeks since María was kidnapped, and we needed a short rest, but now Julia's disappearance has again thrown the whole base into emergency search mode."

*Abuelita took time with me in the garden, yet that was before the compound went on lockdown.*

Speeding through the coastal village, the jeep pushed ahead. Teresa maneuvered around school-age children playfully darting into the road. The kids laughed, and sounds of their mothers and grandmothers scolding them came from inside the huts.

"Children are at home during the day, kept away from inland schools." Roberto waved at the huts. "We think the kids are isolated so the village can keep its indigenous culture."

Gabe nodded.

Teresa filled Gabe in as much as she could on the wild ride, telling her leaders thought the culture was best preserved by keeping children in home schools except for special emergency situations, even though it usually meant setbacks in conventional education for disadvantaged youth. Of course, any children showing aptitude on educational tests would be given placements at city boarding schools paid for by taxpayers' money. Villagers let them go.

Here on the outskirts, the isolated and impoverished villagers were especially suspicious of intruders. They trusted only their own connections, legal or not. Illegal business could include anything from placing bets to hiding kidnapping victims for a price. Needy villagers might do anything, including committing a crime to keep cash coming in. Fortunately for New Day: Women, Teresa explained, she'd made friends with people who lived on the lagoon when she'd kayaked for recreation through the canals.

"If anything smells suspicious, I'll stop at a few locations and get a sense of the action," said Teresa. "If the traffickers bribed someone to stash the girls, I'll offer more cash than they did and negotiate for their lives."

Gabe's mouth went dry.

Teresa pointed out some doors, and Roberto banged on them until someone came out to deal with her. Roberto kept his gun ready, and Gabe felt antsy watching.

At one hut, no one answered for a long couple of minutes, but Roberto kept pounding. A sleepy-looking man finally came to the door, and Roberto asked to come in and search the premises with Teresa.

Gabe waited expectantly. The two came back to the van with no success or new information, ready to move on to the next hut.

"Are you going to let me help? I know how to handle a gun." Gabe stretched the truth, thinking of the compound range instruction.

"This is not your average city street, Gabe." Teresa pronounced and set her jaw.

Roberto lifted his eyebrows, but Gabe couldn't get a read on him, which made her even more impatient.

"You probably have an extra gun or two in this jeep, but you're thinking my abuelita wouldn't go for me using it."

"Not at all." Teresa wound around a tight turn of the village's dusty road.

"If you're not saying no?"

"And she's not saying yes." Roberto retorted.

Gabe gave Roberto a questioning glance. "Do you have a .22?" Gabe asked Teresa.

"No, but there's a .38 right under the back seat. Thought you'd never ask."

Gabe reached for the gun.

"Girls with guns are nothing new around here." Roberto was curt. "I hoped not to see you packing so soon, Gabe, but I'll back you both up."

New Day: Women's blue-team search party rattled along the dirt street, stopping to check on all of Teresa's known sources and to stick their noses in a few other places. Only one resident acted like they had disturbed the peace. The others seemed to have heard friendly buzz about Teresa from her village connections. Gabe held the .38 close inside her jacket pocket.

While Roberto backed up Teresa, Gabe surveyed the local activity and kept an eye on the jeep. A villager Teresa talked with said he'd seen someone of Julia's description in one of the kayaks bound for the lagoon. At that time, he hadn't known whether she was a local or a tourist.

Suddenly, Gabe saw a man dart in front of them, holding a girl with dark hair by the arm, and she hastily pulled her gun.

# chapter 43

"JULIA!" GABE SHOUTED AND aimed her gun at the man with the girl.

Teresa and Roberto grabbed their guns but kept them lowered.

The girl gasped at the sight of Gabe's gun, and the couple turned to them in shock. The girl was clearly not Julia.

Gabe's hand shook.

"Whoa!" Teresa shouted. "Not so fast, Gabe! That's not Julia!"

Roberto made their apologies to the couple while Teresa turned to Gabe. "Are you shaking? You said you've used a .22."

"I did. Once. And, I had a few hours at the range."

"Guns are our last resort. We don't want to create a scene with the villagers we've cultivated relationships with. Maybe you like to stir things up where you're from?"

"Not me."

Teresa holstered her gun with the ease of a professional.

Gabe wondered how many times Teresa had used a gun and if she'd ever killed anybody. She'd looked so cool driving the van and at the awards ceremony. Now, this was Teresa on steroids, and her criticism of the near altercation made Gabe anxious. She felt she might not survive to get back to Mamacita and José. She didn't want to die in Colombia and have them think she'd deserted them and disappeared as suddenly as Abuelita.

"Want to go back? Are you too scared?" Teresa sounded stern.

"I can't even with you right now." Gabe quivered slightly.

"You can't *even* with me?!" Teresa looked over her shoulder at Gabe, but Roberto looked at her reassuringly.

"Hurry." Teresa jumped out. "We'll take a kayak and sweep the mangrove canals and the island. No stone left unturned." She found a kayak stashed in the undergrowth and motioned for the others to get in and grab a paddle.

As they navigated through the natural canals, snowy egrets seemed to swoop down at every turn. One egret with a long wingspan flew toward them with wings outstretched and touched ground, quietly prancing on an island with its head bobbing along, a yellow peak atop a thin white neck. Its spindly legs moved forward on knobby knees. The bird's head and neck moved back and forth, and its whole body turned as if to sense what draft would take it up to soar again. It shied away, hiding behind a rock, then rocked forward with a zap, clamping a lizard in its mouth and swallowing it down, its snowy neck bulging.

The group of three paddled effortlessly like a trained crew.

"Undisturbed nature surrounds us. I'm always astonished at the tangled mangrove roots, how they intertwine, yet still leave room for the kayak to zip through." Teresa was in the zone.

Roberto's head moved from side to side. He looked lost in the natural wonder.

"Is it always like this?" Gabe responded to Roberto's movements but didn't like the way her voice squeaked.

Teresa looked around. "Always."

"Creation reflects a divine hand." Roberto mused.

Teresa dropped her chin. "Nature speaks."

*The divine spirit I'm drawn to.*

Roberto looked over his shoulder. "You're quiet, Gabe."

Gabe nodded. In the glint of the sun on the spray with each stroke of the paddle, she could see reflected faces of family, students, homies. They would love kayaking, slipping through the water, observing natural life in the mangroves.

"We're making fast work of this." Roberto interrupted her reverie. "Let's take a look at the peninsula."

Emerging from the canals, they burst into a clear blue pool of water. It looked heavenly, enchanted. They paused, put their paddles down, and rested for a second.

"Back there with the gun … it was all my fault." The confession felt good for her soul.

"It's all right." Teresa held up one hand. "This first and only time."

Gabe nodded at Teresa's forgiveness.

"Don't worry. You're the one I'd want beside me in a fight." Roberto tried to settle her.

Gabe shivered. "I don't think so."

"I know you have fierceness in you, and you're my medic." Gabe took the compliment.

Roberto looked sideways at Gabe.

Teresa winked. "They make the men strong and smooth in Colombia, like the liquor."

"I wouldn't know about either, Teresa." Gabe stuck her legs under the seat.

This time Roberto blushed.

"You sew a mean stitch." He pointed to his arm.

"Thank you, Roberto. I'm determined. My spirit animal is a jaguar, fastest jungle animal, a beautiful cat."

"Mighty feline jaguar roaming Colombian wilds, Gabe?" He turned and tapped her knee.

"You tease, Roberto. You're smart, but I suppose you're a tamarin—a cotton-top monkey!" Teresa, laughed.

"Teresa, that's *you*, swinging around from place to place."

"Yeah, I do admire the tamarins. I'm Teresa the Tamarin."

"Actually … I am … wait for it." Roberto paused, looking up at the sky to see a bird. "I am an Andean condor."

"The bird on the Colombian flag?"

"Largest bird in the world, our national bird." Teresa chimed in, flapping her wings.

Gabe chatted with them about animals and spirits. The wildlife and spiritual world captivated her, since she came from a concrete jungle of mean streets, and the team seemed to enjoy her newfound openness. She giggled a bit and then straightened up when several texts beeped, one right after another on all three phones.

"From Central. Let's get back!" Teresa signaled them to whip the kayak around. For several minutes, no one spoke as they exerted every muscle to get the kayak back to shore in double time.

Once on shore, they hopped into the jeep, catching their breath. Teresa pulled a one-eighty, leaving skid tracks in the dirt and excitement on the faces of spectating local kids.

Roberto read aloud, and Gabe saw the same text on her phone: "Green team, activity from informant. Possible abduction of two girls downtown."

Gabe gasped. "Two? Alive?"

"Julia and maybe María. A twofer." Teresa advised them they'd reach downtown before Micah's interior unit did so her group could meet them.

"Shush." Roberto was on alert.

"Gabe has clearance. The yellow team found the traffickers' hiding spot in a rural area outside of an inland town. They're in a thatched-hut cooking area for drug manufacturers. Yellow team checked the ashes of the fire the criminals set to cover their tracks. They pulled a matchbook from Fiero Club."

"Teresa, what does Abuelita make of it?"

"Micah's instinct is that Julia and María may have been held there, then transferred to the club when the heat settled."

"Two rescues for one trip. Let's go! The system is working." Roberto pumped his fists.

"Green team has the lead. We're backup. No guns unless I say so." Teresa glared at Gabe.

Gabe slid down slightly in the back seat. She missed her homegirls who might understand her aggressive ways. *At least homegirls give me respect. Teresa. Says she's a tamarin, acts like a wildcat.*

She could see how Teresa's decisiveness made her popular, but this was the first time at New Day: Women when Gabe felt accusations coming down on her. And they stung. She needed to show Teresa more smarts and finesse on the mission.

"Take care. Female tamarins, aggressive species." Roberto secretly relayed his tip to Gabe.

*Could Teresa report me for insubordination and improper use of a firearm to, of all people, my own abuela?"*

"Gabe, we may need your med skills." Teresa's words helped Gabe calm down.

Teresa gunned the jeep and headed toward the night-club row.

"I run by those nightclubs. Fiero Club gets a lot of traffic."

"Yes, Gabe." Teresa looked grim. "It will tonight."

# chapter 44

TERESA'S BLUE TEAM ARRIVED at their destination two blocks away from the club, and her jeep slid into an inconspicuous parking space. Up ahead, Jessie and her green group unloaded the van and stealthily moved toward the club. Jessie signaled Teresa's blue team to move forward.

Gabe, Teresa, and Roberto gathered in the side alley near Fiero Club, while Jessie and her group took first position nearest the target location. At the door to the nightclub with the blazing red banner stood a man with a white-gray beard dressed in a military vest and indigo jeans. Waving his hands, he spat as he shouted at a younger man attired in shorts and T-shirt. After a heated monologue, the older tough guy shoved the newbie into the club and ventured out into the street.

The slithering nightclub crowd congregated along the row, waiting for doors to open, but tonight looked more disorganized than other nights. Gabe checked a text alert from surveillance: "Club owners dine out. Young subordinates in charge."

What luck! The rescue teams nodded at each other.

Jessie ran down the street, drew her weapon and bounded into the nightclub. Ernesto, her right-hand man, stood guard outside the Fiero Club as Teresa, Roberto, and Gabe followed close behind. Gabe felt tentative because of Teresa's reprimand of her gun use earlier.

On her downtown Cartagena jogging route, she had noticed the dark alleys and hidden club corridors seemed perfect places to hide contraband. Men in suits at these clubs looked like management or bodyguards. From her time at Club Jupiter in California, Gabe remembered the owners' soundproofed suites, where any illicit business could be transacted, and no one would be the wiser if young women screamed from inside.

On the cavernous nightclub's first floor, she heard techno music and saw bodies of men and women warming up, whipping around the poles. She turned her head to keep the scene out of her eyesight. She thought of Julia, who might be imprisoned in this immoral atmosphere. It surprised her how much her thinking and actions had improved while working at New Day: Women. Before, she wouldn't flinch at spending some time frolicking at a shady nightclub.

Pressing ahead, Gabe followed her team up and around a dark corner to an office. Locked. Jessie and Ernesto kicked it in and walked inside while Teresa and Gabe followed, with Roberto posted outside. They heard cries from behind an interior door. Again locked. Jessie and Ernesto threw their shoulders against the door, but it didn't budge. They stepped back, exhausted.

Gabe motioned at the lock with her gun, and Teresa lifted hers and shot the lock, blowing it to pieces. Jessie and Ernesto burst in and moved someone out of the cavernous area. A disheveled girl with long, stringy hair and hollow eyes met them inside. The weak girl was not Julia, but from the photos she'd seen, Gabe thought she might be María. The cave contained steel, human-size cages with padlocks.

"We have one in handcuffs here. María." After Jessie's announcement, it took both Ernesto and her to move María out. The girl tried to stand but slipped into Ernesto's arms.

Jessie directed Teresa and Gabe. "Go in for the other one."

"Julia?"

"It's me! No handcuffs." Julia showed her free arms. "I picked the lock. Gabe showed me after class. I hoped to help María to unlock hers. How did you find us?"

"Micah found a clue. Jessie's satellites picked up traffic here." Teresa whispered inside.

"Top guys left to celebrate." Roberto informed the group in a low voice.

"I got names and codes."

"Good, Julia." Teresa affirmed her as she removed María's handcuffs.

"Julia," Gabe carefully patted her shoulder, "you make rescue easy."

Roberto gave a concerned look at his smartwatch.

Teresa alerted them with a wary look. "Cover us, Roberto. Downstairs."

Roberto touched Gabe's hand as he left. Gabe checked the girls' conditions.

From downstairs came the sounds of a scuffle. A thump. Footsteps resonated up the stairway. Teresa and Jessie signaled to Ernesto not to shoot yet, and Gabe thought it smart to avoid friendly fire in the close quarters. She'd placed her gun on the floor to get her medic gear. Shadows of the club guards moved toward them. Six muscular young men burst into the room. They wrestled the outnumbered Teresa, Jessie, Ernesto, and Gabe to the ground.

One man grabbed the two kidnapped girls and threw them back into a cage, locking them up together. Another locked Gabe in the second cage. They secured the cages with a strong steel cable and then wrapped leather around the wrists of Teresa, Jessie, and Ernesto, dragging them down the back hall.

"We'll come back for you, Gabe!" Teresa gasped out the words as one of the men yanked her along.

After the shouts and echoes of a struggle died out, Gabe concentrated but couldn't hear anything else. Were the others dead, and Roberto too? She could scarcely think.

*We're trapped.* Gabe's heart pounded. "Julia? María?" She fought to control the surge of adrenalin. With her training, she could help them.

She looked around her cage. If she was cramped, Julia and María must be having trouble even breathing in their tight space. She tried to pick the lock, but she couldn't do anything about the steel cable.

"I'm here." It was Julia. "María's hurt."

"Keep any weight off María. Breathe. Count six in, six out. And as you do, pray." Gabe coached the girls while they kept counts, breathing together until Julia said María looked like she was ready to pass out.

*What next?* Trapped again after almost finding freedom, now the two trafficked girls seemed resigned. And here Gabe was one of them. Had she come this far to lose her calling and her life? Would escaping her history be a dream that *never* came true?

It seemed like an hour had passed, but Gabe's watch showed only several minutes had gone by. She heard feet dragging, coming toward them in the front hallway. She squirmed and thrashed, jolting the lock, desperately trying to find a way out.

"Gabe?"

"Roberto? What—?"

"I was knocked out. They left me for dead." Roberto's feet unsteadily scraped against the floor.

"Are the armed men still down there?" Gabe asked.

"No. They left. Up here?"

"I don't think so."

Julia whimpered.

Roberto staggered toward the office, banged some desk drawers open, pulled out a strong cutting tool and sliced through the cage cables while Julia stifled her exclamations and María held her injured wrist.

"Gabe?"

"Coming, María." Freed, Gabe wrapped María's wrist while Roberto carefully checked down the back hall.

He motioned to Gabe, and she followed.

Teresa, Jessie, and Ernesto lay in a crumpled pile, knocked out, and roped with leather straps to a water pipe. Roberto untied them while Gabe roused them to consciousness with water drops.

"Quick." Teresa slurred her words. "I heard the bad guys say their van is coming … guards out drinking. They thought I was all the way out, but I wasn't."

*The guards' celebration or a setup?*

Roberto and Gabe steadied the rescuers as they came to. After adjusting their eyes to the lighting, they moved on shaky legs around the office to help Julia and María get out of the cages. The trafficked girls stood up, testing their legs.

Quietly, green and blue teams moved the girls out of the near-empty club. They split the girls up, loading María into the van and Julia into the jeep. In the jeep, Gabe belted Julia into the seat beside her and covered her trembling torso with a blanket. After shaking off her headache, Teresa drove off, expertly navigating the maze of the city streets and looking at her phone's GPS with Roberto spotting cross-traffic and shouting, "Clear!" The jeep followed the van according to plan.

"Julia, have you eaten anything?" When Julia shook her head, Gabe handed her orange juice, beef jerky, and emergency rations from a plastic bag. "Eat slowly."

Teresa accelerated.

"Where are we going? I heard a crazy tale about a safe house."

"Julia, it's not so wild. Hang on. We're splitting up from Jessie." Teresa's jeep careened around the corner onto a completely different route than the van had taken.

Gabe's eyebrows raised. "Safe house is ready." Gabe announced the text she'd picked up on the smartphone.

"I know that car!" Roberto pointed at a souped-up gray sedan coming up behind them. "I just saw the video of this gray sedan shooting at me and the guards at the compound."

The sedan pulled up close to their rear, but Teresa shifted into high gear, made a quick right turn, and left the perpetrators in a cloud of flying road dust and pebbles. The sedan's engine sputtered and then gained speed, getting closer to them. Men leaned out windows with AK-47s and shot at the jeep.

Gabe gulped and ducked. Again, just when her dream of rising above her past was starting to come true, her very life—and the lives of those she'd come to love—hovered close to danger. *What will these men do if they capture us? Unspeakable violence.*

Roberto returned the volley as best he could.

Teresa floored the bouncing jeep. Cheetah fast, it leaped forward with another burst. Gabe shielded Julia, who had dropped to the floor.

The attackers closed in.

# chapter 45

TERESA SPED AHEAD TO what looked like a man-made mountain entrance, with Roberto firing enough ammo to keep the gunmen at bay. A van appeared a distance behind the sedan. More human traffickers.

"Roberto, Gabe, shoot while I swerve." Teresa directed her team.

Gabe carefully returned rounds. She noticed Roberto shot like a pro marksman. Even while the jeep changed directions abruptly twice, and they fought to maintain balance, shots fired damaged the traffickers' van's windshield and tires, slowing it down.

Teresa saw their hesitancy in her rearview mirror. She pressed a button on her window visor. The jeep lunged forward as Roberto and Gabe held their fire. A large natural or unnatural elevation on a section of the mountain seemed to rise up. Gabe grinned.

*The safe house.*

The cartel was on their tail, closing in on them. It looked like they aimed to come into the mountain-side safe house after them.

When Teresa's jeep reached the safe house a few car lengths ahead, the mountain rose completely up. The tunnel opened wide. Then just as quickly as it rose up, the mountain door entrance smashed down to the ground blocking the cartel. When they jumped out of the jeep, helping hands wrapped heavy coats around the girls to keep them from going into shock, and Jessie herded them down into a shadowy passage. Teresa explained an old cartel had utilized the underground passageways until the current regime ran them out of town. Then the three women activists and their group adapted the space for their use and set up a rustic but sophisticated defense system.

A clinic was down a passageway second from the right. Inside, Gabe noticed María and Julia, who both looked much calmer with Dr. Martínez and nurses attending to them.

Jessie explained they'd set up a barricade at the entrance to trip up foes and get video feed of possible attackers. In an alcove full of computers and IT equipment, Jessie's camera screens showed footage from hundreds of cameras. A hacker friend helped Jessie years ago to acquire police cameras footage on the happenings in the city and outskirts at all times.

"We had surveillance video of most important parts of the city. Once the mayor realized our early success, he wanted to work with us on some of his tougher crime cases, so it wasn't hard to gain more camera access." Jessie could only relate this in sound bites to Gabe.

"Is this the front entrance camera?" Gabe pointed to one of Jessie's screens. She and Jessie looked to see the mountain had risen the height of a man, and the intruders moved forward from where they'd stationed themselves to wait about three football fields length away.

"The entrance! Let's go!" Jessie led while Teresa, Gabe and Roberto sprinted from the alcove to the front.

"The door came down so fast, it sprang back up some." Teresa made sure Jessie heard.

Jessie's team took the lead position, while Teresa guided Roberto and Gabe to defensive posts near the tunnel entrance. Teresa equipped them with artillery from Micah's intimidating closet full of specialty items she'd collected in case of an assault. Gabe figured Roberto's crew of gate and wall guards had stayed back to defend the New Day: Women compound.

Gabe felt more serene than she had in a while. Then a stealthy movement came from the brush outside the tunnel. The van was parked where they could see part of it, and they expected at least six men inside. Ernesto returned from checking on María and Julia in the makeshift tunnel clinic. He took a hurried look at Jessie surveying screens, then rushed to back up the defenders at the front entrance.

Gabe stood guard, hidden behind the door to the entrance, while Roberto and Ernesto took point at the tunnel's opening. They had Abuelita's walk-in cave closet full of guns and ammo at their feet, an impressive stockpile. Gabe knew if they rounded up all the guns in her former gang Middle Town's section of Santa Ana, California, it wouldn't rival her abuela's stash. Abuelita had a war chest worthy of an avenging angel. Gabe filed her hard questions away for later.

"Are Abuelita and her team nearby?"

Roberto shook his head. "Gabe, not yet." The yellow team was still on their way to the safe house, a long trip from the Colombian interior.

*What if Abuelita had trouble enroute? Would she arrive safely?*

Roberto carried an AK-47, and Gabe grasped her .38, resisting the temptation to pick up another heavy automatic, the type she'd seen used in Santa Ana gang war zones. Jessie yelled out the feed from the safe house tunnel camera: "Gunmen a hundred yards away!"

Just then, a loud explosion at the tunnel opening slammed Gabe and Roberto into each other.

Jessie surveyed the feed from the cameras, "More explosives! A man with a beard and bodyguards." Jessie waved her arms.

Teresa was up too close. "Teresa!" Gabe gave a jungle yell. Teresa moved back.

"Gabe, get back more!" Roberto pushed her back so he could move quickly. He lifted the AK-47 and charged at the entrance.

With the cartel's traffickers and henchmen outside the safe house entrance, another explosive hit the tunnel. It looked like the attackers were ready to use everything, including missiles. Hit by debris, Roberto winced, grabbed his injured arm while being hurled backward. Teresa and Gabe moved him to the side, then checked to see he wasn't critical. Ernesto picked Roberto up to take him to Dr. Martínez. Jessie moved into forward position with a weapon. As a hand grenade was thrown into the tunnel, Gabe's eyes were fixed on it. She tried to move away. The grenade landed at her feet. She held her breath. *Would she be blown to pieces?*

She felt her face. It hadn't exploded. The pin was not pulled!

"My abuelita will hate me." Gabe muttered to Jessie, and then she pulled the tab and threw the grenade back at the intruders. "That's for playing with explosives!"

The intruders were stymied and some wounded, but in the confusion, one unarmed attacker came forward. Gabe recognized the rude human trafficker who Gabe wanted to fight for terrifying her and Teresa in the Cartagena hotel corridors! His gun had just been knocked away. He broke through the guarded entrance and came at Gabe mano a mano, hand to hand. *Now is my chance!* Gabe centered herself. To her side, Teresa and Jessie, occupied with the attack, couldn't rush over to Gabe, but they raised their guns in case Gabe faltered. The trafficker reached down to try to pull out a small knife from his shoe. Before he could reach his weapon, she lifted her knee up to place it in his groin with perfect form. When he clenched himself and doubled over, she came in for the kill, pounding his head and neck with her clenched fists. He fell to the ground.

Teresa tied the attacker's hands. Jessie held one grenade thrower at gunpoint and dragged him into an interrogation room in the tunnel for questioning. Most of the trafficking crew who had advanced now crept away to find cover, and soon, the sound of a sedan and a van backing up and the squeal of tires. As they split out, Gabe watched Teresa and Jessie fire at the van's tires, the rubber already weakened by Roberto's efforts. *Teresa and Jessie have the stuff of combat vets. The vehicles may limp to the side of the road some miles from here.* She shook all over, but the fight felt clean.

After Abuelita's team from the interior made it to the safe house an hour later, Gabe overheard Jessie briefing her on recent events, from Fiero Club to Gabe's grenade volley. Abuelita didn't seem surprised or angry, and Gabe sighed in relief.

Abuelita then slipped into the room housing the central intelligence. Gabe came nearer and watched her set to work unlocking the system's tapes of the recent activity Jessie had locked after the perpetrators' retreat. Gabe came up softly behind her and while Abuelita used a file to get through a lock, crawl into a secure area, and type codes into the main safe house computer.

*What was Abuelita finding and typing?*

"You're not just the brains." Gabe approached her.

Abuelita jumped. "We teach brains and brawn. Well done." Abuelita gave Gabe a hug. "More than a *little* brawn, Gabe—your fireworks and fighting."

"Well, you set this all up. You and your friends, working with accomplished women—or maybe I should say *accomplices*—to help other women."

"You turn a phrase. I have my reasons. I ran, like you."

"Not like me. Tell me why."

"I did time." The three words fell flat. "No one knew but your Mamacita."

"She didn't tell us, but I guessed after I got here. What were you in for?"

"A little snatch and grab that went south, then defending myself against a provoked attack in prison."

Gabe shrugged. "I could tell. You with a system the mayor admires, Teresa and Jessie moving like con women. Why the secrecy?"

"I didn't want my bad example in front of you, so I left after I spent years in the big house." Abuelita explained how Teresa and Jessie entered the prison after her. Together, they learned skills to give marginalized women a new chance. "Women like you. That counts for something."

"It does, Abuelita. You have the network. You're a trail-blazer helping put a stop to human trafficking. The girls call you Micah, but your real name is Michaela, like Michael. You're named after an angel."

"Oh, sweet Gabe, Gabriela, you're the messenger angel. You came here to carry a message of hope for women. I wanted to come back to you as a whole person with integrity and vision. It became hard to leave with the women here needing me for their safety, their very lives. Then I heard through my network you were in trouble. Petra reached out to the women's network to ask me for help."

"You found a way." Gabe's bruised hand touched her grandmother's. "That's all that matters."

# chapter 46

BACK AT THE BASE a few days later, Gabe stood shoulder-to-shoulder with Abuelita, pausing to talk before self-defense class.

Excited screams went out from the girls and women who had remained at the compound as they scrambled to get to the returning teams. First one and then another came at them, arms outstretched. María gave Isabel a huge whoop and hug, hopping and embracing. Julia gave the next girl a squeeze, looking into her eyes. Then the next and the next. Gabe couldn't help but plunge into the big group, which by now was jumping up and down like a winning basketball team.

"Huddle!" Micah yelled, joining in. Julia and María threw their arms around Gabe's abuelita and pulled her into the center of the fracas.

"Let's hear it for Julia! And María!"

Julia threw her arms around her fellow survivor. "This is a happy huddle!"

"For Gabe and the rescuers!" Julia and María started the chant.

"You are New Day: Women!" Micah shouted.

"It's a new day for me. You came for me." A tear trickled down Maria's face.

"Abuelita! Abuelita!" The group gave a cheer, calling Micah for the first time by the name Gabe had for her.

Gabe beamed. How could anyone be so happy? Inside she knew she needed to learn to trust more. Layers of hurt—what would it take to curb her anger?

At the end of class, Roberto interrupted Micah with a communiqué. He gave Gabe a nod toward the compound garden as if to say he'd be waiting for her there. An invitation to talk together? She responded with a smile. Maybe he would teach her the "Amazing Grace" song, the one his mother taught him, and they would eat *pepitos* and drink *té*

"Walk with me." Abuelita motioned for Gabe to accompany her through the compound.

"So now you see how we work. You'll stay to help?"

"Your girls Julia and María are here now, Abuelita. I love all these girls. I'm happy they're safe now. I love that you study the Bible with Pastor Pérez and Roberto's mother—"

"Then you must follow your heart and stay."

"I'm growing to love this country, Colombia, but you would love our family and friends. This isn't my real home."

"It could be—for a while longer at least."

"Maybe … Someday. Look. You control these women. Not me."

"You feel controlled?"

"Your tactic of surprise. Getting me to the mayor's event, engineering frantic meetings, demanding women take classes to become fighters, pushing and isolating them. You breed rebels."

"Rebels? They're defenders. Defenders! Capable of defending themselves. I thought you could see the plan, *mija*—protect women, teach self-defense, duplicate systems. So many girls are in danger."

"The kidnapped girls aren't safe here now."

"*Exactamente.* You, of anyone, should understand. Julia will go to stay at her uncle's place in Costa Rica, and María will join her cousins in Panamá. They'll teach, establish other sites, help other at-risk women. From country to country."

"Rescued to rescuers."

"Stay here. You fit in this good work."

Gabe looked to make sure no one was within earshot. "I could tell you'd done time because you had to learn these skills somewhere. The system is slick. Jailhouse tactics. Jessie's hacking. Teresa's reconnaissance. Your safe cracking. You operate at a high level. I'll give you that."

"You're back-peddling? Good. The system is what I can do for others. I do expect more from you than I'm able to do. Your medicine, for example. You'll be a medical professional."

"Ah, but the Alma family, your family needs help. I was in juvie. Your nephew is in jail. New Day women are loyal, but they're not family."

"I left you because I was ashamed."

"If you loved the Alma family, you would've contacted us. We would've visited you. Locked up or not."

Abuelita looked touched. "It would've been too hard to visit prison. You all needed to live your lives without a stain on you. You're growing. In years to come you'll be a doctor, and New Day helped."

"You can see I love helping."

"You've equipped the girls to be strong and to teach." Abuelita opened the door, observing students staying after class practicing kicks and jabs with Julia and María at the front of the group.

When Gabe stepped in, the young women stared at her until one gave her another fist bump. Then another clapped her hands, and soon they were all clapping. "Gabe! Gabe!" Apparently, word about her fight at the tunnel entrance was getting around.

Gabe nodded. "They'll do you proud in Costa Rica, Panamá, wherever you send them. In Colombia, also."

"They want to uphold their coach's reputation."

"Slamming that bad hombre gave me more satisfaction than any other fight."

"Why do you think that is, Gabe?"

"I had a cause."

"Stay, Gabriela." Abuelita implored another time. "You're a part of this." She wrung her hands. "What about Roberto? You two have grown close in Cartagena. Have you heard of a *hania*? It means happy, delightful. It's a girl who changes a boy's life forever. She makes him believe in the idea of love, and without a *hania*, life is not worth living."

Gabe choked up. "Roberto means a lot to me. If it's meant to be—"

"Our toughest guard is emotional around you. He'll be an educator soon."

"If his feelings are true, he can wait."

"Why leave people who care about you? So, you want to give up and let the traffickers win? Well go, just go!" She waved Gabe away.

"Abuelita, José will need help with recovery. His sentence for the storage unit substances should be over. He has bad connections."

"I'm sorry to hear." Abuelita's face looked sincere.

"I can stay here two months more. You saved your New Day: Women family. I need to save mine."

Gabe would miss this place. As Abuelita calmed, Gabe told her about discovering snowy egrets, scarlet macaws, and ornate hawks in the mangrove canals, the shrill bird calls beckoning, that slight sparkle of the air, and her heightened senses. She was shaking with enthusiasm.

"Don't count me out, Abuelita. I may be back."

"I am counting on it. Something else you may have forgotten, but I didn't, Gabe."

Gabe could think of many areas in which Abuelita was ahead of her, but her grandmother chimed, "Today's date!"

"Today's date?"

"Happy birthday! You're seventeen today!"

"I do feel a whole lot like seventeen, finally."

"I'll bet you do. Rescuing girls, fighting traffickers. It does age one." Abuelita pushed back her silver-white hair. "I think I'll take a needed break and reconcile with my daughter and my grandson . . . and my great-granddaughter Luz! Others here can mind the work a while. I'd like to come home with you."

"Abuelita."

Abuelita reached out for her granddaughter.

Gabe hugged her then pulled away softly. "I almost forgot. I have plans."

"I won't keep you." Abuelita winked.

# chapter 47

G ABE DECIDED TO TELL Petra what happened to Julia
and María—their capture, rescue, and commission to
help New Day: Women reach out to women in other countries.

*Homegirl, I hear your prayer.*

It came in the still quiet before the call. The whisper.
Gabe was still.

Was this the living spirit she had prayed to? Was this
Jesus the one she and Abuelita once worshipped together
in church and Roberto's mother believed in? Gabe thought
back to the natural world she experienced as a representation
of the glory of God.

Gabe put in Petra's number, and she answered.

"Petra, I've been praying ..."

"Good."

"I have a nudge I need to leave."

"Gabe, your words have a familiar ring—as in when you
left here for there."

"José is getting out of jail. And Abuelita—"

"Abuelita is welcome."

Gabe thought of Abuelita's influence with the international women's network.

"You'll teach more self-defense here." Petra declared to her.

"I'd like to do that. More outdoors."

"Also, your units and grades allow you early admission at the state university. The buzz is you've become even more adept at medicine. *Most* of those here who tried to take you out are locked up. You'd have a good new association at college."

"It's a lot to ask to enter state university, Petra."

"It's not all free. You'll work part-time in the school medical center."

"Thank you, but I can't leave Mamacita in the barrio with me at college."

"Who do you think asked around to find your med center job? Don't sell your mother short. She's lined up a place for your family near campus."

Gabe grew misty-eyed.

"She wants it for you. She's prayed for you, homegirl. You'd be surprised how your homegirls are improving in school. Some kickbox. Some go to the corner church with a café and bookstore."

Gabe was startled. Mamacita was another homegirl who prayed, and God had answered. God had spoken to her. The prayer was for all the homegirls. Mamacita, Abuelita, and Julia were her homegirls. Olivia, Petra, Rosa, and all those who waited.

*Homegirl, I hear your prayer.* The whisper seemed louder, as if accompanied by the brush of wax palm leaves.

What was the song she remembered? Gabe hummed a few bars, thinking, "How sweet the sound."

For two months, Gabe worked with her students on their self-defense form, technique, and strategy until each looked like a professional teacher. If they followed protocol, they could foil predators in South America and throughout the world. The number of women helped would greatly increase as Abuelita and her winning strategy spread across the continents.

Kayaking in the mangrove canals remained her favorite memory, and when Roberto surprised her with a couple of return visits to La Boquilla, kayaking on its waterways while teaching her names of local species, she knew he'd stay gentle on her mind.

She'd gained a working knowledge with indigenous plants and longed to learn more about western medicine through regulation pre-med and med school. Along the way, her sadness had lifted. *How had she come so far with so little perceived effort?* When she looked at her reflection in the beveled mirror at the medical clinic, soon-to-be Dr. Gabriela Alma peered back at her.

Gabe felt a tug to return to Cartagena someday, reinforced perhaps by Roberto's cheerfulness and their sweet evening talks in the garden, moments when warm breezes came up and he quoted his mother's favorite verse, John 3:8: "The wind blows where it wishes and you hear the sound of it, but do not know where it is going; so is everyone who is born of the Spirit."

"*Hania*," Roberto called her, and she looked pleased. *Hania*. Pronounced like the second syllable of Cartagena. Cartagena, this city, a gentle gem changing her life forever. Caring people bringing about a new openness.

It was the evening before she and Abuelita were scheduled to fly out. Gabe remembered what Abuelita told her *hania* meant, though she couldn't believe she could be a delightful young woman whose love made a man's life worth living. Roberto probably didn't have a clue she knew the word. He took her hand like he believed in love.

*She didn't know men like this existed.*

Whipping her hair, the wind wrapped her up in her dress and made her think of what it would be like to dance with him. How silly, but wonderful. She smiled at the thought.

Gabe reasoned Abuelita, Teresa, and Jessie were cocky to think they could save all endangered young women. They were immensely courageous and strong, but realistic? She thought maybe they needed a new recipe with a measure of purpose, prayer, *pepitos*, and *té*, or Colombian cookies.

Gabe looked out the airplane window as it taxied and thought again of Abuelita, Teresa, and Jessie. If Abuelita Micah, the senior leader, and the other two women leaders in their prime were like this now, what had they been like, in and out of the big house? Spunky like Gabe? No, Abuelita might say that. She'd say, at least Gabe has her medical calling confirmed and can focus on becoming a physician, maybe a surgeon.

It felt unreal, sitting in a plane next to her Abuelita, who had been missing in action for so much of Gabe's life. How would Abuelita fit in with the Alma family, and how would they receive her? Who would this larger-than-life, silvery-haired woman become now? Could Micah really help in the neighborhood? Gabe would finally get a chance to find out. Family first. Connect with her niece, Luz. Continue with the healing arts and college pre-med.

She had the moments with Roberto to think about, and who knows, they might add more later as he also worked and studied. Could she finally stop her chase? Gabe leaned back against the headrest and prayed. She felt like God was moving in and through her, speaking and taking her hand like a friend. *I hear you.* She heard the whisper more clearly now.

Was the whisper for her or for others as well? It was for all of them.

Gabe felt the plane's landing gear lift.

The air picked up the message, and it took flight.

Art is the giving by each man of his evidence to the world.
Those who wish to give, love to give,
discover the pleasure of giving.
Those who give, give life.

—Dorothy L. Sayers

# ACKNOWLEDGMENTS

Like a musical theme, this work took several movements in time and tone. Many generous hands helped bring *Gabriela's Chase* to life and are dearly appreciated.

My parents, Faith and Bob, believed this book would be a reality until the days they passed into heaven. Memories of their goodness and generosity inspire me, symbolized by the praying hands sculpture they left our family.

My Schneekluth family members quarterbacked phases of the book project: husband Clark with encouragement and copyreading, sons Kyle and Blake in production as well as communications. Cartagena scenes are from our young family's unforgettable times kayaking in the mangrove canals and exploring the El Castillo, pirate canons and all. Daughters-in-law Alycia and Ava led in art, caring, and marketing. Camden and Collins are gifts. My sister Marilyn encourages my work as writer/professor. Thank you to Verlag.

Award-winning novelist and mentor John Francisco Rechy showed me a writer's eye as he read and penciled through drafts. Nonfiction mentor Gay Talese, said by Tom

Wolfe to be inventor of "new journalism," led me to see the extraordinary within the ordinary. Writers James L.Rubart, Sarah Sundin, James Scott Bell, and Thomas Umstattd, Jr. provided guidance.

Professionals Battalion Chief of Orange County Fire Association Bryan Bear, former Otto Fisher juvenile hall and Orangewood principal Kirk Anderson, former parole officer David French, and youth authority officer Phyllis Nemeth—who devoted numerous hours opening doors and evaluating research for this project—have my highest regard. I'm grateful to have served at the Santa Ana Lighthouse Community Center, Mariners Church.

Notes from beta readers Danna Acevedo, Gloria Bashara, LaShelle Endly, Kris Hollowaty, and Cheri Maniz fleshed out the characters and provided clarity. Author Dolley Carlson introduced me to her sharp professionals, Candice L. Davis editor and Kimberly Martin at Jera. Samuel Sutton, senior graphics designer, lent the cover thrill and color.

Support and prayers also helped usher this book into the world: Campbells, Franklins, Geigers, Jantzs, Millers, Ochs, Townsends, women's Refresh group, ACFW, Women of Vision book club, fiction book club as well as others. To God for it all.

I hope this work serves well.

Thank you anyone who has ever prayed for me.

Here is to all who seek, believe, and never give up.

# DISCUSSION QUESTIONS

1. Setting plays a major role in this novel. What details about life in Santa Ana, California, and Cartagena, Colombia, are new for you? How do you compare the cities? What influence does each environment have on Gabriela's (Gabe's) attitudes and actions?

2. Gabe finds herself in dangerous situations. Do any of these encounters made you uncomfortable? If so, which ones and why? Are Gabe's actions in menacing situations justifiable? Why or why not?

3. Gabe has a far-reaching career goal. How would you describe what she wants to achieve?

4. How does the disappearance of her grandmother, the deportation of her father, and the death of a brother impact Gabe? When she discovers Abuelita, is their relationship intact?

5. Running is a part of Gabe's training for boxing, yet how is this theme carried through in her self-defense teaching and life decisions?

6. Mamacita and Aunt Olivia support Gabe's efforts to surmount challenges and pursue medicine. How do they rely

on love and faith to rise above the hard times? In what scenes does this show that even broken, dysfunctional families can overcome negative patterns?

7. The value of community is a theme in the novel. How do Petra and Coach Al at the Grace Community Center help give Gabe's life focus?

8. How does New Day: Women in Cartagena, Colombia offer her a path forward? What giftedness does Gabe use to give back?

9. In what situations do you see Gabe's medical aptitude and skills revealed?

10. Both physical and psychological pain invade Gabe's life. Do you sympathize with her and her students in specific incidences in the novel? Is pain a challenge for young adults, if so, what are coping mechanisms?

11. At different times, both Ramón and Roberto vie for Gabe's affection? How do they differ? How does her insecurity tempt her to succumb to tainted love with Ramón? How does he try to traffic her as a mule and attempt to entice her into his business? How is this relationship resolved, at least for the moment?

12. How might the light romantic interest with Roberto in Colombia follow the "Beauty and the Beast" motif with Gabe as the heroine healer and Roberto as the burly guard of the compound?

13. Roberto worked as a guard at a Tanzanian compound, so he is familiar with danger. Is this what attracts Gabe? What are Roberto's personality qualities she discovers while tending to his wound? What do Gabe and Roberto have in common, and how do they differ?

14. One of my favorite activities is kayaking through mangrove canals in Cartagena. Did you connect with Gabe's appreciation of the natural habitat of exotic birds and creatures in the rescue scene at *La Boquilla*? How does this infuse some joy into her relationship with Roberto and the others?

15. In some scenarios, nameless Kafkaesque figures come after Gabe to crush her. Sometimes they are shadows. The opponent in the underground, ultimate fight may be created by a futuristic mechanism. What do you make of the apparition in her juvie cell? Do any of these elements portend real trouble or are they magic realism?

16. Would it be realistic to have a compound such as New Day: Women to help endangered women in other countries? What skills would women administrators of these facilities have? What knowledge or classes would help at-risk girls succeed in life? Is this Petra's "homegirl's heaven"?

17. Trafficking and kidnapping are adversities for the young people in the city of Cartagena. What are the three check-points Gabe teaches the girls to use to evaluate and identify possible predators? How do online and in-person stalking of young people appear in your sphere? Is your community involved in the effort against human traffickers and human smugglers?

18. Wind is a recurring motif in the story. What did you notice about this? How does nature express itself and how does Gabe respond? Are these spiritual elements?

19. What do you think is the significance of the title *Gabriela's Chase*?

20. How do you expect Gabe's future will unfold?

# POLVOROSAS RECIPE

Colombian Butter and Sugar Cookies
Recipe from Danna Acevedo

The perfect cookie to pair with coffee, the name *polvorosas comes* from the Spanish word *polvo*, which translates to "powder" in English.

Prep Time: 15 minutes
Cook Time: 15 minutes
Total Time: 30 minutes
Servings: 12

Ingredients:
    1 ½ cups unsalted butter (3 sticks)
    ½ cup sugar
    2 cups all-purpose flour
    ½ cup powdered sugar
    ½ teaspoon vanilla extract

Instructions:

1. Preheat the oven to 350 F.
2. To clarify the butter, place unsalted butter in a medium pot over low heat until it is melted.

3. Let it simmer until the foam goes to the top of the melted butter.
4. Remove the pan from the heat and let stand for about 5 minutes.
5. Skim the foam from the top and discard. Pour what remains into a bowl using a fine mesh strainer.
6. With an electric mixer, beat the butter for about 3 minutes. Add the sugar and vanilla and beat until well blended. Add the flour and continue beating for 2 minutes.
7. Form the dough into a ball. Wrap in plastic and place in the fridge for about 30 minutes.
8. Roll 2 tablespoons of dough between your palms into balls. Place the balls on a large, greased baking sheet about 1/2-inch apart. Flatten the balls using your hands.
9. Bake the cookies until golden on top, about 15 minutes. Let them cool for about 5 minutes on the baking sheet. Dust the cookies with the powdered sugar.

Pro Tips:
Use a quality butter.
Allow the cookies to cool completely before storing them in an airtight container at room temperature.

Nutrition:
Calories: 312 calories
Carbohydrates: 29 grams
Protein: 2 grams
Fat: 23 grams

Nutrition information is only an estimate.

# ABOUT THE AUTHOR

 *Gabriela's Chase* is Sherilyn Faith's debut novel. She has published short fiction and nonfiction, and of her many plays, one was produced internationally. With a master's in writing from the University of Southern California and a master's in literature from the University of California, she has taught at the university level. Sherilyn served as panelist on Iowa Visiting Artists' "The Visionary Role of Literature" (with Maxine Hong Kingston and Marsha Norman) and delivered papers on C. S. Lewis at the Festival of Faith and Writing, Grand Rapids. She was awarded best feature column from California Presswomen. She loves her family and the outdoors, enjoying walking trails, water sports, and ecotourism. Find her blog at www.sherilynfaith.com.